Intimate Abduction

Ann Carol Ulrich

Intimate Abduction

First book in
The Space Trilogy

by Ann Carol Ulrich

Earth Star Publications

ISBN 978-0-944851-02-9

Second Edition

First Printing, November 2021
Second Printing, February 2025

DEDICATION

This second edition of the original novel
is dedicated to my late husband,
Ethan G. Miller (1934-2008)

Contents

PART I

The Gathering

— 1 —

Mission of Mercy

"Amazing." Preejhna Chiyuub stood with grayish-white fingers pressed against the panel beneath the viewing screen.

"Shall we pull away now, commander?"

Preejhna Chiyuub sighed. "Not just yet. I so enjoy these spectral variations."

The shuttle helmsman was gentle in his reproach. "It is well past dawn, commander. There is much risk of staying this low..."

"Yes, I know." The Preejhna continued to gaze out over the landscape. "The Terrans call this Autumn," she commented. "Isn't it splendid?"

A tall masculine figure entered through the bubble hatchway and stopped as his eyes fell on the Preejhna.

"Serassan is here, commander," announced the helmsman.

Turning, the Preejhna flashed official greetings to the unusually lofty Estronian. His head, like her own, was large and bald. The skin on his body was grayish-white. He wore the one-piece uniform of an astronaut with its Earth-Star insignia that identified his mission. His eyes were a particularly deep color of blue, sloping widely toward the sides of his scalp. The two nostril holes opened and closed in regular breaths. The lipless mouth line moved at the corners as he regarded her.

"You summoned me, commander?" he asked.

Preejhna Chiyuub beckoned him to the viewing screen. Daylight had broken over the horizon and the ship hovered steadily over a dense, colorful forest of rolling hills. "Isn't it an amazing view?" she commented.

Serassan noticed the shrug of the helmsman. "There are Terrans who do not appreciate it as you do," he replied. "But ... if the Preejhna will excuse me for being so bold ... isn't it rather risky of us to be this visible during daylight?"

The Preejhna signaled to the helmsman. In a moment the shuttle lifted away as if it had been sucked into a vacuum. The next thing the viewing screen showed was the bright arc of the planet's skirting as they pulled away from the atmosphere.

"Please sit down," the commander told Serassan. They took seats across from each other. "I want to know your honest opinion about this mission."

The tall Estronian clasped his grayish fingers and looked his commander sternly in the eye. "The Terrans need our help." His large slanted blue eyes shifted past her, toward Earth's sloping rim. "They are on the brink of disaster, as we and others have known for quite some time."

He looked back at her and continued. "It is also true that we need Terrans. Through our mutual need of each other, we can help a few of them, and perhaps fulfill Estron's mission as well."

The Preejhna grimaced. "You speak of *need*." She stood up and paced the floor. "It has come to my attention, Serassan, that there are those among the crew who would take advantage of our role as *saviors* in order to fulfill their own selfish needs." She stopped pacing to stare at him. "I am not accusing *you,* of course. I've always trusted and respected you, Serassan. Some of your fellow guides, however ..."

The tall Estronian stroked the patch of grayish skin that connected his colossal head to the narrow shoulders. "Are you expressing doubt that we can carry out this mission, commander?"

"I have little doubt, Serassan. However, I *do* wonder sometimes if we are doing the right thing."

"But we have come this far." Serassan's deep blue eyes widened. This was not good that the Preejhna was having doubts—not at this late stage of the mission. He had already begun taking preparations for his physical transformation.

The Preejhna stood with her thin back to him as she stared at the screen. The ship was leaving Earth behind. "You have already made contact with your Terrans," she stated. "The stage is being set. Your physiological and biochemical transition has already begun. Yet it is not too late for us to abandon the mission." She slowly turned around to face him, her face giving nothing away.

"Our mission is in an ethical one," Serassan insisted, "a merciful one. Are you forgetting that there are those who would *directly* interfere with Earth's politics? We and other members in the Federation have been fighting to keep the perpetrators from meeting their goals. It is not as though we are changing anything overall."

"This entire situation is so … so volatile." The Preejhna shook her head sadly. Then she sighed. "I suppose you are right. We must do our part to help. Yet we risk so *much*."

"But what do we risk?" demanded Serassan.

She studied him a moment, then replied, "Trust."

"Eventually we will have their trust, commander."

"Then, to be sure we have it, none of us must show weakness." The Preejhna's voice became harsh. "If the Terrans suspect that our intentions are dishonorable... "

Serassan jumped up from his seat. "I beg your pardon. How can you say that? The Earth Star mission is saving a chosen number of otherwise damned individuals ..."

"That is all!" interrupted the Preejhna in her sharp voice. "I did not intend to argue with you, Serassan. Leave with this advice. Any guide who uses this mission as a vent for his sexual frustrations will answer to the high command."

Without further comment, the tall Estronian sighed, then turned and departed. Preejhna Chiyuub watched the hatch close behind him. She suspected the helmsman of harboring an amused reaction, but as she turned around to probe his thoughts she found he had instinctively blocked his mind.

— 2 —

The Man in the Next Seat

The auditorium was filling up fast. Johanna Dobbs glanced at her watch. Six minutes before eight. It was close to curtain time, yet people continued to pour down the aisles, and the ushers were busy helping patrons find their seats.

"Quite a crowd tonight," Manley murmured beside her.

Johanna smiled at her brother and leafed through her program. "Imagine a Russian ballet company coming to *our* little city," she commented.

Her brother sighed indifferently. It was obvious to Johanna that Manley would rather be at home right now, in front of the television. "One ballet group is like any other," he mumbled.

"Oh, but you're wrong," said Johanna. "They're on tour from the Soviet Union. They're one of the top ballet companies in the world."

Manley grunted.

Johanna closed her program. She had to admit, it had been unexpected when Manley called her that afternoon. "Come on, get out of the house. It'll do you a world of good," he had said over the phone. Hadn't it been only this morning she had read in the paper that the ballet was in town, and hadn't she wished there was some way she could attend?

"Some customer gave me the tickets," Manley had explained on their way to the Civic Center. "Even when I told the guy the ballet isn't my idea of an entertaining evening, he insisted I take them. And I knew Doris wouldn't want to go. You know how *she* is."

Doris was Manley's wife. Johanna considered her sister-in-law to be uncultured and frumpy. Why Manley had married Doris in the first place was beyond Johanna's realm of logic. Manley might prefer a basketball game over the ballet, but at least he attempted to show a slight interest for Johanna's sake. Doris was just plain ignorant.

"Manley, it was very thoughtful of you to invite me," said Johanna. "You know I love the ballet."

"Well, I knew you'd get a kick out of going," he replied. "Otherwise I might have gone and traded the tickets in."

Johanna couldn't help wondering why someone would give Manley tickets to the ballet. She watched him out of the corner of her eye. He still treated her as if she were the skinny, frail, dark-haired 12-year-old she had been when their parents had been killed in an auto accident.

Eleven years her senior, Manley still took care of her. At 45 he was overweight and balding. He worked across town as a salesman at a used car lot. That's where he had gotten the tickets for tonight's performance.

Johanna reached for her coat, which she had laid over the empty seat next to her, as someone pressed in from the aisle. Glancing up, she noticed a tall man in a brown suit. His hair was coarse and black. He sat down in the seat next to her and for a second their eyes met. She noticed the wide-set, almost slanted look. The deep blue color seemed unusual for some reason. He smiled at her warmly.

Startled, Johanna returned the smile, then quickly looked at the program in her lap.

"What?" Manley nudged her with his elbow.

Johanna turned to her brother. "Nothing. Everything's fine."

"You sure?"

Before she could reassure him, the lights in the auditorium dimmed and the murmur of the patrons died down. Johanna directed her attention to the stage as the curtains parted and the house went dark. A chill darted up her spine. She could hardly wait for it to begin.

She noticed the stranger next to her sat very still. Apparently no one had come with him. She wondered why he had come alone. Then some familiar strains of Tchaikovsky pulled her from the distraction of the tall man's presence. Johanna soon lost herself in the ballet.

Intermission followed the first act. As the house lights came on, Manley yawned in his seat. People started to get up and to saunter out to the lobby for refreshments. "Maybe I ought to give Doris a call," said Manley. "She'll be mad as hell having to get up to answer the phone, but at least she'll know we're thinking of her."

Not we, thought Johanna. *Leave the 'we' out, Manley.* It was then that Johanna noticed the seat next to her was vacant. She had been so totally absorbed in the ballet, she hadn't noticed the tall stranger get up and leave.

"I think I'll stretch my legs." Manley eased his way out to the aisle.

Johanna sat back and crossed her legs. Watching the couples, both young and old, she wondered what it would have been like had she come with someone other than her brother. Suppose she had come as the guest of the tall man who had sat down beside her? When had he left? It seemed strange that she hadn't even noticed that.

She evened out her skirt over her knees and examined her legs. She had nice legs. Maybe when that tall man returned to his seat he would notice. What was she thinking? *Oh Johanna, you dimwit. You're 34 years old, going on 90. Men don't notice you anymore. None have ever been good enough for you, didn't you learn that a long time ago? The only one who ever treated you decently was Manley.*

If there was one thing Johanna could count on, it was her brother. He was always there for her. When something went wrong with the car, or the plumbing, or the time the furnace's pilot light had gone out, Manley was only a phone call away. He had taken care of her since she was a little girl. He had been more father and mother to her combined than her own foster parents.

Marrying Doris had been his biggest mistake. Funny, Manley had never seen it that way. He had met Doris in the used car lot, of all places. She had bought a used car from Manley. Two weeks later they were man and wife. Only Doris hadn't realized at the time she would have to share Manley's devotion with Manley's sister. That did not go over well, Johanna remembered. The resentment between her sister-in-law and herself had been present since Manley's wedding day.

Johanna uncrossed her legs as Manley squeezed past her to go back to his seat. He had changed his mind about calling home.

"It's too bad Doris didn't come," Johanna fibbed.

Manley sat down. "Oh? Is it that good?"

"It's *excellent*." It had been so long since Johanna had been to the ballet, anything would seem better than average. She glanced to her side to find no sign of the tall man. People were on their way back to their seats. In a couple of minutes the second act would begin.

"If you say so." Manley folded his arms and looked bored.

Johanna glanced around, then said, "If you don't mind, I think I'm going to find the restroom." She took her purse, stood up and started for the aisle.

When Johanna came out of the ladies' room, she was alone. The hall was dark and deserted except for the concessionaire and an usher standing with his back toward her at the door to the auditorium. Music played and she realized the second act must have already started.

11

The usher stopped her as she attempted to pass him. "Excuse me, ma'am," he whispered. He placed a restraining hand on her sleeve. "Intermission before Act III is about to begin. If you could wait just one minute, you won't disturb anyone."

Johanna stared at the young man. "Act III? But didn't we just have intermission?" she asked.

The usher gave her a blank look and glanced at his watch. "Half an hour ago."

How could she have missed the whole second act? All she had done was visit the restroom. She hadn't been gone more than two minutes.

The scene ended and the audience filled the auditorium with resounding applause as the house lights came on again. Johanna brushed past the usher and zigzagged her way through the slow charge of people heading for the lobby. When she got to her row, she found Manley looking distraught.

"Johanna, where were you?"

She let some people out before she slipped into her place. She noticed the seat where the tall man had sat was still vacant.

"Are you all right?" Manley's look of concern startled Johanna.

"Perfectly," she replied.

"When you didn't come back to your seat, I started to get worried about you. Were you in the bathroom all this time?"

"What do you mean *all this time?*" Johanna noticed a lot of people getting up to stretch their legs. "I wasn't gone more than..."

"But you missed the whole second act," Manley cried.

"That's impossible!"

Manley shook his head stubbornly. "I was ready to go check on you."

"Manley, I don't know what you're talking about."

Her brother sighed in futility as she scanned her program. She couldn't believe she had been gone more than a few minutes. She glanced at her watch and her breath caught in her throat. It was past 9:30. How could it be that late?

"Are you feeling all right? Do you want to go home?" asked Manley.

Johanna stared into his caring brown eyes and, for the first time in her life, wondered if she was in her right mind. Thinking back to her trip to the restroom, she discovered she didn't remember any details of what she had done. "Well ... now that you mention it, I ... I do feel kind of strange," she murmured. She was on the verge of letting Manley talk her into leaving when suddenly the man whose seat was next to hers returned. As he lowered himself into place, his sleeve bumped her elbow.

"Oh, pardon me," he said in a pleasant, deep tone with a foreign accent.

Johanna turned to the tall stranger. Her pulse raced as her eyes met his and their penetrating depth. There was a familiar, kind look in them that seemed to hold her. Finally, Johanna was able to tear her gaze back to her hands and her lap.

"Please pardon me for being so bold," the man said. She detected more of the foreign accent. Middle Eastern, perhaps? She couldn't tell. "It's just that I ..." He didn't finish. Instead, he cleared his throat and stared ahead. "Are you enjoying the ballet?" he concluded.

Johanna wished he had finished what he had started to say. It seemed he had been on the verge of saying something she had always wanted to hear. *It's just that I ... never saw anyone as beautiful as you,* or ... *I can't take my eyes off of you. Please tell me your name.* But he was simply a stranger trying to make polite conversation.

When she didn't reply right away, he turned and smiled. "Well, how are you liking it?" he asked gently.

Johanna felt a tingle. "I'm enjoying it immensely," she told him.

"Well, are you ready, Johanna? Let's go." Manley stood up.

Johanna frowned at her brother. "But, Manley ..."

"Johanna, you said you felt ..."

"I want to *stay.*" Johanna couldn't help but notice the tall man watching them. "I feel fine now. Really."

A loud sigh of defeat escaped Manley as he sat back down.

There was a scuffle behind the curtains just as the music to the third act began. Somebody stopped the recording, and the audience began to mumble.

"I wonder what's happening," commented Johanna.

Manley stuck out his lower lip and shrugged. The man sitting next to Johanna stood up and left once again. Johanna watched him as he made his way to the aisle and out. It seemed he sure couldn't sit still for very long. Strange, but pleasant. No, *intriguing.* And very *sexy.* What was she thinking? *Such thoughts!* What was happening to her?

Someone came out on stage just then and announced that one of the leading ballerinas had become ill and there would be a substitute in the evening's program. Within minutes the music began again. But Johanna watched the rest of the ballet in a fog. The tall man did not return to his seat again, and she grew unusually tired. She was actually glad when it came time for Manley to drive her home.

"Now, are you sure you're all right?" Manley sat in the driver's seat with the motor idling as Johanna stepped out of the car.

"Don't worry about me, Manley." She waved him off, and Manley's car drove slowly away. The snow was still falling from that afternoon, and had accumulated a couple of inches. Johanna went inside and took off her coat.

The house she lived in was a rather drab, two-story Victorian—one of the oldest in the neighborhood. She had plenty of room, even if it wasn't fancy. It was here that she worked, giving music lessons during the day, composing at night. The outside world did not lure her away from where she was comfortable and secure.

Johanna did not feel like turning on the set to see what the late movie was tonight. As she was getting out of her clothes, she happened to notice her reflection in the bedroom mirror. She walked over and studied herself. Could she have been a ballerina? The slender figure, the narrow neck ... except for the crow's feet under the gentle brown eyes, and the gently bulging thighs, she might pass for someone in her 20s. But heck, she was too short to be a ballerina. Still ... Johanna gathered up her dark hair and pulled it tight so that her forehead was bare and her triangular face stood out.

Ridiculous, Johanna, you look absolutely silly. She let her hair fall to its natural state, just touching her shoulders, then shook her head. She reached for the brush on her dresser top and began stroking. That's when she noticed something wasn't quite right.

"What is *this?*" she murmured aloud and replaced the brush. She leaned toward the mirror and touched the area on her face just under her nostrils. *That* had never been there before, at least not that she had noticed. A tiny white slit showed from just beneath her nose, exactly in the center. Strange that she had not seen it before. What could it have been from? Why, it was a scar! It looked as if someone had taken a knife and carefully parted her nostrils. She was not imagining it. It was definitely a scar. But how had she gotten it? Was it possible it had always been there, since she was a child, and she had just now noticed it?

"It must have been there are all along," reasoned Johanna. Pulling on her nightgown, she dismissed the discovery as one of life's trivialities, unaware of how much—even at this moment—it would change her life.

— 3 —

Speak No Evil

Johanna opened her eyes and greeted the light of day. She had finally succeeded at getting some sleep. It seemed she had lain awake most the night, unable to settle down. As tired as she had been, her dreams were one series of disturbing images after another. Parts of the ballet had replayed in her mind, complete with orchestra. Then she would see the face of the dark-haired stranger whose seat had been next to hers. He kept invading her dreams.

Underneath her bed were the fur-lined slippers she wore first thing in the morning. Johanna filled them with her feet, then reached for her robe. Suddenly an image of the tall stranger bending over her face with a small glittering object caused her to shudder. She blinked her eyes and clutched the robe to her bosom. It seemed so real, like a memory. Yet it had only been her dream. She strained to recall more, but fragments surfaced, then sank again before she could make any sense out of them.

In the kitchen Johanna turned on her radio. She enjoyed listening to the beautiful music station. Strains of *Shangri-La* played while she emptied stale water from her tea kettle. While the new water heated on the stove, Johanna went to the front door to get her newspaper. A cold blast of air swept in as she stepped outside.

Children with lunch pails and backpacks passed by on the sidewalk on their way to school. The bus stop was only a block from her house. Johanna saw Mrs. Scott, the neighbor lady, shoveling snow off the sidewalk in front of the house next door. She had a lot of energy for a woman close to 80. Mrs. Scott wore a gray tweed coat with a scarf on her head.

Johanna picked up the rolled-up newspaper as two little girls walked by on their way to school. They laughed, and she wasn't sure, but it sounded like

15

they were speaking Russian, or Portuguese, or Swahili. She looked up at them in surprise. As their voices faded, she shrugged. Probably a class assignment. Amazing what they taught kids in the lower grades these days.

Mrs. Scott spotted Johanna and waved.

"Good morning, Vera," Johanna called out to her. Mrs. Scott cocked her head and cupped a mittened hand to her ear. Johanna called out a little louder, "I just said good morning!"

When there was still no response, she continued, "It's a beautiful morning, isn't it? The sun's sparkling on the snow. The air is so crisp, and the sky is radiant."

Mrs. Scott just stared at her, not moving a muscle. Johanna shivered and went back into the house with her paper. It seemed the least Mrs. Scott could have done was say good morning back to her. It wasn't like the neighbor woman to react in that strange way. She was usually over friendly, if anything.

The tea kettle let loose with its shrill whistle. Johanna laid the paper on the table and chose a mug from the cupboard. She hummed to the radio as she made the coffee. Today was Wednesday. That meant she had only two pupils coming in the afternoon for piano lessons. She had most of the day to herself and could spend as much or as little time as she wanted on her composition.

She carried the coffee to the table and set it down next to the morning paper. At first, she thought her eyes had blurred, but when she looked again, she realized she couldn't read a word that was printed.

The headline read:

Mmev shasrik xigir tw plujyipeqkenl

The picture of the President shaking hands with the Chinese ambassador was clear, but the words under it were meaningless. She couldn't even pronounce them. She grabbed up the paper and her eyes scanned the page. The columns of words were mixed up and undecipherable.

Abandoning her cup of coffee, Johanna whipped through page after page of the entire edition, but nothing was readable—not even a single ad. There wasn't a thing she could comprehend.

"What kind of a joke is this?" Johanna sank into a chair at the kitchen table. It was as though the typesetting machines had gone berserk at the *City Times*. But then ... suddenly she chuckled and sighed with relief. "Of course ... Manley." He often teased her about the time she spent working on crossword puzzles. He must have gotten up early and planted this bogus paper on her doorstep. That was it, she was certain. "He's probably home right now, chuckling to himself," she said.

She drew the coffee cup to her lips. Doris might have put him up to it, yet Johanna figured Doris didn't have the brains to think up something this crafty.

She examined the front page of the paper. "But how did he ... where could he have ... oh, what it must have cost him!"

She was still chuckling over the practical joke when the telephone rang. Johanna answered it. "Hello," she said into the receiver.

"*Juxbrilkur yopchashxh.*"

"*What?*" Johanna pulled the phone away from her ear.

Then, realizing whose voice it was, she burst out laughing. "Oh hello, Manley. I should have known that it was you. Are you crazy? April first is still two months away. How did you get off playing a joke like that on your only sister?"

"*Snofguget havnuxork, whurfmeeb shtatsdenfilo looperhank!*"

Johanna quit laughing. "Manley, what do you do, make it up as you go, or did you have it all written down on a piece of paper?"

More jargon followed, and Manley's voice grew louder and more forceful. Johanna pulled the receiver from her ear until he calmed down. Then, with a sigh, she spoke into the phone, "Manley ... that's enough. Be serious now. The joke's over."

"*Swoffensockfeld brorgen yulp!*"

Johanna started to lose her patience. "Knock it off, Manley!"

There was silence for a moment, and then she heard the voice of her sister-in-law, Doris Dobbs. "*Quispenulper marbenvanch hulpfiss,*" the woman blurted.

"Doris? Oh no, not you, too. I should have known you were in on it. Doris, enough is enough. Let me speak to Manley."

"*Thratenbelk xastupdig klojmid renkelstimp!*" Doris cried in alarm.

Then Manley came back on the line, yelling and carrying on worse than before. Finally, Johanna could take no more of his nonsense and hung up.

"They're perverted!" she cried. She went back to her coffee, but her mood was broken. The whole thing was rather disgusting. It had been a joke gone sour, and now there was no crossword to do.

She went to get a magazine, so she could have it at the table while she sipped at the coffee. She stopped before she reached the table. Every printed word on the magazine cover was scrambled and undecipherable, just like the newspaper. She paged through it and found the same.

Johanna dropped the magazine as if it were full of maggots. She picked up some other publications. All of them were the same way. She recognized which magazines they were from their colors and pictures—none of *that* had changed—yet every printed word was in jargon.

Next, she went to her bookshelf, desperate in her search. She knew the covers. Her beloved *Tales of Canterbury* was now *Ɀmƿreggooghsƙy Ʂawziƙ Ʋrauƿlooch*. Her record albums—her favorite works of Beethoven—all encoded. There was no way Manley could have accomplished all of this.

Johanna could only stand and stare. A wave of fear clutched her as she eased herself onto the couch. "Something is going on here," she murmured to herself. *Either that, Johanna, or you are going mad.* There had to be some logical explanation for all this.

At last, she gathered her wits enough to walk back into the kitchen. When she picked up her coffee cup, the black liquid within was cold. She took one bitter sip, then poured the rest down the drain.

"I'll try Manley again," Johanna decided. She went to the phone and started to dial, but stopped when she saw the strange marks where the numbers used to be. A cry escaped her throat, and her breath came irregularly as she tried to remember what the numbers were on the dial.

Trembling fingers worked out a pattern, but as she lifted the receiver to her ear, an annoying whine sounded. Johanna slammed the phone down, then hesitantly lifted it again.

"I must talk to someone," she murmured, "*anyone!*" She knew if she could hit the zero, she'd get an operator. After two attempts, Johanna heard the familiar ringing tone. Someone answered almost immediately.

"*Ɀhurwasqbrl,*" the female voice said.

Startled, Johanna didn't know how to respond.

"*Ǥeenstrƿlimz xabfabujrƿ bwunhrawj,*" the voice continued.

Johanna's voice cracked as she replied, "Operator? Please ... help me. I ..."

A gush of gibberish broke in. Johanna dropped the phone back into place and felt hot tears on her eyelids. She struggled to retain control of her emotions. This was no time to go to pieces.

Maybe if she went back to bed and got up again, she'd discover all of this had just been a bad dream. It couldn't be real. She did go back to bed, but she didn't sleep. She lay for what seemed hours and listened to the faraway music from the kitchen radio.

The doorbell rang at 4 o'clock that afternoon. Johanna had managed to collect her wits enough to get dressed. She hadn't been hungry enough to fix herself lunch and she hadn't eaten any breakfast, so now her stomach churned. She shut off the kitchen radio. The hard clicking of her heels on the bare kitchen floor echoed throughout the house as she anxiously made her way to answer the front door.

The Gilchrist children stood in their winter coats, hats and mittens, with their piano books under their arms. They looked up at Johanna in expectation. Johanna noticed Mrs. Gilchrist sitting in her car, and stepped out onto the porch to wave at the children's mother. She tried to get the woman's attention, but Mrs. Gilchrist wasn't looking in Johanna's direction as she backed down the driveway.

Turning to her pupils, Johanna held the door open. "Donny ... Margaret, come in." They said nothing, but stared up at her silently. "How are you today?" She was afraid to ask.

Neither of them answered her. Johanna beckoned them in and closed the door. They made no move to take off their coats.

Johanna swallowed the lump in her throat as she forced herself to remain calm. "Well, who's going to be first today? Donny, did you practice this week?"

The little boy's mouth dropped open and his sister looked from Johanna to her brother with wide eyes.

Johanna's nerves tightened, but she tried to act normal. "Oh, I see. Well, Margaret, we'll start with you. I know you always practice. Take off your coats, children. Come into the drawing room and we'll get started."

When the children remained rooted to the floor, Johanna stared at them in disbelief. What was going on here? Why did she have this feeling that something dreadful was going to happen? When she reached out and tried to lead Margaret by the shoulder, the little girl resisted and clung to the arm of her brother. Both stared up in fear at Johanna.

A quaver crept into Johanna's voice. "What is the matter with you children today?" she chided. The Gilchrist children were usually anything but timid. Margaret, especially, loved to show off in front of her brother how well she had prepared for her piano lesson.

Donny swallowed, then spoke, "*Ĕmdeerst frícklope gruden*," he said in a small voice.

Margaret's lip trembled, then she told him, "*Ozten seegelstimp wooshtreb plafften.*"

Johanna felt goose bumps break out on her arms. "Oh my God!" she exclaimed. Her hands felt her face. "It can't be."

Margaret started to cry.

Johanna reached out to comfort her student. "Oh no, Margaret, please don't cry."

But Margaret sobbed louder. Donny's eyes bulged in terror. Suddenly, they both dropped their piano books on the living room floor and ran out the front door. Johanna watched them stumble down the porch steps and run across the snow-covered lawn of her front yard.

"Donny! Margaret!" she called after them. It was no use. They were already in the next block. She stooped to pick up the John Schaum Book I and II, printed in scrambled letters.

The telephone rang. At first, she was eager to answer it, to talk to someone—*anyone*—who could speak to her in a civil tongue. She hurried over and snatched up the receiver. She was afraid to speak. Suddenly, it seemed the worst thing she could possibly do was talk.

Manley's voice on the other end flung out sentences in such mixed-up language that Johanna dropped the phone and watched it dangle on its cord.

Her mind in a frenzy, Johanna stood and stared at the room around her. What should she do? Something was terribly wrong here. The Gilchrist kids had not understood a word she had said to them. Manley was on the line, yelling.

"I'm losing my mind!" Johanna screamed.

She needed to calm herself, so she raced over to her piano and plunged into her latest composition. She played faster and harder. She was soon pounding the keyboard. She squeezed her eyes shut, forcing only the sound of the music through her harried brain. Sweat dripped down her back. Her muscles craved rest and her fingers burned as the ivory grew slippery beneath her touch.

She ended the composition in a series of banging chords. She was exhausted, and when she finally let go, she slumped forward. Her nose touched the black keys and she felt the blood surge through her arms. Remembering the predicament she was in, she fell into sobbing. She was unable to erase from her memory those awful nonsensical words, those puzzled, frightened looks. She understood now why Mrs. Scott had only stared at her this morning, and why the girls on their way to the bus stop had seemed so strange.

Not much later, a knock on the front door startled Johanna back to the present. Sniffling, she got up from the piano bench. She wiped her nose and cheeks with her sleeve as she stumbled to the door. Maybe the Gilchrist children had come back for their piano books, or perhaps it was Mrs. Gilchrist already. How would she ever explain that Donny and Margaret had run away? Then she heard Manley's voice calling from outside.

"Oh Manley, thank God!" Johanna opened the door to find both her brother and Doris standing on the porch. Both looked concerned.

"Manley, I don't know what's happening to me. I've never been so scared!"

Her brother and his wife exchanged puzzled glances, then slowly entered the house. Doris, in her squat fashion, sort of cowered behind Manley, who reached out to Johanna. Sympathy flooded his face.

"Manley, speak to me!" Johanna sobbed as she fell into his arms. "Tell me I'm the same as before! Oh Manley, please help me!"

Manley turned to the woman behind him and muttered some meaningless words. Her brother led Johanna to the couch and made her lie down. Apparently Doris was using the telephone. Amidst her cries of frustration, Johanna watched as her brother and his wife merely exchanged knowing, sad looks.

— 4 —

The Losing Battle

Barbara Wetzel, M.D., stepped out of the elevator and approached the nurses' station on the east wing. It had been a long day and she had hoped to cut out early. What a relief it would be when the new doctor came on staff. Sixteen-hour days were for residents and interns, not 32-year-old women psychiatrists. She had been on her way out, in fact, when they paged her to Admitting.

Barbara swept her hand through a lock of light-colored hair that had escaped the barrette, then reached for the chart on the counter. The patient was in isolation. That was standard practice when someone was admitted against their will. Tucking the chart under her arm, Dr. Wetzel headed down the hall to the room where the new patient waited.

When she had spoken with the patient's brother, he had appeared extremely upset. "Please, doctor, you've got to help my sister," he had implored. "Yesterday she was as normal as you or I. Today ... she's a babbling idiot!" The initial examination had ruled out stroke. Obviously, this was a case of sudden hysteria. Something must have occurred to bring on the condition. All Barbara had to do was find out what that was.

She came to the room and slowly opened the door. The patient sat on the bed. The woman, in her mid-30s, had dark brown hair, parted in the center and drawn back. Her startled brown eyes met Barbara's, then turned away as if in embarrassment. There were some telltale signs of crying on the patient's cheeks, and her eyelids appeared puffy and red.

Dr. Wetzel glanced down at her chart. She read the name—Johanna Dobbs. The patient was 34 years old. Occupation: concert pianist, retired.

"Miss Dobbs? My name is Doctor Wetzel. I'm here to help you ..."

Guttural, incomprehensible sounds gushed from the patient's lips as she reached out for the doctor.

"*Yik pulkgrib nooklduhl shnowtztrumf!*"

Barbara drew back in surprise, but immediately composed herself. The brother had mentioned a babbling idiot. An interesting symptom indeed. Dr. Wetzel wrote on her chart, "*Patient is speaking in unintelligible syllables.*" Then she said out loud, "Tell me, Miss Dobbs, can you understand what I am saying?"

More gibberish burst forth and the patient in the gray hospital gown displayed a look of frustration, even anger. Miss Dobbs pointed to the door. More sounds emerged from her throat.

Barbara decided to make a stab at conversation. "If you can understand me, Miss Dobbs, please give me a sign. Raise your hand to show you understand me," she directed.

Miss Dobbs continued in the strange tongue. Her pleading looks and gestures convinced Barbara that this was a patient completely out of touch with reality. *Just like someone else*, she thought. Had she come across evidence of a brand new mental disorder? Barbara scribbled on the chart, her mind racing. This was a fantastic opportunity. One case had not been sufficient cause, but *two* ... She smiled as she imagined the response from her colleagues when she wrote the article on Wetzel's Syndrome.

The babbling continued, rising in volume and intensity. Barbara started for the door. Suddenly, the patient rushed past her in an attempt to flee from the room. Barbara had been expecting the move, however, and caught Miss Dobbs by the arm. Without hesitation, Dr. Wetzel left the room and locked the patient safely within. As she finished making the entries in the chart, she could hear the door knob rattling and the muffled cries of nonsensical sounds coming from the isolation room. This was indeed a wonderful coincidence. What did Miss Dobbs have in common with Mr. Piedmont?

With renewed hope, Barbara held her blond head high and walked on down the hallway.

The room Johanna was in had bare white walls and no windows. She detested the ugly gray gown the nurse had dressed her in. She knew exactly where she was. Manley had brought her to Reeve Memorial State Hospital. She had been too exhausted and upset from crying to resist. What use was it to protest? They couldn't understand her, no more than she could make out anything anyone else said.

When the woman doctor had come to the room, Johanna had hoped by some miracle of fate she could make somebody understand her predicament.

The doctor was fairly young, blond and attractive. Her plump cheeks gave her a baby doll look, yet her manner had been professional. When Johanna tried to explain who she was and that all she wanted was to go home, the doctor had reacted as if Johanna had laid a curse on her.

Now she felt trapped, a prisoner in this room. For how long? Where was Manley? Why had he left her here? Whatever had happened to her, Johanna did not know. She felt lost, betrayed, confused.

After the doctor left her alone in the room again, Johanna wondered if she would ever see the outside of these walls again. The idea horrified her. She knew she wasn't crazy now, but if she stayed in the hospital, she'd go crazy for sure. Of that she was certain.

"This can't be happening to me," she said aloud. "I don't belong in the hospital. I'm the same as before. It's the rest of the world that's flipped out." Yet she could not erase the small patch of doubt that was festering in the back of her mind.

Within minutes a nurse and an orderly came to Johanna's room with a wheelchair. Her first reaction was one of hope. Was she to be released? Was Manley waiting outside to take her home? She eagerly cooperated as they seated her and rolled her out of the room. But it soon became apparent that the hospital had no intention of releasing her.

Johanna was taken to an elevator and the nurse pushed the arrow that pointed upward. When Johanna began to protest, the orderly held her down. She tried to convince him and the nurse that she didn't want to go up, but they spoke to each other in words that didn't make sense.

When the elevator doors opened, the nurse called out and two more orderlies appeared to keep Johanna from breaking away. Then they accompanied her on her journey to what she gathered must be the hospital's psychiatric ward. A gate separated the hall from the rest of the floor. They passed a room in which a woman was causing a commotion. The yelling frightened Johanna.

Her new room was larger than the one downstairs. The wallpaper was bright and colorful, and there was a window, two beds, a dresser, table, overhead lamp, television, and a tiny restroom. Johanna noticed right away the bars that covered the outside of the window. "Oh no." She began to wail as tears burned her chapped cheeks. She realized there was no escape here either. She could cry and plead until she was exhausted. No one listened or understood. No one cared. The nurse helped Johanna into her bed and offered a pill and a glass of water, which Johanna refused.

After much tongue-wagging, another nurse soon arrived with a hypodermic needle. Johanna shrieked when she saw it. She hated needles, but she hated the thought of being drugged even more. What would she find when she woke up?

It was no use fighting. The nurses held her down and injected her. She barely felt the sting in her arm, and before she knew it, weariness overcame her and she sank as she hit the pillow.

When Johanna awoke, the light of morning flowed in through the window of her room. She was groggy and at first a little confused about where she was. She could hear the patter of footsteps outside the room, then realized she was still in the hospital. She had slept uninterrupted the whole night, and now her stomach churned for something to eat.

A rustle of movement in the room startled Johanna. Propping her head on her elbow, she saw that somebody was asleep in the other bed. Johanna sat up and tried to see who it was. The yellow bed quilt covered a rather large woman with a mess of light brown hair. A fat white arm lay prostrate near the head, and the sound of deep breathing signified the roommate was still asleep.

Johanna laid back and sighed. She reflected over her situation and wondered if she would see Manley today. Would the blond woman doctor return? Was somebody going to try to help her, or was the whole thing useless? Perhaps she would spend the rest of her days in this hospital, or some institution like it.

"No! No ... I'm not crazy!" Johanna cried out. She closed her eyes and tried to think back to when it had all begun. Yesterday morning seemed an age ago. Everything had been normal until she had stepped outside onto her porch to get the morning paper, and had overheard the schoolgirls on their way to the bus stop. Then Mrs. Scott's stare. Then the scrambled newspaper gibberish ... the maddening phone call from Manley.

"What has happened to me?" Johanna clutched her head and felt her face. She was still the same person. She had to cling to that fact. Whatever altered state she was in, she was still Johanna Dobbs—not long ago a traveling concert pianist. Her hand slid over her lips and suddenly she remembered the scar below her nose. It hadn't been there two days ago. What did it mean?

"Ŝegyen grulƙ ... marʄzen xɦøøsɦ." The words had come from the woman in the other bed.

Johanna watched the woman sit up in her bed. "What? What did you say?" The woman had a large, round face with sunken gray eyes, thin lips, and a round nose. From the way the woman squinted at her, Johanna could tell that her roommate could not understand what she had said.

The woman spoke some more gibberish, and Johanna sighed helplessly. "Don't bother," she said. "I think you're going to find out that I'm not someone you can talk to."

The yellow bedspread flew back, and Johanna's large roommate plunged onto her bed in defiance. She muttered some words in anger, then turned her back on Johanna.

"Same to you," grumbled Johanna. The woman reminded her of a cousin she had. Maybe it was because she was fat, or perhaps it was the light brown hair that made Johanna think of Francine. She would probably never know the woman's true identity, so why not refer to her roommate as Francine?

"Francine," she called out, "oh, Francine ... what are you here for? I sure hope it's nothing too serious. I don't relish the idea of being in a psycho ward, you know."

The woman did not answer. She did not seem to get upset at all, and it felt good to Johanna to be able to say mean things that nobody could understand.

"Did anyone ever tell you how fat you are, Francine?" Johanna suddenly burst into laughter. This was absurd, but it released a lot of tension. "I mean, you are literally obese." She laughed louder.

Suddenly, she heard a chuckle from the other bed. Johanna waited to see if there would be further reaction. After a minute Francine chuckled again. Then the woman giggled and said something that must have been terribly amusing. Johanna couldn't understand a word, but Francine's laughter continued and it was contagious. When she glanced over at the fat woman on the other bed, their eyes met and suddenly both of them laughed. Johanna felt exhilarated at the release, but Francine just kept laughing, harder and harder.

"That's enough, Francine." Johanna fought to catch her breath. "Oh ... if Manley could see me now ... at the funny farm!" She finally managed to quit laughing, but Francine did not stop. Johanna could not imagine what was so funny that the woman had to keep laughing until she could hardly breathe.

Suddenly, the door opened and two nurses hurried toward Francine's bed. Johanna realized then that her roommate was in some kind of distress. The heavy woman gasped and wheezed as the nurses attempted to calm her down. After a moment, Johanna noticed Francine's laughter had turned to tears. The massive shoulders shook with each sob.

Nobody paid any attention to Johanna as she quietly got out of her bed and started for the door. She needed to find out where the exit was. Before she reached the door, however, one of the nurses lurched out, caught her arm and restrained her. Johanna tried to resist, but it only made the nurse angry. She was pushed into the small bathroom and could hear Francine still causing a commotion in their room. While Johanna took care of her personal needs, she wondered if it was going to be like this from now on. Would her every action be monitored by these policemen and women in white attire?

When Johanna returned to her bed, she found Francine had been sedated and was lying calmly on her back, her chest rising and falling with each breath. Her sunken eyes peered at Johanna, then turned to the ceiling. She seemed to be in a miserable state.

Before long, breakfast arrived on a tray. The attendant, a thin, red-haired woman dotted with freckles, drew the curtain around Francine's bed, which gave Johanna a welcome feeling of privacy. She ate because she was hungry, not having had anything since early yesterday. She wondered when someone would come and talk with her. She wanted to find out how long she would have to remain here. Could they treat her condition—if it was a condition? There must be some way she could rationally communicate with somebody.

When Freckles came for her tray, Johanna tried to ask questions, but the thin woman's eyes darted up and down suspiciously. Freckles paid no attention and left the room. When Johanna got up, she discovered the door was locked.

Once again, fear welled up inside Johanna. With her bodily needs satisfied for the time being, her predicament came back to haunt her. She banged on the door and called out for someone to come and help her. She wanted Manley. She cried her brother's name over and over, until she sank to her knees, sobbing. Loud snores from Francine's bed signified that her roommate was oblivious to Johanna's outcries.

After what seemed a long time, the door opened and Freckles picked her up and helped her to bed. Out came another hypodermic needle. Johanna squealed in protest, but soon lapsed into oblivion as black shadows swam before her eyes.

She was still under when the young woman doctor came to see her. Johanna was barely aware of the blond woman's presence, but she remembered the chubby-cheeked face and the mixed-up words that prodded her in an attempt to rouse her from the stupor. Johanna managed to mumble, "Sleep. I want to sleep," and "Manley. I want Manley. I want to go ... home." Then the doctor left and she slept on.

Another time she remembered Manley's face. Perhaps it had been only a dream, but she thought he had come to visit her. She also could hear the whiny voice of Doris in the room. Although she did not see her sister-in-law's pudgy face, the smell of cheap perfume confirmed Johanna's suspicion that Doris must have accompanied Manley on the visit. She wanted so desperately to talk to him, but she was so out of it, she couldn't even get any words out. And then he was gone.

Her dreams were scattered and nonsensical. She dreamed of the ballet at the civic center. She dreamed of sitting in the audience with Manley. They were waiting a long time for something to happen. The ballet had been delayed. Something had gone wrong backstage. Johanna dreamed that the audience was getting restless, so she climbed up on the stage and performed her composition on the piano.

Although she had played it perfectly many times before, in the dream she kept making mistakes. Her fingers found the piano keys much larger than normal. The black keys were too high and stretched her fingers until they hurt. Frustrated, Johanna began to cry. "I *can't*," she sobbed over and over.

Then she looked up and there, standing over her, was the tall, black-haired man who had sat next to her at the ballet. His deep blue eyes stared kindly into hers. "Don't be afraid," he said in a soothing voice. "This won't hurt, I promise you. It will all be over before you know."

His face was close—too close. She was afraid. His hand moved over her face, and then a curtain closed over her eyes. A prick above her lip caused Johanna to wake with a start.

— 5 —

A Cry For Help

It was morning again, but Johanna didn't know the day. Somehow it felt as though several days had passed since she had arrived in this room. She was groggy again and weak. Despair settled over her and she whimpered for several minutes before she heard sharp words thrown at her from the next bed. Francine was awake.

"I can't help it, Francine." Johanna sobbed. Hot tears streamed down her cheeks. "It's so awful. I don't want to be here. I don't want them to stick any more drugs into me."

Francine came over and stood over Johanna's bed, her large figure clad in a faded blue robe. There was pity on the heavy woman's pudgy face as she stared down at Johanna, who continued to cry. Hesitantly, Francine put her hand on Johanna's head and smoothed her hair. She mumbled a few words of jargon, but the tone of her voice was unmistakable: Francine was expressing human compassion.

"Oh, Francine ..." Johanna managed a smile as the heavy hand with stubby fingers lifted from her head. "Thank you. I don't know what your problem is, or why you are here, but I'm glad I have someone to talk to." She looked up into the deeply set gray eyes. "I know you can't understand me."

Johanna sat up in bed and rubbed her face.

Francine continued to stare at her. "*Trumpledeck shissjdeguass*," she told Johanna softly.

In the days that followed, Johanna cried and shrieked in protest whenever the hospital staff came to her room. In vain she pleaded with the woman doctor, but when that got her nowhere, a nurse would show up and inject her with another sedative. During these phases of semi-consciousness, Johanna was aware that Manley visited her. He would sit by her bed and hold her hand. She noticed the smell of cheap perfume was no longer in the air. Apparently Doris had stopped visiting altogether.

Afraid that her brother would also lose interest in her and quit coming, Johanna knew she had to do something. She was sick of lying in this bed hour after hour, day after day, controlled by chemicals. All she wanted was to scream and make herself heard.

She fantasized an escape, where she evaded the nurses, leaped from the room, and ran down the hall toward the nearest window. There she would crash through the glass and fling her body, with its flapping gray gown, downward against the ice-covered pavement of the parking lot.

Johanna clenched her fists and teeth. She knew she was too weak to get out of this bed, let alone ward off the hypodermic needle. Yet she couldn't go on this way another day. She was already going insane, thinking of suicide.

Then, it finally dawned on Johanna that if she remained calm and passive, the injections might stop. Weren't they drugging her because of her loud outbursts and panic attacks? What if she cooperated? What if she went along with this crazy scenario and simply gave in to despair?

"I'll stop. I'll be good. I'll do anything they want," Johanna cried desperately into her pillow that morning. "Just, please God, no more shots. No more drugs. I'll do what they want me to do. I'll shut up."

Johanna's plan of resignation worked. When the doctor came to her room on rounds, Johanna sat up in bed and stared calmly into space. She showed no resistance whatsoever as the nurse went through the morning ritual of washing. The woman doctor wrote lots of notes on her clipboard and smiled in a pleased way as if, at last, Johanna was making progress.

What progress? Johanna churned inside. She was not defeated. Not yet. She simply had to make the doctor and attendants think that she had given in to this insanity. She was determined to find some way out of this mess she was in, if she had to do it all alone. But Johanna knew she could do nothing if the drug treatments continued. So she submitted to the expectations of her caretakers. She would decide what to do when her head was clear and in the proper perspective.

That afternoon, after she was served lunch on a tray in her room, the skinny, red-haired attendant Johanna had named Freckles helped Johanna get dressed. Now, instead of the ugly gray gown, Johanna wore a beige type of leisure suit that zippered and hung on her slender figure slightly better than pajamas. She kept her slippers as Freckles helped her walk down the hall. They passed the nurses' station and came to a large room where many people were gathered. Johanna felt weak after her long confinement, but was ecstatic to find different walls, different faces. She guessed the room to be the recreation hall of the psychiatric ward. A male attendant with light-colored hair and a banana nose stood guard near the doorway and exchanged some banter with Freckles.

Francine was there, watching a soap opera on the color television. When Johanna came through the door, Francine looked up at her and smiled. She came over to greet Johanna and offered her hand. Johanna followed her roommate to an armchair in front of the TV viewing area. A large-bosomed African American woman with wild hair sat watching the show. Her huge dark cheeks sagged beneath blood-shot eyes and her mouth seemed to wear a permanent frown. She noticed Johanna approach and a spark of fear caused the lady to cringe.

Glancing around the room, Johanna studied the others. She was startled by a tall, lanky man with a crew cut, crawling along the floor in the far corner of the recreation hall. At first she thought he might be a maintenance man, but she could see right away that he wasn't right. She recognized the leisure suit that all the patients wore. He seemed unaware of anyone else in the room as he seemed to be collecting things on the floor.

A pale young man in his early 20s, with auburn hair and a dull look in his eyes, sat in a wooden rocker and rocked with his hands gripped tightly to the arms of the chair. He, too, seemed to be in a world of his own. Johanna noticed a man sitting at a card table who seemed to be puzzling over a deck of cards. He was about her age, she guessed. He had brown hair, a mustache, and appeared normal. She wondered why he was here.

Some chatter broke loose as Johanna saw a shriveled-up old lady with gray, unbrushed hair, calling out to a tiny, red-haired woman in her 40s. The old lady was wiry and quick, and moved in jerks. Her eyes darted suspiciously around the room, but she directed her speech toward the younger woman, who ignored the hag. The red-haired lady, in fact, held her thin head high and had a haughty air about her. She had been reading a book near the fireplace and now closed it tightly against her narrow breast. The old gray-haired lady began swinging her arms and growling, but the younger woman continued to ignore her.

Suddenly, Francine whimpered. Johanna turned her attention back to the television. A young female character was crying on TV. Johanna noticed Francine had tears running down her cheeks. As Francine continued to cry, Johanna's attention was drawn to the black lady next to her. A low moaning sound came from her thick lips. Soon they had a duet going, the black lady chanting in a sorrowful way, and Francine crying louder and holding her head. All this over a stupid soap opera?

Johanna looked to see if the banana-nosed attendant at the door would do anything about the crying women. Freckles had already left and Banana Nose paged through a magazine, unconcerned. This seemed to be standard behavior. At least the attendant was not interested in what was happening between Francine and the other lady.

Then, something caught Johanna's eye. In the back of the room, behind the card table where the normal-looking young man in his 30s was shuffling cards, Johanna saw an old upright piano. Her pulse quickened. "A piano! Oh my God." She immediately stood up and moved across the room. She hadn't touched a piano in weeks, it seemed. Her fingers ached to play it, just to run her hand up a scale or two.

Johanna sat down on the old rickety bench and stared lovingly at the keyboard. It was like meeting an old friend. A smile spread across her face as she lifted her hands to the ivory.

"Gaoohhhwww! Cheee-laaa! Mahupo queee. Stoobvudfack!"

Johanna shrieked in alarm. The rancid smell of urine struck her. She drew back as the shriveled-up, gray-haired lady shoved her. Another blow sent Johanna reeling off the piano bench. She landed on the hard oak floorboards, skinning her elbow. It burned as she scrambled up again. Johanna rubbed her arm as the old patient plunged down against the keyboard. Cacophonous tones chilled the room as the old lady pounded and pounded as hard as she could.

"Stop it!" Johanna cried out. "Please, don't pound!" She couldn't hear herself over the noise.

Everyone in the room looked in their direction. The old lady would not stop. She pounded the piano harder and harder.

Francine came over to see if Johanna was all right. The tears still streamed down Francine's cheeks. She sobbed as she pointed at the piano and shook her head. Francine appeared to be warning Johanna against any future attempts to play the piano, otherwise the shriveled-up old lady would go berserk. What a strange bunch this was.

As Johanna took her seat near the television, she scanned the room again and studied the different patients. Francine and the black lady cried harder, even though Johanna noticed the soap opera they had been watching was over and a game show was on. Why couldn't they stop crying? Francine, in particular, seemed to be getting worse, just like she had that day in their room when Johanna had first met her.

The man with the crew cut had worked his way over to the fireplace now and was busy picking up dust from the hearth. It was then that Johanna noticed a stout man she hadn't seen before, sitting quietly in a recliner next to the fireplace. This man was older, maybe 55 or 60, of medium height but round, with short reddish hair, a coarse red-gray beard, and wire-rimmed glasses. He sat reading, not too concerned about the other people in the room, and every so often he scribbled something in a notebook.

Francine's cries rose to screams. Some of the other patients began to react to the disturbance. The petite, red-haired lady shouted something and stuck her nose in the air. The black lady seemed to be pleading with Francine to quiet down. The normal-looking man playing cards just stared. He seemed to notice Johanna for the first time, but he didn't smile or acknowledge her look at all.

"Francine ... what's the matter?" Johanna stood up and went to her roommate. "Can I help? Calm down, Francine."

Her words meant nothing, it was obvious. Francine soon caught the sympathetic look in Johanna's eyes and her face exploded in anger. She jumped up and started running around the room. She wailed and she shouted and stomped her feet. Her crying had turned into a temper tantrum. Johanna shrank away out of fear.

The black woman started to chant. It reminded Johanna of a spiritual. The woman moaned louder and faster as Francine's screams mounted. Johanna huddled in her chair and pressed her hands against her ears. This was madness. These people were insane and they were driving her mad as well. She didn't belong here among them. Before long, Banana Nose returned to the room with a nurse, who removed Francine from the room. In a few moments, as Francine's screams diminished in the corridor, the recreation hall calmed down. Even the black woman's chantings subsided.

Hang on, Johanna, she told herself, *you've got to. You've got to adjust to this ... to these people, or you'll end up in isolation again. You can't let that happen. You've got to maintain your sanity.* But she wasn't sure she could do that. She knew it wasn't going to be an easy task, not with the constant influence of these weirdos around her.

Johanna came to the recreation hall every day. There wasn't much else for her to do because she soon grew tired of looking at books and magazines in her room, where all she could understand were the photos. Television upset her. The altered speech frustrated her. She longed for music, for the touch and sound of the piano. And each time she got close to the instrument, the old lady with the wrinkled skin and unbrushed gray hair came over and threw a fit.

Johanna did not want to cause a scene, but on the other hand, her need to play music was pressing. She listened to the radio whenever she could. Although she couldn't understand any of the talking, it was still her only link to her old world, the only thing that kept her from flipping out completely. She tried not to think of what lay ahead, what the future held in store for her. In the meantime, she felt cranky, unsettled, restless.

In the few brief days she had gone to the recreation hall, she learned the behavior patterns and eccentricities of some of the regular patients. It grew into a game. She gave the patients names, like she had Francine.

She named the big black lady Wanda, whom she guessed was suffering from paranoia. Wanda seemed to be very withdrawn. She regarded the others, including Johanna, as "suspicious." It was as though Wanda was afraid everyone was possessed of demons and wanted to hurt her. Wanda's closest friend was Francine, and together they would sit and watch soap operas most the day.

Francine was also Johanna's closest thing to a friend, yet Francine frightened her when she went into one of her wild episodes. Johanna came to the conclusion that her roommate must undoubtedly be a manic-depressive, or bi-polar—a person who is either very high or very low. That explained Francine's uncontrollable laughter, temper tantrums, and panicked crying spells. When Francine was "normal," she was the gentlest, sweetest, most compassionate person in the hospital.

After watching the petite lady with red hair and the snobbish expressions, Johanna came to refer to her as Her Highness. She couldn't think of any name other than Lady Jane. "Her Highness" fit the woman to a tee. She would have nothing to do with anybody. She acted as though she were some kind of queen, or untouchable. Johanna had heard of inferiority complexes, but obviously Her Highness was just the opposite. Johanna surmised that her family must have committed her because Her Highness was unbearable to live with.

Then there was the silly, tall man with the crew cut who crept along the floor. He wasn't always on the floor, hunting "woollies," as Johanna called them. Sometimes he sat or reclined, but he did not interact with the other patients. He seemed to have hallucinations at times, when he'd smile or giggle for no reason, and quite often he would carry on a conversation in gibberish, all by himself. Johanna decided to call him William.

The young man who rocked all day she named Charley. He was apparently autistic. Johanna wondered how long he had been that way. If he wasn't sitting in the rocking chair, he would pretend he was in one. He loved to rock back and forth ... rarely stopping.

The normal-looking man who had played cards by himself that first day was by no means normal, Johanna decided. She wasn't sure why he was in a psychiatric ward, but her guess was that he might have been a hostage at some time in his life. He acted normal until outsiders came to visit, or the doctor stopped in, or nurses wanted to help with something. Then he'd clam up and act very paranoid, as if they were going to torture him.

The old lady who hated the piano so much, Johanna decided to call Melody.

Melody had very violent tendencies. She was unpredictable and picked fights among the other patients. So far, Johanna had seen nothing too serious, but she avoided Melody as much as she could. The old hag frightened her more than any other patient in the room.

Then there was the older bearded man who sat with his pen and his notebook. He never said anything. He seemed content to sit and observe. Johanna caught him staring at her one afternoon, as if he was trying to figure out why she was here. She longed to converse with him, with *anybody!*

But she already knew it was a futile hope that anyone could understand a word she'd say. The few words she had spoken in the recreation hall had been during outbursts of violence or emotional disruptions on the part of other patients. She knew it was best not to stir things up by opening her mouth. She didn't have a name for this older gentleman. She was still thinking of one. Maybe one day she would approach him, though. He had such a kind look.

Manley came every afternoon to see her. She looked forward to his visits, but his attempts to talk with her upset them both. As she had with the woman doctor, Johanna soon gave up even trying to communicate anything to Manley. She let him sit and ramble on. He was probably telling about his day at the used car lot, or he was unloading all his troubles with his marriage. She didn't know. He always looked worried and this bothered her. She wanted to reassure him that she was still sane, but what was the use?

One morning, while Johanna was walking to the recreation hall, she heard a female voice cry out from one of the rooms. "Please! I'm telling you, I don't belong here!"

Johanna swung around and scanned the corridor in search of the room from which the voice had come.

"Let me out!" cried the female voice from the room.

"I hear you!" Johanna yelled. "I hear you! Where are you?" In her excitement, she couldn't figure out from where the voice had come.

Suddenly, an attendant passing by grabbed Johanna and held her. A gush of strange syllables scolded in her ear. Johanna would not be restrained. She shook away from the attendant's grasp.

"I'm not crazy! Listen! There's someone else here who I understand!"

"Help me! Whoever you are, please help me!" The sobbing voice was a girl's voice. It came from a nearby room in this hall.

Suddenly, Johanna's only objective was to seek out this person who could prove her sanity. She rushed from door to door. She was aware of the attendant calling for help. The next thing she knew, a nurse came up behind her and jabbed a needle into her. The hallway spun as she collapsed onto the floor.

— 6 —

Piedmont

Barbara Wetzel blew her nose into a tissue as she sat beside the bed of her sleeping patient. Her head ached, but the chief of staff had no sympathy. The new doctor had been promised by the end of the week, however. Perhaps then she could get a day off.

Miss Dobbs stirred. Barbara wadded up the wet tissue in her palm. It wouldn't be long before the patient awoke. Too bad they had sedated her again. Such an action just might set Miss Dobbs back, right when it looked as though her condition might be improving.

"What did she do, doctor?"

Dr. Wetzel glanced over at the heavyset patient who shared Miss Dobbs' room. Mrs. Finnegan had been filing her nails. Barbara smiled in a reassuring manner. "She'll be all right, Mrs. Finnegan. Miss Dobbs became violent in the corridor this morning."

"Why? Johanna's usually no trouble at all."

"Tell me, Mrs. Finnegan, how are you and Miss Dobbs getting along?"

The woman put down her nail file and sighed. "Well, considering her problem ... not being able to talk right and all ... I'd say we get along real good. I like Johanna."

Dr. Wetzel reached over to take Miss Dobbs' pulse as her sleeping patient showed further signs of coming to. She wondered what had caused the patient to start screaming in the hallway. Perhaps it was related to her syndrome. It would now be necessary to keep Miss Dobbs under careful observation.

"She's waking up," announced Mrs. Finnegan.

"Yes," said Barbara. "Come on, Johanna, you can wake up now. You're safe and sound, back in your room."

The brown eyes opened and the patient blinked. She shook her head, then focused her gaze on Dr. Wetzel's face. Suddenly, Miss Dobbs bolted up from the bed. A deluge of words flew from her dry lips. Barbara could only tell from the sound of the patient's voice that whatever she was trying to convey, the woman was excited. What on earth was she trying to tell her that was so important?

"Please, calm down, Miss Dobbs," said Dr. Wetzel.

"*Breeklen wrurspgullf schwassvumpliss reejewlivblub cribglitch!*" blurted the desperate patient. Her eyes filled with tears as she gasped and continued to explode in her undecipherable rhetoric.

"Can you make any of that out, doctor?"

Barbara eyed the recorder at the foot of the bed. She was taking down every word, just as she had at the earlier sessions with Miss Dobbs. So far, no one had been able to make any sense out of Miss Dobbs' language. Even experts had been unable, so far, to break the code of jargon.

"What could be so important to her?" Mrs. Finnegan asked.

Dr. Wetzel jotted notes onto her clipboard. *Patient acts like she has had traumatic experience*, she wrote. She watched the imploring brown eyes that now delivered tears down Miss Dobbs' cheeks. The patient continued to babble.

"Doctor! Doctor, help her!" cried Mrs. Finnegan.

Barbara glanced over and saw that Mrs. Finnegan was starting to get worked up by Miss Dobbs' crying spell. It didn't take much to set her off. "Why don't you go down to the recreation room, Mrs. Finnegan?" she suggested.

"No, not without Johanna," replied Mrs. Finnegan. "I don't want to leave her alone like this."

"It's okay, Mrs. Finnegan. You go ahead. I'll take care of her."

The large woman in the other bed began to sob. Dr. Wetzel got up and pushed the button for the nurses' station. This was getting nowhere. Miss Dobbs was obviously agitated. Possibly it was a side effect from the syndrome, then again ...

A thought struck her. The attendant had mentioned some kind of emotional disturbance from Room 411. Had that been the cause of Miss Dobbs' upset? The third patient had arrived just last night at Reeve Memorial. Dr. Wetzel wondered if there was a correlation.

By now Mrs. Finnegan was in a state. Dr. Wetzel went to the door to call a nurse. One was just outside in the hallway. "What took you so long?" Barbara snapped.

The young nurse grimaced. "A disturbance from Room 411, doctor."

"Never mind, I'll go take care of it myself."

"What about Mrs. Finnegan?" asked the nurse.

Dr. Wetzel turned and shrugged. "Standard procedure," she murmured, and hurried on down the corridor.

It was two days before Johanna was allowed to leave her room again. She suffered through another day of being drugged, but her spirits felt alive. She had not hallucinated. She remembered fully that she had heard the voice of a girl calling out in "English." Someone else was apparently being held in this place—someone who was as sane and as trapped as she was. Johanna knew she had to find some way to meet this patient. It might be days before they'd let her out of her room. All Johanna could do was remain calm, be patient, and wait.

That afternoon she was allowed to go to the recreation hall. As the attendant led her past the corridor in which Johanna had heard the girl's voice crying out, she paused and listened for any further signs. All was silent. What if they had removed the other patient? Johanna grew worried. What if the girl was gone? Her only link to communication might be gone from her forever. It was a frightening thought.

Inside the rec hall, Johanna looked around. Not everyone was present this day. Her Highness was reading in the corner. William was picking at his toes. Charley was rocking. Wanda and Francine sat glued in front of the television. The older man with the beard and reddish hair sat writing in his book by the fireplace. But where was the Hostage? Johanna also noticed that Melody, the shriveled-up old lady, was not in the room. Her heart leaped. This meant she had a chance at playing the piano.

Francine waved in greeting to Johanna, who smiled back at her. Nobody else paid any attention as Johanna sauntered over to the upright piano. She sat down carefully, then glanced over her shoulder, just to be sure Melody hadn't slipped into the room. What a relief it was to be able to sit on this bench, rest her fingers against the sleek ivory, and not have that madwoman racing toward her to throw her off.

Johanna felt a surge of emotion and her breath caught in her throat as she played the first chord. The music filled the room and she played the next chord. She was in heaven. She immediately fell into Chopin's *Valse in C-sharp Minor*. The music flowed from her spirit and filled the recreation hall with strains that lit up her very soul. She lost herself in the piece. Her rusty fingers made minor mistakes, but they weren't important. The music was all that mattered. The release of everything pent up inside of her gave way as the colorful tones continued to flow.

Then—like a thunderbolt—something smashed against Johanna's shoulder. The chord ended in a blatant crash of twisted tones as Johanna's hands slipped from the keyboard and her body fell to the floor. She cowered as she saw Melody towering over her in a seething rage. The old woman had fire in her eyes. Johanna covered her head with her hands. She had been so involved in the Chopin, she had not noticed the hag enter the recreation hall.

A man's voice rumbled over Johanna. She dared to look up and saw the Hostage and a male attendant restraining Melody. They dragged her away as the hag continued to bellow in nonsensical spurts.

Johanna picked herself up off the floor and brushed her shoulder, where Melody had struck her. She had a few bruises to contend with now. She jumped in surprise as William came up to her. Scrunching his narrow face, the skinny man reached out and picked dust off Johanna's sleeve. Then he stuck his finger in his mouth and licked his lips.

Traumatized, Johanna scurried away to the fireplace. Her pulse raced and she needed some time to recover her senses. For a couple of minutes, though, she had played the piano. She had actually succeeded at communicating her feelings through music.

"Pssst..."

Startled, Johanna glanced up and saw the stout, red-haired man with the beard motioning toward her. He had never so much as spoken a word to her or anyone before. Yet now he was beckoning to her. She rubbed her shoulder and slowly approached him. She didn't know what to expect. He looked harmless enough, yet ...

"Did she injure you?" His voice was gentle and hushed. He glanced around to see if anyone was paying attention.

Johanna's mouth dropped open in surprise. She couldn't reply.

"It's too bad, really," the man continued. A warm smile spread over his ruddy face. "I wanted to hear more. Your playing was lovely."

Johanna stared, fumbling for the words. "You ... you ..."

"Yes, dear. Draw up a chair. Sit and talk with me for a while. You can't know how long it's been since I've had someone to converse with."

Johanna grabbed the nearest chair and dragged it over beside the recliner. "My God," she finally managed to say, "all this time ... I thought I was the only one."

"The fault is mine," the man said. "If I had paid more attention, I would have heard your speech much earlier. I prefer to keep to myself as much as I can, for obvious reasons." He rolled his eyes toward William, who was now hunting cracks in the wall. Then he smiled at Johanna once again and took her hand in his. The palm was warm and dry. "My name is Piedmont."

Johanna introduced herself quickly. She had a million questions.

"I do not know all the answers," he interrupted. "But listen to me, Johanna.

We must be careful. We must avoid talking when the doctors and nurses are around."

"But why?"

"Trust me. You have only been here a short time. You will learn more as time passes."

Johanna was puzzled. "How long have you been here, Mr. Piedmont?"

"Please, just Piedmont. Call me that or Professor."

"You're a professor?"

"That's right."

"Well, what's happened to us? Are we in some kind of altered state?"

"Shh." He quickly turned away.

High heels clicked across the floor of the room as the woman doctor entered the room. She had just come in with Melody, whom she sat in a chair in front of the television. It looked like the old lady had been given something to sedate her. The doctor left again, and the clicks disappeared down the hall.

Piedmont cleared his throat. "As to your first question, I have been here several months. Since November, I believe. Before that, I taught English classes at the university. It appears I am on an unrequested sabbatical." He smirked to himself.

"What happened to you?"

Piedmont inspected her. "A conspiracy, my dear, that's what."

"What do you mean? What kind of conspiracy?"

"It's too involved. It has taken me months to figure it out, but I believe I am right in suggesting that we are part of a conspiracy."

"On whose part?" Johanna's bewilderment grew. "All I know is that I woke up one morning and suddenly the world was turned inside out. Now I'm a prisoner in this asylum, and I don't think I'm ever getting out! Who is to blame, Piedmont? I want some answers."

"Calm down, Johanna. You'll know soon enough." The professor's face tightened as he noticed someone enter the recreation hall. He signaled to her to keep silent, then picked up his book and pretended to read.

Johanna's mind whirled. She was confused, yet exhilarated to have met Piedmont. He was the first person she had been able to talk to since her incarceration. A nurse had entered the recreation hall and Piedmont made a motion for Johanna to move away. As she did, he twitched a smile and winked an eye at her.

When the coast was clear once again, Johanna pulled her chair close to Piedmont and listened as he related his tale. The change had come over him very suddenly, while he had been lecturing on Milton to a class of college students. It had been very embarrassing for him. His colleagues had brought him to this hospital, convinced he had suffered a mild stroke. Like Johanna, he had been given drugs and had gone through a period of trauma in which he had been convinced he was insane.

"But we are not alone," said Piedmont. He patted her hand. "You are no longer alone."

Johanna remembered the voice she had heard in the corridor a couple of days ago. She told Piedmont about it, then how she had been drugged and kept in her room until today.

Piedmont appeared surprised. "Then there is another," he said. "Things are starting to happen. The time is growing short, Johanna."

Whatever was he talking about? Johanna begged him to elaborate. What was this *conspiracy* he had referred to? Were the doctors and nurses plotting against Piedmont and herself, or was he as paranoid as some of these other patients in the ward? Johanna began to have second thoughts about Piedmont. She began to doubt whether he knew what he was talking about. Just because they spoke the same language didn't mean he was totally rational. For that matter, could she trust herself? Was this some kind of a disease they suffered in which she could expect her own mental faculties to falter?

"Somebody's looking for you." Piedmont nodded toward the door. The attendant Freckles came straight toward them.

Johanna saw that the thin girl wanted to take her somewhere. Johanna wanted to stay and talk some more with Piedmont. She wanted him to explain what he had meant about the conspiracy. Freckles spoke some jargon at Johanna, then pulled her arm to lead her away. Johanna had no choice but to follow. Her shoulder was still sore from Melody pushing her off the piano bench.

When she was out in the corridor, she saw Manley waiting at the nurses' station. It had been days since he had come to visit her. She was happy to see him and grinned. "Oh Manley, it's so good to see you!" Then her smile faded at his look of disappointment.

She no longer cared. She walked with him back to her room, telling him all about Piedmont and the fact that she was not the only person in the world suffering from her malady. Manley was patient and studied her face, but he wore a pained expression the entire time.

— 7 —

The Piano Lesson

The next day when Johanna met Piedmont in the recreation hall, he asked her if she had heard anything further from the mysterious girl from one of the rooms.

Johanna shook her head. "But I'm certain I heard it. Honest, I wouldn't make something like that up."

Piedmont said not to worry, he believed her. "My concern is that they have removed her to someplace else." He stroked his beard as he looked around the room.

"Well," sighed Johanna, "I was kept in my room several days before they let me come here."

"That is probably the reason," Piedmont agreed. "Will you play something on the piano for me today?"

Johanna glanced around the room. Melody was playing cards with the Hostage. "I would, but ..."

Piedmont nodded in understanding. "I know. It is risky for you."

"Why is she so ..." Johanna couldn't think of the right word to describe Melody.

"Explosive?" Piedmont finished.

"If I go near that piano, she becomes a raving maniac."

He sat back and folded his hands in his protruding lap. "Perhaps in her childhood her parents forced her to take piano lessons," Piedmont surmised. "Perhaps she is displaying her frustration at never mastering the instrument and simply can't stand anyone who *can* play."

"Do you know anything else about her?" Johanna asked.

"Not really," said Piedmont. "She was here before I arrived. She was gone for a while, but returned shortly before you arrived. I have a feeling her family tried putting her in a nursing home, so she could be with other elderly people. My guess is she became too violent and they couldn't deal with her."

"Is music the only thing she reacts to?"

"Heavens no. See that lady with the red hair?"

Johanna noticed Her Highness reading a magazine. "Yes."

"She despises the red-haired lady as well. Red will have nothing to do with the others—thinks she's too good for them. Well, your piano maniac loves to tease Red and get a rise out of her."

"What about that man playing cards?" Johanna pointed to the Hostage, shuffling his deck at the table. "Why is he here?"

"Oh, him. The loner. He's perfectly all right, except ... I think he prefers to remain here."

Johanna was puzzled. "He *likes* it here?"

"Ironically, yes," said Piedmont. "He's had visitors off and on. Family, I think, including a wife. Pretty thing. From what I can gather, everyone is trying to convince him to leave. But he won't go. He's afraid of the outside world. Somehow he feels safe within these walls, strange as it may sound."

Johanna confided how she referred to the man as "The Hostage," and Piedmont's eyebrows lifted.

"You could be absolutely right, Johanna. Funny I didn't think of that myself." He reached for his notebook and scribbled something in it.

"What are you writing?" Johanna wanted to know.

"It's my log," he explained. "Someday I'm going to write a book about all this."

"Are you a writer?"

"As a matter of fact, I am. I've published three historical novels and several of my poems have been printed in literary magazines."

"That's wonderful." Johanna was impressed. "I just hope that one day— when we get out of here—someone will be able to read what you write."

Piedmont sighed. "That could be a problem." He looked at her. "By the way, what did you do with your life before you got here?"

Johanna disclosed a little about herself, her lonely existence, writing compositions, teaching music. "It hasn't been a very exciting life," she confessed.

"Oh? Have you performed much?"

Johanna smiled as she remembered back to her late teens. "I was a concert pianist for several years. I even toured in different countries."

"You are very talented. What made you give it up?"

Johanna stared into her lap. She examined the fingers that ached to play the piano again. "To be quite honest, Piedmont, I don't know." She glanced over at the piano longingly, then up at him. "I can't tell you that. My brother ..."

"Ah, the bald man who comes to see you is your brother." Piedmont sighed. "All this time I thought he was your husband." He smiled. "I *thought* you were too young for him."

Johanna blushed. She had never felt young, even compared to Manley. "Thank you."

"Your brother made you give up your career as a concert pianist?"

"Well, not exactly," replied Johanna, "but Manley and I have always been close. I just grew tired of touring and living the stressful life of a concert pianist. I prefer to stay at home and compose."

"I can identify with that," Piedmont assured her. "I never married either."

Johanna started to feel depressed, thinking of her house and her piano and all the things she missed. She needed to change the subject. "Piedmont, what were you talking about yesterday when you mentioned a conspiracy?"

Piedmont started to say something, but noticed something else just then. He motioned toward the other side of the room. "Look," he said.

Johanna saw Melody approach the piano. The old woman had abandoned the card game with The Hostage and was now standing over the keyboard with her messy gray head cocked. A thin, wrinkled hand slowly moved over the keys but did not touch them. Johanna watched the old woman for a couple of minutes as she simply stood and stared at the instrument.

The Hostage called out something to Melody. She spun around and hissed at him, then turned back to the piano.

"How curious," stated Piedmont.

"Has she done this before?" Johanna asked.

"I don't believe so."

Johanna stood up and started walking over to the piano.

"Johanna ... don't," cautioned Piedmont. "Wait ..."

"It's okay," Johanna told him, and continued over. She came up to Melody, half expecting the deranged patient to push her away with a snarl. But the old woman met Johanna's gaze with a look of reluctance. Johanna dared to be bold. She pointed to the keyboard. "Why don't you play it?"

Melody searched Johanna's face. It was as though the old woman were testing her, waiting for the wrong move to provoke an attack. Johanna stood still. She was on her guard, but tried not to show fear. Finally, Melody plopped herself down on the piano bench as Johanna stood over her. Then the old woman placed her hands over the keyboard and hesitated. The room was quiet except for the low hum and mechanized voices on the television.

"Go on ... play something," encouraged Johanna in a compassionate voice.

The next moment Melody plunged herself against the keyboard and filled the recreation hall with a dissonant blast of tones that made Johanna's heart freeze. Over and over, the old woman pounded the chords that rang out in cacophony. A cry escaped the old woman's lips as she doubled over on the piano bench. Although Johanna could not understand the words, it was apparent that Melody was shrieking in frustration.

Johanna touched the old woman on the shoulder to make her stop. Melody turned on her and hot sour breath swept over Johanna's face. Johanna sensed the old woman wanted to play music, but simply didn't know how. And here Johanna stood, *longing* to play music ...

Forgetting any danger to herself, she squeezed in beside the old woman on the piano bench and played a rippling scale up the upper half of the keyboard. She expected the old woman to belt her like she had yesterday, but instead Melody grabbed Johanna's hands and gripped them very hard. There was a pleading look in Melody's eyes—a look that begged for something. A cackle of desperation erupted in the old woman's throat.

Johanna managed to slip her right hand out of the woman's grasp. She took hold of Melody's bony wrist and firmly placed it in the position of the Major C chord. Pressing down, she forced Melody to play the chord. The woman did not protest.

Next, Johanna formed the second chord and did the same. Melody sat, fixed and listening. Johanna played the following chord in the scale. Again, there was no negative reaction on Melody's behalf. When Johanna looked up, there seemed to be light in Melody's gray eyes. "Try it again," Johanna coaxed. She put the woman's hand in the proper position.

This time Melody shook off Johanna's grip and formed the chord with her own fingers. After she was sure she had the position right, Melody pressed down. A soft tone met their ears. Melody's face broke out in a smile. Her toothless grin made her face seem even more wrinkled. She played the chord over and over, and seemed extremely pleased with her accomplishment.

Johanna sighed in relief and glanced around. Everyone in the room stared in their direction. Piedmont smiled with pride. A black-haired man in a white jacket stood in the entrance to the recreation hall. Johanna did not remember seeing this doctor before. He had coarse hair and was tall. He stood next to Banana Nose, the attendant, as they both went over some charts.

Melody grew tired of playing the chord and dropped her hands. She chuckled to herself and spoke some jargon to Johanna, then got up off the piano bench. Johanna took this as a signal that now it was *her* turn to play something.

"All right," said Johanna. "How about some Beethoven? I'm in the mood for some old-fashioned Beethoven." She started to play *Fur Elise*. She hadn't gotten as far as the third measure when she heard Melody screech. Next, the old woman grabbed Johanna's hair and tried to drag her off the piano bench, calling out in angry gibberish.

Johanna squealed from pain and struggled with the old woman as others gathered around to pull the hag off of her. When Piedmont and The Hostage and some others had managed to pull Melody away, Johanna found herself sprawled on the hard oak floor, whining from the pain of a scratch on her neck. Her scalp felt like it was on fire.

"Oh, God! She's impossible!" Johanna cried out. "Keep her away from me!" She sobbed in humiliation. It was not so much the fact that she had been attacked by a madwoman as it was the fact that Melody had prevented her from carrying out her greatest need—to *play the piano.*

A strong arm helped Johanna to her feet. Through her tears, she noticed the white jacket and black hair. The doctor who had been standing in the recreation hall entrance examined her. Johanna recognized him right away and drew back, startled. She recognized those unusual blue eyes. It was the face of the man who had sat beside her on the night of the ballet—the night before she had been brought to this hospital.

Johanna gasped. "It's *you!*"

The doctor only stared at Johanna. It was obvious he did not remember her. In jargon he gave some orders to Banana Nose, who left immediately with Melody, who was still carrying on in her raspy, cackly voice. Then the doctor spoke to the other patients gathered around, and they all went back to what they were doing. In his familiar deep voice, the doctor spoke more gibberish, this time directed at Johanna, and he led her away, outside of the recreation hall.

Johanna glanced over at Piedmont before she left. He stared with a look of concern as the doctor led her out. Still shaken from the episode, sobs escaped Johanna's throat as the doctor escorted her to a small examining room near the nurses' station. The pungent odor of Mercurochrome dominated the small chamber with its white walls and fluorescent lighting.

The doctor helped Johanna onto the table. A nurse came in and spoke to the doctor, who gave some orders Johanna could not decipher. Then the doctor and the nurse treated the scratch on Johanna's neck. It stung when the antiseptic touched the wound. The cotton felt cool, and then the nurse applied a bandage.

Johanna continued to sob, although she was trying desperately to calm down. Her shock at seeing the doctor and recognizing him was part of it. She wondered why he acted as though he did not know her. Perhaps he really did not remember her. Why should he, after all? She was nothing to him. Just because she had found *him* attractive ...

Johanna wanted to go back to the recreation hall after being treated. She wanted to finish playing Beethoven. The melody of *Fur Elise* was still strong in her head. It needed to come out for everyone to hear. She also wanted to talk to Piedmont. There were questions she needed to have him answer.

But the nurse was given instructions to take Johanna back to her room. Protesting did not a shred of good, so to avoid being injected again, Johanna cooperated and went with the nurse. She was given a pill, which she guessed was a sleeping tablet, and put to bed, where she cried herself softly into a slumber.

— 8 —

Night Visitor

Johanna was grateful to find Piedmont in the recreation hall the next day. She discovered he had been worried about her skirmish from the day before. "You must promise me you won't try anything like that again," said Piedmont, referring to Johanna's attempt to teach Melody how to play the piano. "She's much too dangerous. Much too unpredictable."

"I know, it was stupid of me," Johanna admitted, "but you have to admit, for a couple of minutes I did get through to her. It was exciting. Oh, if only I could have a chance to play that piano when Melody isn't around."

"You deserve that," Piedmont added.

Johanna looked around the room. Francine and Wanda sat in front of the TV set as usual. Charley sat in his rocker and rolled forward and back in a continuous rhythm. The Hostage dealt his cards in front of him while William hunted "woollies" on the floor. Her Highness was trying to read, but Melody kept moving her chair closer to the red-haired woman, who would move hers an inch further. Johanna wondered how long Red would put up with Melody's pestering before an altercation occurred. She and Piedmont, at least, had privacy in their own little corner of the room, next to the fireplace. Johanna gazed longingly at the piano.

"I see you are wearing a bandage," Piedmont remarked.

"It's just a scratch from the old woman," Johanna explained. "The doctor treated it, and I was taken back to my room. That reminds me, Piedmont. About that new doctor ..." She stopped. She was about to tell Piedmont how she had seen the man before at the ballet. She shrugged. "Never mind."

"Oh, you mean Doctor Serassan."

Johanna looked up in surprise. "How do you know his name?"

Piedmont patted Johanna's hand. "It's not important. He's not new here either. He was on temporary assignment a while back. Looks like he's landed himself a full-time job at this hospital."

"Oh, did you know him before?"

"Before?"

"You know. Before you came here."

Piedmont caught the interest in her eye and squinted. "Did you?"

She shook her head. "Of course not."

"Well," resumed Piedmont, "he's not to be trusted."

"Why do you say that?"

Piedmont lowered his voice. "He's part of the .... conspiracy."

Johanna wondered whether the bearded man was slipping into paranoia again. She didn't understand what this *conspiracy* was that Piedmont kept referring to. She was about to ask him more about it when a crash sounded from across the room.

With a shriek, Her Highness began hitting Melody over the head with her book. The violent old woman attacked the red-haired woman, and curses flew from both their mouths. As the two of them struggled on the floor, Johanna saw Francine get into the act. Her large roommate put herself between the quarreling couple and tried to put an end to the violence.

"Oh no! Francine!" Johanna jumped up and ran to call the attendant, who must have slipped off to the restroom. In the skirmish a chair that had fallen lost one its wooden legs. The old woman grabbed for the leg and began to beat Francine with it as the fat woman cowered on the floor. Her Highness stood up and screamed. The Hostage got up from the table and tried to overpower Melody, but the hag was quick and agile. She turned on him next and hit him with her club, then turned back to bludgeon Francine.

"Help! Please!" Johanna cried into the corridor. "Somebody!"

Banana Nose popped his head out of the restroom just then. The tall doctor appeared from down the hall and came running. Johanna pointed, and the two men took charge of the situation. They managed to restrain Melody. Amidst a lot of her shrieking and gasping, Dr. Serassan loaded a hypodermic needle and inserted it in Melody's shoulder. Within seconds, the woman sagged. Banana Nose and another nurse carried her out of the room.

Johanna stood close by as Dr. Serassan knelt beside Francine, who lay unconscious on the floor. Blood matted Francine's hair next to her ear. Her Highness began throwing out angry phrases at Dr. Serassan, as if all this was *his* fault. Wanda began chanting in her spiritual fashion, bowing and moaning as if in prayer. The Hostage seemed to be the coolest. He spoke with the doctor, and the two of them lifted the heavy injured woman up to the couch.

Next, two nurses rushed in. Johanna moved out of the way. Sickened by the sight of blood and the horror of what had just transpired, she joined Piedmont, who had sat watching from his chair. He met Johanna's look with a sad sigh. Only William and Charley went about their usual habits without so much as a glance at the others.

"She's hurt badly," Johanna whispered to Piedmont.

"I can see that," he replied.

"They've got to do something about that horrid woman." Johanna shuddered. "Oh, poor Francine." She buried her head in her arms, but the awful memory was still vivid in her mind. When she looked up, they had brought in a wheeled cart and were lifting Francine onto it. Dr. Serassan stayed at Francine's side as they rolled her out.

"I don't know what they can do." Piedmont sighed.

"She should be locked up," said Johanna. "They should put her away and throw away the key!" She trembled.

Piedmont put his arm around Johanna to comfort her. "There, there. Take it easy."

Wanda roamed around the room, moaning. The Hostage had approached Her Highness and was trying to talk to her, but the red-haired woman refused to look at him. She paced back and forth with her arms crossed, still angry.

"Get your mind off it," Piedmont suggested. "Look. There's the piano. The old woman's gone ... at least for today. Why don't you go on over and play something?"

Johanna looked up at him. She felt too shook up to play the piano right now. "I can't," she murmured.

Wanda wailed just then, and it sent a chill of fear up Johanna's spine. She couldn't take any more of Wanda's weird chanting, or the snappy outbursts of anger from Her Highness. So she got up and went over to the piano. She sat down. Glancing over her shoulder, she made sure Melody really was gone from the room. Then she plunged in and played *Fur Elise,* as she had yesterday.

At first she played rapidly, as though in a race to get through the piece. Then she grew calmer and formed the music so that it expressed the gentleness and beauty it had always given her. When she finished the piece, Johanna was startled to hear a few claps. When she looked up, she saw Piedmont and The Hostage smiling at her from across the room as they applauded her playing.

Her Highness had quieted down and stared crossly at Johanna for a second before opening her book once again. Wanda had returned to the television set, but continued to sniffle. Johanna's relief at finally getting to play a whole piece prompted her to play some more. She immediately fell into a Mozart sonata.

She was interrupted this time by William, who crawled underneath the piano bench. She abruptly stopped playing as he reached one of his thin dirty hands underneath the piano. Afraid that he would grab her foot or provoke her in some obscene manner, Johanna closed the keyboard and stood up.

As she started back to her chair beside Piedmont, she noticed the figure of the tall doctor standing in the doorway of the recreation hall. He stared directly at Johanna. His mouth seemed to be open a little, as if he were in some kind of a daze. Johanna stared back at the piercing, unusual blue eyes. She could feel her heartbeat picking up. Did he recognize her now? Did he remember her from the night of the ballet? She tore her gaze away from him and noticed Piedmont watching the doctor as well. When Johanna looked again, Dr. Serassan had recovered himself and left.

"Now how did that feel?" Piedmont smiled warmly as Johanna rejoined him several minutes later.

"Splendid," she breathed. "I feel a lot better now."

"Notice how the room has settled down," he commented. "Music to soothe the savage breast."

Johanna blushed.

"Curious," muttered Piedmont.

"What is?" asked Johanna.

"Serassan. When you were playing that last piece, he came and listened."

Johanna was puzzled. "So?"

"He just kept staring at you. More reason not to trust him."

"Piedmont, I wish you'd explain what you're talking about," Johanna implored. But it was no use. Piedmont changed the subject. He would not elaborate on Dr. Serassan nor the "conspiracy." But Johanna knew Piedmont was keeping something from her, and she intended to get it out of him, sooner or later.

When Johanna went back to her room, she discovered Francine had been removed. The other woman's belongings had been taken away, and the bed with the yellow spread had been made. Johanna's heart raced as she feared the worst. Was her roommate dead?

"No ... it can't be." Johanna's eyes filled with tears. "Francine, no!" She sobbed for half an hour, until a nurse came to scold her. Although Johanna pointed to the empty bed, the nurse did not seem to comprehend the cause of Johanna's distress.

Johanna spent the evening in her room, listening to her radio. Her heart felt heavy and she thought back over the afternoon and the violence that had resulted in her being alone in this room. She had finally gotten her chance to play the piano, but now she missed her house and her own piano more than ever. She cried some more as she thought of all the things she missed and the fear that she might never see any of those things again.

The door to Johanna's room opened slowly. It was late. She was usually asleep by now. In fact, Johanna found it strange that no one had given her a sleeping tablet tonight. She reached for a tissue to blow her nose as somebody stepped inside. It was Dr. Serassan.

Johanna remembered what Piedmont and told her, that Dr. Serassan could not be trusted. He looked at her, and she wondered what he wanted. Was he going to remove the bandage from her neck? He closed the door quietly behind him, then slowly approached her bed. She was surprised when a trifle smile spread over his sensuous lips.

In that moment she realized he *did* recognize her after all. But why was he moving so slowly? Why had he closed the door as if he didn't want anyone else to know he was here?

Johanna had become accustomed to saying out loud anything she wanted to people. Knowing they couldn't understand her speech, she had grown uninhibited. She met the doctor's smile with a soft smile of her own. "Well, well ... imagine a handsome hunk like you coming to my room this time of night ... perhaps you came to seduce me?"

The doctor stopped smiling and gently reached out to check the bandage on her neck.

"Oh, it's better," Johanna rambled. "I think you can remove the bandage now." He ripped it from her skin and she winced. "Ow ... that hurt." She touched the wound surface, then continued. "I know you can't understand a word I'm saying to you, doctor. But haven't we met somewhere before?" Johanna giggled, as if she were a schoolgirl. It was so much fun doing this to these unsuspecting staff members.

"What a line," she continued, feeling uninhibited. "You know, I think I could actually fall in love with you. Let me tell you a secret ... I've never fallen in love before. But somehow ... I think I could fall in love with someone like *you*. It could be ... interesting." She felt suddenly giddy, flirtatious.

She sat cross-legged on the bed and watched him as he disposed of the bandage without a glance at her. "When I saw you at the ballet that night, something sparked inside of me. Yes, I know it sounds trite. A woman meets a tall, dark stranger. And suddenly her life is turned upside down." Johanna paused as she thought about those words. "But if *that* isn't the understatement of the year." Then her emotions overcame her, and hot tears filled her eyelids. "I wish I could go home," she murmured. She struggled to control herself before a sob broke loose.

The doctor cleared his throat then and spoke. "I apologize if I hurt you," he said with a slightly foreign accent. "I don't think we'll need a new bandage." He looked into Johanna's eyes and seemed to perceive her very thoughts.

Johanna drew back in shock. He had *spoken* to her! A flush of embarrassment covered her face as she recalled the things she had said out loud to him.

Dr. Serassan reached out and took her hand in his. It felt warm and sent a strange sensation of energy throughout her body. "Do not be alarmed, Johanna. I am Serassan."

Johanna's voice felt dry as she struggled to find words. "Yes, I ... I know."

"Good. The nurse told me you had been crying. I suspect you were worried about your roommate."

"Yes." Johanna still could not believe she was actually talking with the doctor. "Yes, h-how *is* Francine?"

Dr. Serassan looked puzzled. "Francine?" Then he understood. "Ah ... yes. She's all right. Mrs. Finnegan—or your Francine—has been moved to another part of the hospital temporarily. It seems she has suffered a skull fracture. But I think she'll come through it."

Johanna sighed with relief. "Thank God."

"Yes." Serassan smiled at her. "It looks like you're going to have this room to yourself for a while."

Johanna shook her head in disbelief. "You can understand me. How can you talk to me? I heard you speak before. You ..."

"Shh." The doctor put a finger on her lips to quiet her.

"But I have so much to ask you," Johanna protested. Her speech became desperate. "You're able to talk to me, but you can also understand everybody else. What does this mean? Why can't *I* communicate with everybody else? What has happened to me, doctor?"

When he smiled, the unusual blue eyes seemed to reach right out at her. She was held in a gaze from which she couldn't turn away. "Do not be afraid, Johanna ..." were the words he spoke in a deep, precise voice she remembered from somewhere else. But where?

"Who ... who are you?" The room seemed to fog up around her all of a sudden.

"There will be time for all your questions later," Serassan told her in a hypnotic voice that seemed to calm her more and more. "Right now you are tired. You need only to sleep."

Johanna tried to fight off the wave of fatigue that had suddenly made her feel impossibly weary. She opened her mouth, but she was too tired to utter any sounds.

"Johanna, there is no cause for alarm," he said. "You are special. Now I want you just to relax." His fingers began stroking her hand. The warmth penetrated her skin, and she could feel a wonderful energy flowing up to her elbows, to her shoulders, into her neck and cheek muscles … relaxing her entire being. She could only stare at him in awe as she felt her head tilt to one side. "There, that's better already." His energy continued to nourish her, to soothe her distressed mind.

"I must know ... I want to know ..." she murmured, forcing the words out in her fatigued state.

"Of course," he interrupted. The strokes continued. The energy flowed and her eyelids grew heavy. "Sleep now, Johanna. You will rest, and it will be better the next time we meet."

She felt her body being carefully laid to rest on the pillow as the warm energy bathed her. She was drifting away.

"Good, you are asleep now." His voice faded away, but she heard these last few words. "*My beloved ... my special one.*" The words echoed in her dreams as she slumbered.

— 9 —

Radya

The girl in Room 411 stood at the window and stared out between the bars. Barbara Wetzel closed the door behind her, and the girl turned and regarded her with apathetic eyes. "And how are you this morning?" the doctor asked.

As expected, the girl said nothing. She hadn't spoken in three days now.

Barbara walked over and put a hand on the girl's slender shoulder. "Come over here and sit down." She led the patient across the room to her bed.

Without resisting, the girl sat and folded her hands in her lap. Stringy blond hair dangled from a center part on her head, and the uncertain blue eyes stared ahead.

Barbara whipped through the pages of notes on her clipboard. Jane Doe had been admitted ten days ago. Still no clue as to her identity. Certainly someone must be wondering where this beautiful child was. As close as they could determine, Jane was in her late teens.

When the police had brought her in, she had been a wreck—totally out of touch with reality. She had been terrified of the doctors and nurses. A physical examination had revealed no evidence of drug abuse. She had not been beaten, yet the authorities had reported picking her up wandering the streets on the worst side of town.

Minutes after they had admitted her, Dr. Wetzel had been called in. The patient had displayed undecipherable speech patterns. Jane Doe had become Barbara's patient from that moment on. Her emotional state had prompted wasted days of drug treatments which Barbara regretted but, nevertheless, found necessary. Now it appeared Miss Doe had passed that barrier that had been a pattern in the first two similar cases.

"I have a treat for you today," said Dr. Wetzel. "No more solitary. You're getting a roommate." Barbara stood up and opened the door to Room 411. Looking out, she summoned an attendant from down the hall. "And that's not all, Jane…"

The girl glanced up slowly, uncertainly, as the red-haired, freckled attendant entered the room.

"Ellen, please escort Jane Doe down to the recreation hall," said Barbara.

"Sure." The freckled attendant took the patient's arm and led her out of the room. "Anything else, Dr. Wetzel?"

"Yes. Let me know when Dr. Serassan arrives. Page me."

"Okay, doctor."

Barbara sat down on the bed and unclasped the barrette from her head. Shaking her hair, she smoothed it and replaced the clip. What a relief it was to have Dr. Serassan on staff. He was quite handsome for an older man, with those remarkable blue eyes and that strange accent. She wasn't sure where he had originated, but his credentials were top-notch. She had worked with him last November, when he was a visiting physician. He took an interest in the patients and had actually taken the time to sit down with her over a cup of coffee while she told him about "Wetzel's Syndrome." He had asked her to keep him informed of any progress she might see in the three patients who had the condition.

Johanna went to the recreation hall early. She had slept peacefully throughout the night. When she had awakened, she remembered the face of Serassan and the shock of knowing he could communicate with her. She was anxious to discuss this new development with the professor, but he wasn't in the recreation hall yet when she arrived.

The Hostage wanted to play cards with Johanna, but she refused him. Yesterday or the day before, she would have been glad to interact with him. He seemed like a friendly, outgoing man, and except for his paranoia around the doctors, nurses and visitors, he was the sanest person there.

Johanna could not get her mind off Serassan. He mystified her. There was something about his eyes. She cringed as she recalled all the things she had blurted out in front of him before she realized he could comprehend every word.

When the door to the recreation hall opened, Johanna looked up, expecting to see Piedmont. Instead, Freckles brought in somebody else. A thin young girl, probably no older than 18 or 19, leaned on the arm of the attendant. The girl, dressed in the telltale leisure suit, had stringy blond hair. Her eyes were wide and fearful as she glanced around at everyone in the room. She had a long, slender neck which reminded Johanna of an ostrich. The girl seemed reluctant to be left in the room. The attendant sat her down next to Charley, who paid no attention as his rocking chair continued to creak in rhythm.

Johanna could see that the new patient was frightened. Johanna wondered if this could be the person she had heard call out that day in the corridor. She had to know for sure. Johanna got up and approached the blond girl, who stared at her timidly.

"Hello," said Johanna. She knelt in front of the girl and smiled.

The girl's doe-like eyes expanded. She continued to stare but said nothing.

Johanna sighed. She had been wrong. The girl obviously couldn't understand her speech. She stood up. "Oh well. I thought you were somebody else." She started back toward her empty chair at the fireplace.

"Wait!"

Johanna spun around. The girl had spoken to her in English. Johanna gasped. "Then you *can* understand!"

The girl closed her eyes and wrung her hands as if a horrible burden had been lifted from her shoulders. "I was beginning to think I was really crazy," she told Johanna. She took hold of Johanna's hands and squeezed them. "You can speak Russian!"

Now it was Johanna's turn to look surprised. "Russian?"

"But of course!" The girl laughed.

Just then Piedmont walked in, carrying his notepad and pen. He stopped abruptly when he saw Johanna with the girl.

Johanna could hardly contain herself. "Piedmont!"

With a glance behind him, Piedmont signaled Johanna to be silent. Then he beckoned her over to their spot by the fireplace.

"Who is that?" asked the girl in reference to the professor.

"Come on. You'll see." Johanna led the girl over, and they all sat down. "Piedmont, this is the girl I was telling you about—the one I heard call out."

Piedmont eyed the girl cautiously. "What is your name?" he asked.

"Oh, this is wonderful!" squealed the girl. "He speaks Russian, too!"

Johanna squinted at them both.

"My name," the girl continued, "yes, I will tell you now. My name is Radinka Yakovna Bjelkova. I live in Moscow. Oh, I cannot tell you how glad I am to be among comrades."

Johanna stared at Piedmont. She was baffled, but Piedmont stroked his beard and nodded. He smiled at Radinka and introduced himself, then Johanna.

"But neither of you are Russian?" Radinka looked perplexed. "Ukrainian, perhaps? You speak so well."

"You are mistaken." Johanna smiled at Radinka. "We are all speaking English."

Piedmont put up his hand. "Johanna, you are *both* mistaken."

"How?" Radinka wanted to know. "I know no other language but my native tongue." She shook her head. "At least it seemed that way until a few weeks ago."

"It is not Russian, nor is it English," Piedmont explained. He gestured to the other people in the room. "*These* people are all speaking English, Johanna. They have not changed. We three have."

Radinka's face shriveled up and tears began to seep from her eyes. "What is happening? Oh dear, it is as I thought. I *am* insane!"

"No, no, you are not," Johanna chided. "None of us are."

"Radinka, please, tell us what happened," said Piedmont.

"Please, call me Radya," the girl insisted, "it is less formal."

"Of course," the professor mumbled. "Radya, how did you get here from Moscow, of all places?"

Radya began to tell her story. She was a ballerina with the Soviet ballet company that had performed at the civic center the same night Johanna had been there. The company was on tour from Moscow to various cities in North America. It was, in fact, Radya's first tour. She had been very excited, but at the same time a little scared. Early in the tour she discovered herself to be homesick. She missed her family terribly, but it was out of the question to be permitted to return home.

The evening of the performance of *Swan Lake* at the Civic Center, Radya had felt fine. One of the principal dancers hurt her ankle while warming up before the third act, and Radya had been picked to replace her. She danced the part to the best of her ability, and everyone told her afterwards how terrific she had been. The following morning, when Radya awoke in the hotel room, she found the three other women who shared the room with her speaking in a foreign tongue. No one could understand a word she said from that point on.

"It was a nightmare," Radya explained. "The others would have nothing to do with me. Even my closest friend, Tanya. Everyone thought it was a trick. They chastised me and acted as though I were doing it to be different, so I could be sent home before we finished the tour. All this I gathered from the way everyone behaved."

"Well, I'm surprised they didn't send you back to the U.S.S.R.," Johanna put in.

"No way," put in Radya. "Instead the directors deserted me."

"They deserted you?" Piedmont looked surprised.

"Rather than risk trouble from the authorities, they took me to your inner city and left me." Sobs choked Radya's voice as she recalled some details obviously disturbing to her. "I still cannot believe it of them. It is my guess they went on to the next stop on the tour and told the authorities I had defected. After several days, the patrols discovered me. And when I could not explain my situation, I was brought here."

"That's terrible." Johanna's heart went out to the young girl. She turned to Piedmont. "But certainly Missing Persons would find out who she was. I've heard of Jane Doe cases, where they put the victim's picture in the newspaper."

Piedmont shook his head. "I have strong doubts about that," he said. "I'm sure our abductors were very careful about picking up the pieces."

"Abductors?" Radya leaned closer. "What abductors?"

"Piedmont, you're holding a lot back," accused Johanna. "I wish you'd tell us what you know." She lowered her voice, then said, "Last night Serassan came to my room."

Piedmont's eyebrows lifted. "And he *spoke* to you?"

Johanna told him briefly about her experience, then she asked, "How many others are there in this hospital who can understand the three of us?"

Piedmont sighed and put his notepad down next to the recliner. "All right. It's time I told you. As far as I know, Serassan is the only contact we have. At least I haven't spoken to anyone else."

"The woman doctor," said Johanna. "Is she in on it?"

"Dr. Wetzel?" Piedmont chuckled. "Heavens no. She's only interested in us because she thinks she's discovered some new kind of mental illness." He sat back and put his feet up. "Serassan gets a kick out of that."

"Who is this Serassan?" Radya demanded.

Piedmont replied that she would meet him shortly. "Mind you, I don't know all the details of the conspiracy. But I do know that Serassan and his organization have the upper hand on us. They got away with *this* much, didn't they?"

"But who are they?" Johanna asked. "What organization?"

"Who could pull off such a stunt as this one?" Radya questioned. "At first I thought this was an American plot to extract information. But even I know you Americans are not capable of such genius."

"Serassan has told me very little," Piedmont admitted. "I only know that he is involved because I was in contact with him just before the transformation happened to me."

Johanna remembered Serassan had sat next to her at the ballet. Had he planned to sit next to her? But why?

Piedmont went on. "The morning before my class on Milton, I met Serassan at the coffee shop I used to frequent. I was in the habit of stopping there each morning for a bit of breakfast. He sat next to me at the counter and we indulged in conversation. One thing led to another and he happened to accompany me to my office. Then I didn't see him again until a few weeks ago, when I saw him here."

Johanna was interested. "Piedmont, you said you came here in November."

"That's right. Serassan was here as a visiting doctor for a few weeks."

"And did he speak to you right away?"

"He observed me for a few days, then confided in me."

"Did he admit anything?" Radya asked. "Do you suppose he put something in your coffee?"

Johanna said she hadn't had any coffee. "I met Serassan the evening of the ballet," she confessed. She told how he had sat next to her in the audience.

"And did anything significant happen that you can recall?" asked Piedmont.

Johanna remembered the confusion she had felt when she'd come out of the ladies' room, only to discover she'd missed an entire act of the ballet. How could that be important? She shook her head.

"No dizzy spells?" prompted Piedmont. "No missing time?"

Johanna stared at him. *That* had to be it. She explained about the visit to the restroom and how half an hour of her life could not be accounted for. "I'll never forget it," she said. "Manley wanted to take me home then. We were going to leave, but then Serassan ... he came and sat down again and I ..." Her finger brushed against her upper lip as she strained to remember. She had stayed because of Serassan. She had wanted to be close to a stranger she had found attractive.

Radya bent her head close to Johanna. "What is that?" she asked and pointed to Johanna's nose.

Johanna looked at her. "What?"

"Your hand was just ..." Radya's eyebrows crinkled. "I have one of those, too." The Russian girl felt under the tip of her nose.

Piedmont bent forward to examine first Radya, then Johanna. "The scar," he announced. "You both have it."

It was then that Johanna noticed the tiny white slit, barely noticeable, under Radinka's nose. It was just like the white slit she had discovered on herself the night of the ballet, after she had gone home and was brushing her hair before bed. "How curious," breathed Johanna. "I don't have any idea where it came from."

There was a tremor in the blond girl's voice. "I just found it in the mirror the other day."

Johanna turned to the professor. "What do you make of it?"

He rubbed his grayish-red mustache. "You cannot see mine. I grew the mustache and beard after I arrived here."

"Can you explain it?" prompted Johanna.

The professor ignored Johanna and turned to Radya. "Did you experience any blackouts on the evening of your performance?"

"Well, I had a dizzy spell," admitted Radya. "It was after the performance, though. However, I credit that to our celebration with vodka." A tinge of pink flooded Radya's cheeks.

"So, Johanna, both you and I saw Serassan before each of our transformations," said Piedmont. "And we know that Serassan was at the ballet the evening Radya performed."

Johanna turned to the Russian dancer. "Did any strange men come up to you at all that night?"

"We are watched closely," said Radya. "It was not possible. What does this Serassan look like?"

Johanna described the doctor, with Piedmont's help.

Radya frowned. "I do not think so. Perhaps if I see him, I will remember."

Johanna mentioned that she recalled Serassan had left his seat twice during the performance. "Once before the intermission," she said, "and later, after I had returned to my seat. He was gone when the ballet ended."

Piedmont lowered his voice. "We must split up now. I see Dr. Wetzel has just come into the room. Radya, it is important that we keep to ourselves as much as we can, as long as the doctors are watching us."

"I understand."

"Johanna, things are starting to make more sense to me now." Piedmont studied her face. "The fact that we both saw Serassan before … and especially your episode of amnesia."

"Do you think it ties in with all this?"

"It is highly probable." Piedmont turned away to retrieve his notepad. "Now … scatter, before she grows suspicious."

Johanna got up and wandered over to the piano while Radya slipped off to another corner. Piedmont had revealed a lot, but there were still so many questions that needed to be answered.

Johanna wanted to speak with Serassan again. She wanted to ask him point blank what was going on. What kind of an organization was Serassan involved with? What was their purpose? What would the future hold in store for herself, Piedmont and the Russian girl?

That night, after Johanna returned to her room, she paced the floor. She had seen nothing of Serassan. The questions tormented her.

Dr. Wetzel, the woman doctor, had met with each of the three of them during the course of the day. She had taken Radya first and spent a good two hours with the Russian ballerina. Then Johanna had sat and listened while Dr.

Wetzel tried to communicate with her. She'd been given paper and pencil to write with, but it was useless. Johanna had ended up doodling on the paper, which seemed to excite the doctor. Johanna was not an artist, but it became entertaining to draw things in front of the doctor, who acted as though Johanna was attempting serious communication.

After forty minutes of that, Johanna grew tired of the game and refused to do anything more for the doctor. She had not been allowed to return to the recreation hall after that.

Manley had not come in three days. Johanna missed her brother. This whole affair had upset him so much, she could tell. Perhaps Doris had convinced him it was best if he just stopped coming. It had to be torturous to Manley, seeing her this way.

She sat on her bed, struggling to remember more about the night of the ballet, when her door opened.

In walked Serassan.

— 10 —

The Conspiracy Unfolds

Johanna's heart thumped with anticipation as the tall man in the white jacket softly closed the door to her room.

"So, you are not asleep yet?" asked Serassan.

"I thought you'd never come," she told him. "I need some answers. Please!"

"Ah, you have been talking with Piedmont again." Serassan came over to stand in front of her. "I had to leave for the day. But I thought I'd come by and check on you, Johanna. How are you?"

She would not be put off. "Why am I here? I know you are responsible for bringing us here."

"By *us* you must mean yourself, Piedmont and the Russian girl," said Serassan. "The credit is not all mine, Johanna. Circumstances are what brought the three of you together. It is merely coincidence that you all ended up at the same hospital."

"We want to know what's going on," begged Johanna. "I don't know how you did it, how you managed to make freaks out of us."

"I understand you perfectly."

"How can Radya, who speaks only Russian, and Piedmont and I, who speak only English, all understand each other? Why does everyone else speak gibberish? Why does everyone think we are crazy?"

Serassan sat down on Francine's unoccupied bed. "Do not become upset. You are speaking my native language—Estronian, if you will."

Johanna stared at him. His eyes were definitely slanted toward the back of his head, but the blue color was what was unusual.

"What is Estronian? I've never heard of it. Who are you? What country are you from?"

"I came to warn you of something." Serassan was evading her question. His eyes stared directly into hers and he did not smile.

"What? You're not answering my question!" Johanna fired.

"I thought you should know." He stood up and walked over to the door.

"Why don't you tell me where you're from?" Johanna persisted.

Serassan opened the door and peeked out, then shut it again and turned to her. "Not now, Johanna. What I wanted to tell you is this. We are letting the old woman return to the recreation hall tomorrow."

Johanna jumped up from the bed. "Are you kidding? You're letting that old hag back among the patients? How can you? She's dangerous!"

Serassan shook his head. "She's been given a lot of medication. As long as we keep giving her the drugs, we can control her. I doubt there will be further attacks on her part, Johanna."

"How can you say that? She almost killed Francine!"

Serassan came over and tried to calm her. "I suspected the news would upset you. That's why I felt I should warn you." He sat down on the bed beside her and gently touched her arm.

Johanna stared at his hand against her skin. It was strangely warm and soothing. Like last night, she immediately felt the prickle of energy that began to flow up to her shoulder. Then she stared into his face. She felt overcome by a mysterious sensation of pleasure, as though she wasn't herself anymore. "Is... is that all you can do? Give people drugs? Is that your answer? The old woman isn't safe to be around, I don't care how many drugs you pump into her."

Serassan drew Johanna closer to him. Her chin came up to the base of his neck and she noticed a peculiar body odor, not altogether unpleasant. It was definitely something she had never smelled before. His face was tanned and smooth. She realized he must have just shaved because there was no indication of any beard growth anywhere on his face. "Please understand one thing," he told her. "I do not condone the methods of healing used at this hospital."

Johanna became aware of her own breathing, which grew rapid and shallow. She had never been this close to a man before. Serassan's presence was like a shield around her. She couldn't help it. She was actually enjoying this contact. Warmth surged throughout her whole body. "But you're ... a doctor."

Serassan slowly shook his head from side to side, all the while his penetrating blue eyes focused on her own.

"You're not?" Johanna stared up at him, not moving. "Are you saying you're *not* a doctor?"

Ignoring her question, he asked, "How would you like to do me a special favor tonight?"

Now Johanna was scared. What did he have in mind? "You're not answering my question," she managed to utter. "If you're not a doctor, why are you here? Everyone thinks you're..."

"What I know and can do is beyond anyone's capability at this hospital," Serassan interrupted. "But no, Johanna, I am not a physician. I carry my anatophysio card, but that's nothing. And I do have expertise in cerebro-surgery." He ran his finger under her nose in a caressing manner and smiled. "That's sort of like a CPR card in your terms."

Johanna opened her mouth, but nothing came out. She had a strong feeling he was talking about something a lot heavier than CPR or first aid. Whatever operation he was working under, it had to be something tremendous, highly advanced, and secretive. She was in awe of him.

"Now, about that special favor," he whispered.

Johanna thought of Piedmont's warning that Serassan could not be trusted. "What kind of favor?" she asked reluctantly.

"Come with me." He took hold of her hand and whispered, "We must be discreet." Then he led her to the door and carefully peeked out into the corridor. Turning back to her, he said, "No one is in sight. Follow me."

Johanna did not protest. Still holding onto his hand, she followed Serassan down the hallway. The lights had been dimmed, and she noticed that the night nurse was not at the nurses' station right now. Serassan again cautioned her to keep quiet as he led her to the recreation hall.

When they got there, it was totally dark inside. Serassan gently pushed Johanna inside, then closed the door behind them and turned on the lights. She was aware of Serassan's breathing. A chill of excitement caused Johanna's heart to flutter. Why had he brought her here?

"Come." Serassan led Johanna to the piano.

She looked up at him in wonder. It was obvious he wanted her to sit down on the bench and play something.

"I didn't want you to risk yourself tomorrow when the old woman is back. I *need* to hear you play."

Without a word, she seated herself on the bench and stared down at the keyboard. When she looked up at him, she saw a hungry look on his face that unnerved her. He motioned her to begin. She thought a moment, then played a theme from a Rachmaninoff concerto. She soon lost herself in the music. She seemed to drift off into time and space, and her music became interwoven with thoughts of herself and Serassan.

She remembered the touch of his hand, the surge of warmth she had felt, the gentle look in his deep blue eyes. Suddenly, she longed to pour her heart out to him, to confess that the things she had blurted out yesterday she had meant.

Johanna was fatigued when she finished playing. She realized she had been playing different pieces for the last hour. It was very late, and Serassan helped her back to her room. She followed as though she were in a daze, as if all this were just a dream. When they got to her room, he helped her back into bed and stood over her for several minutes.

She had so many questions she wanted him to answer. She wanted to thank him for taking her down to the piano. But she felt so sleepy. A warm blanket of soft energy seemed to enshroud her, and her eyes grew heavy. The last thing she remembered was his face bending very close to hers.

The next morning, as Johanna headed for the recreation hall, she passed the room Radya was in. She hesitated as she heard crying. The door was open, so Johanna poked her head in. "Radya, what's wrong?"

The ballerina stood at the barred window. She turned to Johanna with a tear-streaked face. At once the sobs muffled. "Oh, what a relief … it is you, Johanna."

Radya's room was a terrible mess. Whomever she had for a roommate was obviously a sloppy person. Underwear, books, makeup, and magazines seemed to take up half the room. Radya noticed Johanna's stares. "It's terrible, I know. The other despises me. I wish I could room with you, Johanna."

"Why are you crying, Radya?"

The girl had washed her hair, and it hung loose and shimmering about her shoulders. "Because I am frightened." She sobbed again.

Johanna went up to her. "Of course you are. Come sit down." She led the Russian girl over to the bed against the wall. They both sat down. Radya sank into Johanna's arms and let herself be comforted.

"I do not want to be here," she sobbed. "I want to leave this place. I want my mother and father."

"You're not alone," Johanna crooned. She remembered Piedmont had told her those exact words the first day they had met. Then she recalled she had a lot to discuss with Piedmont. "Come on, we can walk down to the recreation hall together."

Suddenly, the door swung open wide and the red-haired lady glared at Johanna and Radya. In a fit of anger, Her Highness picked up a sweater and flung it across the room. A series of garbled phrases emerged. She seemed to be extremely upset about something. Radya continued to sniffle, and huddled closer to Johanna.

"*Ennx briofhg yoocotnz!*" Her Highness screamed. She found a towel on the floor and flung it at them. "*Kivzhum strowpenwr yapneedlist!*"

Johanna hurried Radya out of the room. "That was your roommate?"

"Yes." Radya sniffed.

"Well, Her Highness is certainly moody today." They walked toward the recreation hall. "She must have run out of lipstick or something."

Radya giggled. Now that she felt safe, she could see the situation from a different perspective. She wiped her cheeks and smiled at Johanna. "Thank you, comrade. It's just that she's ... she's so domineering."

"Be thankful you've got *her* for a roommate and not Melody."

"Who is Melody?"

"Don't ask."

"I wish I could have you for a roommate, Johanna. Maybe they'd let us switch."

Johanna made a point to ask Serassan about this possibility the next time she saw him alone. As they entered the recreation hall, she saw Piedmont in his corner by the fireplace, writing in his notebook. Then her heart skipped a beat when she noticed the bedraggled figure of Melody. The old woman was seated in front of the television set with Wanda.

"What's wrong?" Radya asked.

"Oh, nothing." Johanna did not want to worry the girl. They approached Piedmont, and Johanna felt relieved that Serassan had let her play the piano last night. There was no way she would go near the instrument with that woman in the same room.

"Good morning, ladies," Piedmont greeted them.

"You're in a cheery mood for once," said Johanna, and took a seat.

"Radya, you've been crying," Piedmont bemoaned.

"I'm okay now," replied the Russian girl.

Piedmont rolled his eyes toward the TV corner. "Did you see she's back?" he said.

Johanna explained how Serassan had come to her room the previous night to warn her of Melody's return. "Piedmont, he's very strange. Did you know Serassan isn't even a doctor?"

Piedmont tipped his glasses at her. "Go on," he coaxed.

Johanna went on to explain about Serassan denying that he was a physician. "He all but admitted that this whole thing is some kind of a scam," she said. "And he said we were speaking his native language. Now listen to this. He says it's Estronian."

"What is Estronian?" Radya's blue eyes widened.

"I've never heard that before." Piedmont seemed disappointed for some reason. He scratched his beard and frowned as he thought a moment. Then he looked back at Johanna. "What else did our friend tell you?"

Johanna repeated what she could remember, but did not mention how Serassan had held her in his arms. She felt goose bumps as she recalled the new feelings that had come over her. She did not want Piedmont, or Radya, or anybody to know about the intimacy. She did mention how he had sneaked her down to the recreation hall late last night so she could play the piano.

"You are a musician?" Radya seemed delighted.

"Yes, didn't you know? And Piedmont here is an author and a poet."

"Johanna ..." Piedmont was still puzzled about something. "This is truly amazing."

"What is?"

"Serassan has confided in you. That surprises me."

"Well, what do you think?" she prompted. "What did he mean by the language Estronian? Is there such a thing?"

"Perhaps it is some kind of dialect," guessed Radya.

"He's not from around here," said Piedmont.

Johanna leaned forward. "What are you trying to say?"

Piedmont cleared his throat. "Well, I mean ... he couldn't be."

"This Dr. Serassan sounds very mysterious," commented Radya.

"He's definitely that." Piedmont nodded his head thoughtfully. "He's an alien."

Johanna gasped. She shivered as realization struck her.

"An alien?" asked Radya. "From what country?"

"Radya ..." Johanna put her hand on the Russian girl's wrist. "I think what Piedmont is trying to tell us is ... Serassan is not a man from this planet. He comes from ..."

"From another *world*," emphasized Piedmont.

"Impossible," objected Radya. She looked from Johanna to Piedmont in disbelief. "My country has done a study on the subject, and we came to the conclusion that extraterrestrial life merely does not exist."

"Propaganda, dear Radya," replied Piedmont.

"No, it is the truth!" the girl cried out. "A study was done by the government. People who claimed to see ships ... or flying saucers, as you Americans term them ... turned out to be seeing things that could be explained. It was a Yankee plot!"

Johanna watched as Piedmont tried to convince Radya she was mistaken. Apparently the girl's mind was instilled with Soviet brainwashing of many kinds. Perhaps her shock at conceiving of the possibility of the existence of aliens who could manipulate her mind and cause her to be abducted in such a manner was too frightening for the girl to deal with. Johanna herself was having a hard time accepting the idea. She stared down at her hands as thoughts flashed through her head.

Serassan from another world? What world? It would explain a lot of things about him, including his slant-eyed appearance. She knew he was too tall to be Oriental, and his other features did not match that possibility. It would also explain his hypnotic power over her when he looked in her eyes, or touched her and sent a blanket of energy over her entire body. If Piedmont's theory was correct, it opened the door to a lot of new possibilities, Johanna knew. And it left the door open for a great many more questions that had to be answered. She stood up to leave.

"Johanna, where are you going?" asked Piedmont.

Radya had been reduced to tears. She held her blond head in her hands and cried softly into her lap.

"I've got to find him," she said.

"No, it could be dangerous."

"He won't hurt me," she said firmly.

"Johanna, please stay. I know this news has disturbed you. But we don't know yet what we are up against."

Johanna walked away. She left Piedmont to comfort Radya, and walked out into the corridor. Two nurses were gossiping at the nurses' station as she wandered by, pretending to be on her way to the restroom. How could she find Serassan? She hadn't seen him at all this morning. She knew where the coffee room was, the small lounge where the doctors and nurses took their breaks. Perhaps she would find him there.

When she was sure no one was looking, Johanna slipped into that hallway. She heard a female voice laughing. Johanna swung around and ducked into a closet in the hall. Dr. Wetzel came out of the lounge and with her was Serassan. Johanna recognized their voices. Dr. Wetzel was speaking in jargon, and Serassan answered her with a crack of humorous jargon that caused them both to laugh. A moment later, Dr. Wetzel's footsteps clicked on down the hall.

Johanna waited in the dark closet for another half a minute, then slowly opened the door and stepped out. She was about to confront Serassan when, suddenly, she heard another man's voice. Serassan was conversing with somebody else in the lounge. She would have to wait until he was alone to talk with him, she knew. She waited outside the door, scared that at any second a nurse or an attendant would come along and spy her.

In the seconds that followed, her fears slipped away as she recognized the words that comprised Serassan's conversation.

— 11 —

Jail Break

"Thorden, you are my friend," Serassan said in the doctors' lounge, "but you put such a strain on this friendship. How can I get through to you?"

"You must let me see the ballerina." The other man's voice was higher pitched than Serassan's. Johanna, standing unobserved outside the door, detected a sinister edge to it.

Serassan sighed. "I gave my word to the Preejhna Chiyuub. Have you forgotten the purpose of our mission?"

The sinister voice grew impatient. "No, *you* have forgotten the objective of our mission, Serassan. Now that we are within one solar day of departure, I am growing a little tired of your self-righteousness. *I* picked the ballerina. I *want* her, and I'll *have* her."

Serassan's voice was grave. "But you did not qualify for breeding privileges, Thorden. We are not to interfere with the eugenics."

"And what do you call your involvement with that musician?"

"You will leave Johanna out of it."

"Is it not the same thing?" the other demanded. "You possess as much lust and as much craving as anyone else. You know that once we reach the colony, that is it. Why should you care about these Terrans?"

"I fail to see why you don't, Thorden."

The other voice pleaded, "I'm asking only to indulge once. Do not deny me this, Serassan."

"Once was never enough for you, Thorden." Serassan's voice grew stronger. He seemed to be heading toward the doorway. Johanna cringed. "When do we rendezvous with the mother ship?"

"A van will be ready tomorrow. The other Terrans will be assembled, and we will all meet at launch point. The mother ship is due to pick up the cargo within hours. Now ... let me go to her."

"It is against my better judgment," grumbled Serassan.

"If you do not, I will go to the Preejhna with a report on your conduct regarding the musician!"

"Then you may see her!" Anger had risen in Serassan. He was close to the doorway now. Johanna started back down the hall. She had heard enough. "But please try to restrain yourself, Thorden." Serassan's voice trailed off. "I cannot go on covering your tracks ..."

Johanna ducked into the closet again just as the two men's footsteps came down the hall from the doctors' lounge. As they passed, she heard them talking in jargon. Apparently they were disguising themselves to fit in with the rest of the hospital staff. She waited until she was sure they had gone, then stepped out of the closet.

"I must tell Piedmont and Radya," Johanna mumbled to herself. It was vital that they know what was in store for them. Whoever this Thorden was, he frightened Johanna. There was no doubt in her mind that it had been Radya after whom the sinister-sounding alien lusted. Poor Radya was just a child. "I must warn her!"

"*Pitwomp! Haztilmobschluckg weebzduntrimp voofpinsp!*"

Johanna turned in the direction of the voice. A nurse hurried toward her, screaming for help. Johanna started to run in the opposite direction, but a male attendant jumped out from one of the rooms and grabbed her.

"No! Let me go!"

The nurse gave instructions, and the attendant took Johanna back to her room. There she was locked in. There was no chance of meeting with Piedmont now.

Johanna stared out her window through the bars. Hot tears filled her eyes. How was she going to end up? Piedmont had been right after all. She knew from the conversation between Serassan and Thorden that they had to be aliens. They had spoken of launch point and a mother ship. Were they planning to take her on that ship somewhere? It sounded like they were planning to take her and the others to the launch point tomorrow. How was she going to warn Piedmont and Radya?

I've got to get out of here, Johanna decided as she stared out the window. Snow still covered the ground down below, but the sun was shining. She knew spring was in the air because folded buds covered the tree branch right outside the window. How she longed to be outside in the fresh air again. "I'm going to get out of here," she told herself. "I don't care what it takes. Nobody's taking me to some distant planet against my will. I'll escape, that's what I'll do. There must be some way."

She walked back toward the door, but it was still locked. Johanna fell to her knees and let the sobs come. At least they had not sedated her. But getting out was going to be a hell of an effort. How could she pull it off?

"I'll find a way," she sniffed, getting up. She went over to her bed and sat down. She began to think of a plan. Then she wrung her hands and stared up at the ceiling as another thought crossed her mind. Even if she did manage to escape from this hospital, what was she going to do then?

A knock on the door alerted Johanna. She sat up straight in her bed. It had to be Serassan. The nurses just barged in at any old time. She wiped her cheek and smoothed her dark hair, which she had let fall over her shoulders for once. She called out, "Come in!"

To her disappointment, it was not Serassan, but the attendant Freckles with her lunch tray. Johanna's hopes sank as she realized they were going to keep her confined to this room, probably for the rest of the day. There would be no chance for her to warn Piedmont and Radya. Without a word, Freckles brought the tray over to the bed.

This is it, Johanna told herself with a glance at the open door. *If I don't make a run for it now, I may not get another chance.* She began to moan to get the attendant's attention.

"*Unk siss brazzenjort yipfralvog,*" chided Freckles and removed the lid on the lunch tray.

Johanna clasped her heart and moaned louder. She rolled her eyes as if in great pain.

Freckles stared at her, but did not move.

Johanna let her body go limp. She fell back against the wall as her eyes rolled backward. She lay still and waited for Freckles to react.

A series of exclamations erupted from the attendant's mouth. Freckles reached for the nurses' call button, but Johanna had pulled the wires out of the wall. Johanna heard footsteps running across the room toward the door. Freckles had left to get help.

Without a moment's hesitation, Johanna sprang to her feet. She darted for the door, glanced out, and saw no one in sight, then fled down the hall toward the doctors' lounge. She would hide in the closet until she had figured a way to get out. Taking the elevator was impossible, even if there wasn't a gate to bar her escape. It was right next to the nurses' station. Someone was bound to see her and stop her if she went that way.

Before she turned the corner, she heard humming. A large dirty laundry cart stood outside the door to one of the patient's rooms. Johanna noticed the maid inside, changing the beds. Looking around her, she realized no one had seen her so far. She might not be so lucky so close to the lounge.

On the spur of the moment, she made a decision. Johanna climbed into the laundry cart and crouched low, pulling dirty sheets and clothing over her. The bottom of the cart was gritty. The sheet touching her face was wet and smelled strongly of urine. Worse yet, her nose was greeted with a pungent odor that must have been a mixture of human sweat and defecation. She cringed as her stomach whirled in rebellion.

Outside the cart, she heard a commotion in the hall. Freckles was obviously telling someone about Johanna's alleged fainting spell. The footsteps faded, and then Johanna felt a load of blankets and towels dumped on top of her. She prayed the maid would not look too closely. The cart moved down the hall, and Johanna heard angry voices as they passed her room. The other voice was that of Dr. Wetzel, who was apparently chewing out Freckles for leaving the door wide open. Johanna held her breath and tried not to gag.

A man's voice rang out, and the cart stopped. Someone spoke to the maid, who answered laconically. Johanna recognized the man's voice as that of Thorden, the sinister alien. Dr. Wetzel called out, and Thorden abruptly walked away. The cart rolled once again.

This time Johanna heard the ding of a bell. A moment later, she was wheeled onto the elevator. The maid continued to hum as the doors slid shut. Then the elevator shaft fell rapidly. No one but the maid was in the elevator, Johanna guessed. She wondered where they were headed. Would the maid stop on the next floor? Would Johanna be delayed in her attempt to leave the hospital? She couldn't remain in this soiled laundry cart for long. If she did, she might soil it some more.

It was a long ride on the elevator. When it stopped again, the doors opened and Johanna heard voices, then laughter. The maid said something to the voices, then chuckled. The doors closed and the elevator continued downward.

Suddenly, it stopped. The doors opened, and the maid pushed out the laundry cart. Johanna felt herself moving. As they continued on, Johanna became aware of the loud noise of machines. Then the maid stopped and let out a loud sigh.

Another woman's voice greeted the maid and a conversation ensued. Johanna listened to the gibberish, wondering where she was. The machines thrashed all around them. A minute later, the maid and the other woman's voice trailed off. The two had apparently walked away.

Johanna clawed through the sheets and towels to fresh air. She saw she was in an enclosed room. The antiseptic smell of laundry detergent greeted her nostrils this time as she poked her head up above the cart's rim to see where she was. The cement walls and beams told her she was in the hospital's basement. Washing machines surrounded her. Johanna jerked when she saw a man in janitor's fatigues with his back toward her. He was bald and short, crouched beside a machine. A toolbox lay open at his side. Johanna could see no one else in the area.

She couldn't take a chance on anyone finding her. She'd have to risk being seen by the man. It was better than someone finding her later beside this cart. Besides, the filthy sheets had nauseated her. Johanna carefully climbed out of the cart and ducked behind it so that it was between her and the man repairing the laundry unit. She huddled there a few seconds, trying to think of what she should do next. She couldn't stay here long. Someone from her floor was bound to figure out how she had escaped. Before long, they would call out and conduct a thorough search for her.

Johanna ventured out from her hiding place. She managed to reach the doorway to the laundry room without the janitor seeing her. No one was in the hallway. Glancing down at her leisure suit and slippers, Johanna realized she couldn't go anywhere dressed this way without arousing suspicion. She started down the hallway toward a red exit sign. She found a locker room near the exit. Again luck was on her side. No one was in it. Johanna entered and started opening locker doors to see if she could find something more suitable to wear. A man's jacket hung in the first door she opened. She slammed it and continued her search.

Voices in the hallway startled Johanna. She froze, then came to her senses and hid behind a large post. She saw two figures walk past on their way to the exit. They hadn't even looked in.

Johanna was about to continue ransacking the lockers when she noticed a rack of uniforms hanging on the wall. Candystriper and blue lady uniforms dominated the rack as well as a white lab jacket.

Johanna struggled with the zipper to her leisure suit. She climbed out of it and threw it behind the rack. Over her bra and panties she pulled on a blue lady's dress that was about two sizes too large. Then she put on the lab jacket. At least now she was in a dress, and the white jacket — though it was of thin fabric — would help keep her warm outside.

"Too bad there aren't any shoes or boots," Johanna grumbled. She still had on her gray slippers, but she couldn't waste any more time. She had to leave the hospital now. She stepped out into the hallway once more and headed directly for the exit.

Climbing the stairway to the main floor, a worrisome thought crossed her mind. What if they'd alerted security and guards were at all the entrances? At least she was at a side exit and wouldn't have to leave the building through the lobby, where she'd appear conspicuous.

A middle-aged, gray-haired lady came through the door as Johanna went out. The lady smiled and greeted Johanna, who merely nodded. No one else was in her way. Johanna felt the sun shine on her face and bare hands as the frigid March air greeted her for the first time in several weeks. She was free at last, but she couldn't stop to count her blessings. At least not yet. She was still on the hospital premises. Any second now she could be spotted.

Johanna headed for the parking lot. Her slippers touched the crusty snow as she took a shortcut across the white blanketed lawn. The ceaseless whisper of distant traffic came from the nearby expressway. A few people walked from the parking lot, but nobody seemed to pay attention to her. Johanna kept on, all the time worried that soon someone would be at her heels.

As she crossed the parking lot, Johanna's eyes skimmed the different colored vehicles. People didn't leave their cars unlocked anymore. It wasn't worth bothering to stop and see if anyone had left their keys. She hurried on. Not until she had reached the street did she begin to feel that she had successfully accomplished her task.

By then she slowed down to catch her breath. Carbon dioxide puffs appeared and disintegrated from her breath as she walked along the sidewalk. This was a busy section close to the expressway, far from downtown. Although there was much traffic, there were few pedestrians.

Johanna started to feel cold. She dug her fingers into the thin, thready pockets of the white lab jacket. Her toes were beginning to feel numb. She knew downtown was a long walk. What she needed was a ride.

If only I could hail a cab, Johanna thought. She searched the cars and trucks that passed her both ways. Not a taxi among them. And even if she could successfully hail one, how was she supposed to explain to the driver where she wanted to go? Johanna continued to plod along. Her lip quivered from the cold and she pulled the collar of the lab jacket tighter against her throat.

She thought about hitchhiking. She had never done such a thing in her life, though. She wasn't even sure how one went about hitchhiking. Standing on the curb, Johanna held out her thumb to passing cars. She noticed only a few heads turn toward her. Nobody bothered to stop for her.

After a couple of minutes of this, Johanna turned and continued to walk faster. The sun had gone behind a cloud and the air prickled her exposed skin. "It's okay," she told herself, "Johanna, you managed to get out of that hospital and that's all that matters."

Soon the sidewalk ended. Johanna came to an intersection where two sets of railroad tracks crossed the busy road. Large, dilapidated warehouses stood like wary strangers around her. Rock piles and broken lumber from demolition sites were layered with crusty patches of gritty snow. She knew these tracks led directly downtown, but walking along them in her slippers was not a comforting thought.

Pausing to appease her sore ankles, Johanna noticed a large, shiny black Mercedes as it drew to a stop across the road. She saw two men inside, both looking her way. She couldn't be sure, but the men appeared to have stopped because of her. Afraid that they were police, notified of her escape from the hospital, Johanna quickly glanced around to see where she could hide. Fortunately, they had been heading in the opposite direction. Time was to her advantage.

She gave up on the railroad track idea and continued down the side of the road, picking up her pace.

When she dared to peek over her shoulder, Johanna saw one of the men from the black Mercedes standing outside the car, watching her. He was dressed in a black suit and tie, with a hat and dark sunglasses. There was something menacing about him that she couldn't put her finger on. Her instinct told her to flee. She began to run.

She hadn't gone far when an ache in her chest, caused from the cold air, forced her to slow down. Her breathing came in gasps as she looked behind her. The black Mercedes had pulled away from the curb and was signaling to make a turn. They were going to follow her! Panic seized Johanna and she started to run again. There was nowhere to hide. The men in black were bound to catch up to her.

The screech of bus wheels caused Johanna to spin around. A city bus drew up beside her and halted. The doors hissed open and the bus driver stared out at Johanna. She sighed in relief and ran over. Thank God!

The bus driver asked her a question in gibberish. Johanna tensed up. She couldn't answer him. Worse yet, she realized she had no money. How was she going to pay the bus fare? The driver signaled Johanna to get on the bus. The doors closed and he spoke to her again.

Johanna felt her face collapse. She was cold and hugged herself. She shook her head slowly and showed him her hands, which didn't even carry a purse. He seemed to get the message instantly. Rubbing his chin, the bus driver studied Johanna a long moment. He asked her something which she couldn't understand.

"Please," Johanna implored, close to tears, "don't make me get off the bus. I need to go downtown."

An elderly lady in a plaid coat and wool scarf stood up from her seat at the front of the bus. She extended a wrinkled hand which held some coins. Johanna stared into the wrinkled face and the brown eyes that appeared larger than normal beneath a pair of thick, rimless glasses. The old lady smiled and nodded, showing crooked, off-color teeth. It was clear to Johanna that this woman insisted on giving her the fare.

Johanna reached out and let the old lady drop the coins into her hand. She was grateful to the old lady and wanted to thank her, but didn't dare. The faces of all the other bus riders were focused on the handout, some of them obviously appalled. Before Johanna could even smile at her benefactor, the woman returned to her seat.

The bus driver spoke impatiently. Johanna handed him the money. He counted it, then put the exact fare into his meter. As Johanna turned to find a seat in which to sit, the bus driver grabbed her arm. Then he gave her a couple of dimes, or what Johanna guessed were dimes. She recognized the familiar face of the president, but the writing was, of course, garbled.

Closing her palm over the change, Johanna found a seat at the rear of the bus. People continued to stare at her. A child said something out loud and a moment later the mother hushed the child. Johanna guessed the child had noticed her wet slippers.

The bus drove toward downtown. Johanna sat in her seat and watched out the window, grateful to be where it was warm, and thinking about what she would do when she got downtown. Where could she go?

Manley was her only hope. She would go to Manley. She would call him. She had two dimes. She could find a pay phone and call him at home. There was no one else to turn to, she realized.

Settling back against the vinyl seat, Johanna sighed. She felt dirty from being in the laundry cart and noticed some of the terrible scent had rubbed off on her. Her stomach grumbled. She hadn't eaten lunch and she was hungry. She decided to get off at the heart of downtown and find a restaurant and tidy up in the washroom.

After several minutes, the bus circled familiar territory. Johanna got off with a couple of other people. She clutched the money in her hand, which felt hot and sweaty. Then she looked around at the buzzing traffic and the people bundled up in coats and hats. She realized how out of place she must look in the white lab jacket and gray slippers. It was vital to get inside some place soon.

Johanna noticed a storefront that resembled a small restaurant she had eaten in once with Manley. She hurried over and slipped inside. The smell of Italian food and the sudden warmth of the indoor heat encompassed her as she looked right, then left, in search of the washroom.

Piped-in music greeted her ears. Johanna followed a woman who seemed headed for the ladies' room. Sure enough, inside she found two sinks and three stalls. A small girl in pigtails was drying her hands at the automatic blower. The rushing sound echoed in the small, tiled room.

While Johanna washed, she studied herself in the mirror. Her hair looked as though she hadn't brushed it that morning. Her face was pale and drawn. Her lips were chapped and felt worse from the cold, dry air outside. She scrubbed with the soap, then removed the white lab jacket and stuffed it into the trash barrel. The blue lady's uniform did not fit her that well, but at least she wouldn't be as conspicuous as she would wearing the jacket.

As she emerged from the ladies' room, Johanna envisioned a plate of hot, steaming lasagna. She could see people seated in the dining room, sipping wine. Wonderful smells of hot bread and spicy Italian sauces and other tantalizing delicacies made her yearn for food. *Forget it, Johanna, you have no money*, she taunted herself. Then she sighed. She could always eat first, then manage to get up and go to the ladies' room but not come back. Then she shook her head. That wasn't right either. She couldn't bring herself to be dishonest. *Though you did take these clothes*, she reminded herself, *and if you hadn't, would you have gotten this far?*

Temptation won over and Johanna let a hostess in a low-necked yellow blouse lead her to a single table in the dining room. A few patrons glanced up as Johanna entered. At least no one seemed bothered by her strange attire. Even if they did, Johanna felt too hungry and too tired to care what anybody thought. She sat down and the hostess handed her a cardboard menu. As Johanna turned it over and over in her hands, she saw she couldn't read a word on the menu.

"*Bwopf ladgrix shwan zophah rawkplick?*" the hostess asked Johanna.

Confused, Johanna nodded. To her surprise, the hostess smiled, then walked away. Johanna studied the menu and then set it aside. She saw what other people were eating and her mouth watered. The two coins were still in the palm of her hand, and she turned them over and over, wondering how she was going to order her meal.

When the waitress came, Johanna opened her mouth to speak and pointed to her ear and shook her head. She wanted to convey to the waitress that she was a deaf-mute and thus would not be able to order her meal in the expected manner. This puzzled the waitress, but the woman smiled politely and pointed to different items on the menu. Johanna guessed a lot and the meal got ordered. After the waitress left, Johanna wondered what she was going to have for lunch.

She had seen a telephone in the lobby area of the restaurant. Johanna got up and went to it. She would call Manley and somehow make him understand that she needed him to come for her. How she was to accomplish this, she didn't know. It was much too far to walk from downtown to Manley's home, and she knew of no buses that could take her in that vicinity.

Johanna inserted the dimes and listened for the dial tone as she put the receiver to her ear. Then she stared at the buttons on the telephone. The numbers were squiggles. It would take more guess work. Counting out the buttons carefully to make sure she didn't hit the wrong one by mistake, she dialed Manley's and Doris's number from her memory, hoping it was right.

To her relief, the dimes dropped down into oblivion. A second later, she heard the phone ringing at the other end.

— 12 —

Narcotic of the Mind

Johanna stood and wiggled her wet toes as she held the telephone receiver to her ear. The gray slippers were soaked from the snow. She trembled as she heard the rattling buzz of the phone ringing on the other end of the line. "Please be home, Manley," she prayed.

It rang six times before Johanna heard the click of someone picking up the line. She sighed with relief. "*Leegash brisilch myen schorfg.*" It was Doris's voice.

Johanna panicked. It was just her luck to get Doris on the line. She didn't know what to do, so she said nothing.

"*Premjaquib horg zilgug vimyecktar,*" Doris said into the phone.

Johanna let out a sob, then said, "Doris? Is ... is Manley there?"

Doris cried out in alarm. Johanna hoped her sister-in-law would at least recognize that it was her. If she did, she could summon Manley to the phone, and somehow perhaps ...

"*Dwopneef oogruc destpeesh mubzool brenhuljiv weensh crooblik!*"

"Doris, please ... it's me, Johanna. Please get Manley. I need to speak to him. It's urgent!"

A young businessman in a beige suit coat stood next to Johanna, apparently waiting to use the telephone. He eyed her suspiciously.

Doris flung a torrent of gibberish at her. In the background Johanna thought she heard Manley's voice calling out. Before she could try to convey anything further, Doris hung up.

"Oh no ... *no!*" Johanna whined as she stared at the receiver in her hand. The stupid woman! The connection was broken, and Johanna had no more coins. Even if Manley did figure out she had called, he would have no way of knowing from where she had called. Johanna slammed the phone down and spun around.

The businessman took a step backward as his eyes swept her unkempt figure.

Sniffing, Johanna stepped away from the phone booth. There was nothing left to do but go back into the dining room. Perhaps after a decent meal she could think of something else. She would walk to Manley's house, or die trying.

For the first time in her life, Johanna hated her sister-in-law with a passion. How could Doris do such a thing? She had to have known it was Johanna on the line, and that she needed to talk to Manley. She took her seat and found a tossed salad at her place.

Johanna ate the salad and thought back about the resentment she and Doris had felt toward one another over the past couple of years.

When Manley started taking Doris out, Johanna thought the relationship between the two would pass. Manley dated few girls and then only sparingly. He had never been serious about any of them. When he announced to Johanna that he and Doris were getting married, Johanna had been more than a little surprised. Doris did not seem to be Manley's type. She was obese, dumpy, and lackadaisical about her appearance. What Manley saw in Doris had puzzled Johanna from the beginning, until she found out that Doris had money.

Johanna doubted that Manley truly loved Doris. From the beginning, she knew he was only interested in her money. Manley, on the other hand, was on the obese side himself, over 40, losing his hair. He wasn't the most eligible bachelor, that was for sure. Perhaps he had realized he had better latch onto a good thing while he still had a fighting chance. So he had married Doris.

And ever since, there had been the developing tension between Johanna and her sister-in-law. Doris accused Manley of paying too much attention to his sister. "It's not healthy," she had once spit out in one of their three-way quarrels. "Your love for your sister goes beyond the normal scheme of things," Doris had told Manley. "Too bad there are laws about such matters. I think you prefer Johanna over me!"

Johanna sighed as she leaned her head on her hand. She left some tomatoes in the bottom of the dish. The lettuce liner looked wilted or she might have eaten that. Now that she thought about it, Doris had a point. Manley had been her protector throughout her life. He was always there when she needed him. In fact, he worshiped her.

During her concert career, when she had been on tour, Manley had always managed to come along when he could. He escorted her everywhere. If some dashing young admirer had wanted to approach her, there was no opportunity because Manley stepped in. He felt it was his duty, yet his *duty*—Johanna realized—had gone *beyond the normal scheme of things,* as Doris had stated.

But she hadn't minded. Not then. It was what she was used to. It had become very convenient to have a brother who took charge of her life for her. Losing their parents at such an early age as they had, Manley had taken over as father, friend and escort. And when he had married Doris, things did not change that much. He was still there for her.

Johanna's stomach growled with hunger. She looked around. Where was her main dish? She was starved. *Oh Manley,* she thought to herself, *what is this mess I've gotten myself into? How did it come about? And what part do Serassan and his sneaky-sounding friend Thorden play in it? Am I going to be able to speak and understand only Estronian the rest of my life?*

She stared into her glass of water as she remembered the conversation she had overheard in the doctors' lounge. Just when she had been starting to like Serassan—like him a *lot*—now to find out his intentions were not in her favor. He and Thorden said they were planning to meet the mother ship in a day. They were going to transport the cargo. Were Piedmont, Radya and herself the cargo Serassan was intending to transport?

A flurry of movement caught Johanna's attention. There was a scuffle at the entrance of the dining room. Then she saw her waitress, carrying an empty tray. The waitress pointed in Johanna's direction. Suddenly, two police officers barged into the room. Other diners grew silent as the men in blue uniforms rushed toward Johanna's table.

Johanna did not resist arrest. There was no point. As they handcuffed her, she heard so much jargon that her head swam. No doubt her appearance had betrayed her. That or the man standing next to her at the phone booth had alerted somebody as to her speech.

Johanna sobbed in despair as the police led her out to a waiting squad car.

Johanna sulked in her hospital room the rest of the afternoon. She knew they weren't going to let her out, so she could forget about speaking to Piedmont and Radya. To her surprise, while she was eating her supper, Manley came to see her.

As hungry as she had been, she abandoned the meal and embraced her brother. He held her for a long moment, then drew back and stared at her helplessly. He looked even more worried now than he had the many times before.

"Manley, I wish you wouldn't look at me that way," Johanna told him. "You look at me like I'm crazy. I'm really not, you know. I just don't know how to get through to you."

When she spoke to him, he never said anything anymore. He just stared in pity. At least he listened, despite the fact he couldn't understand her speech.

"It's a plot, you see," Johanna tried to explain. Gestures did little to put across her meaning, but she used them just the same. "It's like Piedmont said, a conspiracy. I'm not really sure what it's all about yet, but ..." She sniffed as tears seeped into her eyes. "But I have a feeling ... oh Manley ... I have a feeling I'm never going to see you again." The sobs broke loose, and she fell into his arms again. "I don't want to be away from you, dear brother. Just hold me. Hold me one last time."

Johanna looked up and found a nurse tapping Manley's shoulder. The nurse spoke to Manley sternly, and reluctantly he left. She stared at her brother longingly before he went. "Goodbye, Manley. Take care of yourself, no matter what."

He shrugged, wiped the tear from his eye, then went out the door.

"Dr. Wetzel? Please ... do you have a minute?"

Barbara Wetzel regarded the heavyset man with the receding hairline. "What is it, Mr. Dobbs? Someone is waiting for me down in the lobby."

"What's going on with my sister? What caused her to run away today? I thought you said she was getting better."

Barbara beckoned him over to some seats next to the elevator. Her date would have to wait five minutes longer. "Apparently Johanna panicked about something."

"What? She tried so hard to tell me what was troubling her. Doctor, I think I understand why she tried to get away. I feel terrible that Johanna has to be kept in this awful place."

Barbara's eyebrows lifted. *What did this man think this was—a dungeon?* She was proud of the conditions here at Reeve Memorial. "Mr. Dobbs, all I can tell you is this. I believe another patient was the cause of your sister's panic today. You see, we have this elderly woman who has attacked Johanna in the past. She's ..."

"*Attacked* her?" Manley's face wore a look of horror.

Barbara went on. "It's not what you think. We removed the woman a couple of days ago, and she is being given heavy medication. She can't hurt Johanna now. We're doing everything possible to ..."

"What have I done?" Manley stood up, the blood rising in his temples. "That does it. I'm getting my sister out of here."

Barbara grabbed his arm before he could get away. "Mr. Dobbs, wait a minute. You can't."

"I thought this was the solution," he raged. "I only wanted Johanna to get better. I thought by sending her here, you people could defeat whatever devil is inside of her." His voice cracked as sobs choked him. "God!"

Barbara felt pity for him, but she felt her own hopelessness as well. She was no closer to finding the answer than before, but how could she admit this? "Please ... Mr. Dobbs ..."

Manley buried his face in one of his fat white hands. "I only want Johanna to get better and come back and live as my sister again. It's ... it's just no good without her." He sobbed again.

"Well ..." Barbara sighed. She was afraid he might carry out his threat and have his sister released. "Maybe there is something you should know," she said with reluctance. "We are removing Johanna from this hospital tomorrow. She is being transferred to a facility with some patients who have similar symptoms."

Manley stared at Dr. Wetzel. "You're ... *what?* Who said you could take my sister anywhere?"

"It's only temporary ... for a day or so. It's ... it's experimental therapy." Barbara forced a smile to reassure him. "If you want to discuss it, I suggest you speak to Dr. Serassan. He is organizing the effort. Don't worry, Mr. Dobbs. Your sister will be back here before Wednesday, and I am confident that a breakthrough is about to occur in her case."

It was late that same night. The lights were out, but Johanna could not sleep. She tossed in her bed and thought over the day's events. They seemed astronomical after so many boring days in this ward. Mostly, she worried about what tomorrow would bring.

The door opened slowly, and Johanna waited. She listened as Serassan entered her room. Her heart began to pound as she closed her eyes to feign sleep. Maybe when he realized she was asleep, he would go away.

For several moments Johanna waited. She heard the soft squeak of his shoes on the floor as he approached the bed. She even heard his breathing. It frightened her. He was not of this Earth, after all. Beneath the covers her body quivered. She couldn't help it. She prayed he would not notice it.

Suddenly, Johanna felt hot air against her cheek. He must be crouching beside her bed. Still, she pretended to be unaware. She didn't want to give Serassan the satisfaction of acknowledging his alien presence. How dare he abduct her and cause her to suffer all she had these last weeks?

"Ahh ... awaken, sweet one." The voice was *not* Serassan's.

Johanna opened her eyes. Before her was a squarish head. She couldn't see well enough to make out the details of his face in the dark. She gave a cry of alarm and jerked up from the sheets.

"Be quiet," he said in a husky voice that Johanna recognized as the voice of Thorden from the lounge. A loathing toward the alien filled her and she fought to move away. For some reason she felt paralyzed and couldn't even turn her eyes away.

"What do you want?" The words came from her, but her lips could not move. She only heard her own voice in her head.

Thorden laughed sardonically as he bent ever closer. "You, Earth woman," he crooned in a tone that sent shivers up Johanna's spine.

"No! Don't touch me!" her mind's voice cried out.

The door to her room swung open just then. Light from the hallway flooded in. "Thorden!" a voice thundered from across the room.

Suddenly, Johanna was free and dropped back onto her bed. Serassan stepped into the room and his tall form came into full view.

The other man stood up straight and faced Serassan. He had narrow eyes and a large, crooked nose. His hair was short and light in color. "Serassan, what are you doing here?" he muttered in a gruff voice.

Johanna could feel the rumble of rage that seemed to emanate from Serassan as he stared fixedly at his opponent. "*Leave* here," he commanded.

Thorden threw his arms out at his sides. A playful smile stretched across his ugly face. "Anything you say. I was just making my acquaintance with the musician."

"I said *leave*." Serassan's voice remained calm, but it held the same note of firmness that commanded his colleague to depart.

Without hesitation Thorden left. Johanna sat up in bed and reached over to turn on her bedside lamp. In the brightness, her squinting eyes met the piercing look in Serassan's as he approached her side.

"Did he harm you, Johanna?"

She placed a hand over her chest. Her heart was still beating fast. "I don't think so." She averted her eyes.

"I'll deal with him later." Serassan reached for her hand and held it in his warm palm. The calming sensation of energy immediately soothed her. She couldn't help but relax, but her mind still rebelled. She remembered the conversation she had overheard.

"You know of Thorden already," Serassan told her as he looked deeply into her eyes. "Yes, I can see it now. What you heard. You are frightened, but you need not be."

Johanna sensed he was probing her mind.

"Why did you try to escape today?" asked Serassan.

The soothing sensation continued. Johanna swallowed, but she was still confused. How could she trust this alien?

"Please tell me, Johanna. Where did you think you could go?" Although the question demanded an answer, his tone was gentle. He looked on her with compassion as he continued to stroke her fingers.

"I don't want to be a prisoner," Johanna blurted out loud. "I was going to find my brother Manley. He would have helped me."

"Helped you? Like he did when he left you here?"

Johanna shook her head stubbornly. "Piedmont said ..."

"You've been listening to Piedmont again, I see." Serassan smiled slightly. "Well, rest assured, Piedmont may be intelligent for a Terran, but he does not yet fully comprehend our plan."

Johanna dared to look him in the eye. "Serassan, what *is* your plan? Why have you done this to us?"

"You mean, to you, Piedmont, and Radya?"

"Yes. And the others."

"Others?"

"You spoke of others. I overhead Thorden say there were others to be gathered and taken to some launch point."

"Of course there are others, Johanna. Others like yourself, Piedmont, and Radya, gathered from all over your planet. And in a short time you will all be embarking on a journey."

"What kind of journey? Where are you taking us?"

"Is it important that you know this now?" Serassan looked grieved.

"You've kept us in the dark too long," Johanna scolded. "I need to know for the sake of my own sanity! Where are we going?"

He patted her hand and withdrew from her side. "To Karos." He stood up. "Now get up, Johanna. We have some place to go."

"Where?"

He pulled her to her feet. She found her robe on the foot of the bed and Serassan helped her put it on. "I must hear you play music one more time," he told her. "This could be your final chance until we reach the mother ship."

Johanna stuck her toes into her slippers, then followed Serassan to the door. He peeked out to make sure the hall was empty, then together they made their way down to the recreation room.

This time there was a night nurse at the station. She watched them, but Serassan said something to her. Johanna glanced over and saw that he had put the nurse into some kind of trance. *How powerful was this man*, she wondered, who had come to her room and rescued her from that malicious Thorden?

She felt strangely secure at Serassan's side. As much as she knew she was his prisoner, she couldn't help feeling safe and even comfortable next to him. He understood more than anyone else in this hospital her need to play the piano.

When they reached the recreation hall, it was the same as the night before. Serassan switched on the lights, closed the door, and listened intently as she played many pieces from memory. Her frustrations, fears, even her temporary happiness at being with this unusual man came out in her released emotions as she made the music in her head and heart come alive for him. It had, after all, been a trying day both physically and mentally. She finally leaned over on the keyboard and moaned as sweat dripped down her back.

Serassan lifted her slender frame from the bench and drew her to him. "Incredible," he murmured in her ear. "Johanna, promise me ... you must promise you'll never leave me."

Even in her lassitude, Johanna glanced up at him. His deep blue eyes had a glassy appearance. His mouth hung open and his shoulders heaved, as if he, too, had been exhausted by her efforts.

"Never leave me," he pleaded. "I could not bear it."

— 13 —

M.I.B.s at Large

Johanna awoke to the rattle of her breakfast tray. The attendant who had brought it was someone new on the floor. Deciding to be bold, Johanna sat up in bed and said, "Good morning."

The woman scowled and left the room. Johanna didn't care. She lifted the lid on her tray and welcomed the warm aroma of scrambled eggs and toast. Steam whirled above the cup of black coffee. She replaced the lid and snuggled back upon her pillow. Breakfast could wait. She wanted to remember last night. She felt good. No matter what the attendant thought, Johanna considered it a good morning. She had slept well.

Her dreams had been full of Serassan. After she had played for him in the recreation hall, he had held her in his arms. He had been so totally moved by her music. Then he had taken her back to her room, where he had put her to bed. Even as fatigued as she was, Johanna remembered the tenderness with which Serassan had looked upon her as he covered her with the spread. When all she had wanted was to curl up and go to sleep after her trying day, Serassan had leaned over and kissed her.

But it had been more than a mere goodnight kiss, Johanna knew. His lips had pressed firmly against her own, and she had responded with intensity. If her passion had surprised Serassan, it had astonished Johanna even more. In seconds she had forgotten how tired she was. Waves of heat had surfaced over her entire body. He was telling her in his mind that he wanted her, and her mind cried out to him in consent. Yet he drew back suddenly, not intending to take the final step in their love-making.

This morning Johanna still felt the wonderful new magic, the strange and impulsive sensations she was experiencing for the first time in her life. She relived the scene in her mind. Although her mind had begged him to stay, he withdrew reluctantly and seemed to be fighting his own urge to kiss her again.

She remembered the look in his blue eyes as he headed for the door. She heard him in her mind. "I don't want to leave, but I must. It would be too easy to give in now. The time is short."

"Serassan ..." she had called after him.

He turned to face her at the door. "Good night, my Johanna," he said without smiling. "Thank you for your performance." And then he was gone.

As she stared across the room now, Johanna smiled to herself. Yesterday she had been frightened of him. Last night he had baffled her, but this morning she *loved* him. As hard as she tried, Johanna could not remember ever being in love with a man before. Oh, perhaps a schoolgirl crush ... there had been Jacques, the dashing young piano instructor, when she had been in seventh grade.

She might have fallen in love with one of the admirers who used to hang around backstage after the concerts, but Manley had always managed to keep them away from her. At the time, she had been grateful. Performances in a different town each night had left little energy for anything but her musical career. Finally, when she had retired from touring to teach and work on compositions, she felt the chance of finding a man with which to settle down was remote.

But now, Manley was not here to protect her. She was head over heels for the man who had been involved in the conspiracy which had brought her to this hospital. He wasn't even a native of this planet, as far as she had been told. He certainly looked and felt human, but he had admitted already that he was an alien.

What did it matter what he was as long as he cared for her? She only knew now that she missed him and wanted to be held in his arms again—and kissed. She wanted to feel those wonderful, thrilling sensations again, and explore what came next.

After her breakfast, Johanna got dressed and took care in brushing her hair. She hadn't forgotten that Piedmont and Radya were probably waiting to hear from her. They would want to know the details of her escape, and her motivation for attempting it in the first place. But when she tried to leave her room, it was locked. When she called for a nurse and tried to explain what she wanted, she realized she was not going to be allowed to visit the recreation hall. In fact, they weren't going to let her out of their sight.

Johanna sank onto her bed. How could she blame them? They were probably afraid she would try to run away again. "Where is Serassan?" she said out loud. "If only I could talk to him, he might let me go, even if it is under guard." She waited for him to come, but he did not.

After lunch, two attendants came to Johanna's room. Seconds later, they wheeled in Francine, who sat in a wheelchair. The blond woman's head was still bandaged, but she smiled over at Johanna when she saw her.

"Francine!" Johanna stood up. "It's so good to see you again!" She watched as they helped Francine into her bed. The woman appeared much weaker than before. She kept looking over at Johanna and smiling. Francine seemed to be happy to be back in the room.

Suddenly, a dark thought crossed Johanna's mind. If Francine was back in the room, how was Serassan going to treat her? Obviously, he wouldn't want anyone else to know he could converse with Johanna. There could be no more intimacy with Francine present.

After the attendants left, Francine turned to Johanna and spoke in gibberish. She seemed to be asking Johanna how she had been.

"I'm okay," Johanna told her. Francine looked at her blankly, but Johanna smiled and went on. "In fact, I'm more than okay. Francine, I'm in love! Do you believe it? Thirty-four years old and I'm in love for the first time in my life." She hugged herself. "It's absolutely wonderful. *He's* wonderful!"

Francine fell into jargon as she gestured and pointed to her head. She seemed to be trying to explain what happened to her after Melody's attack in the recreation hall. Johanna nodded, although she couldn't understand a word. It really was good to have company again.

Later that afternoon, while Francine was taking a nap, and Johanna stood at the window, daydreaming of the outside world, the attendants entered the room with an empty wheelchair. One of them began collecting Johanna's clothes and belongings.

"Hey, what are you doing?" Johanna called out. She started to protest, but one of the attendants grabbed her and forced her into the wheelchair. "What did you do that for?"

Francine stirred in her bed and looked over at Johanna seated in the wheelchair. Francine asked something, and the attendant replied. Suddenly, Francine bolted up in her bed. Her face clouded over as the color burst from her cheeks.

"Am I going some place?" Johanna asked.

With all her things gathered, the attendant turned the chair around and wheeled Johanna out of the door. Francine shouted after her.

Johanna tried to get away, but the attendants pushed her down. "Goodbye, Francine!" she managed to call out as they wheeled her toward the elevator.

She wondered where they were taking her. Why had they packed up all her clothes and things? Had Manley come to take her home? Wanda was in the corridor when Johanna passed. The large woman stared in surprise. The nurses at the nurses' station glanced up briefly and then went on with their duties.

Johanna remembered yesterday's ride down the elevator as they got in.

This time, at least, she didn't have to put up with bad smells.

They stopped at the first floor. The doors opened and the attendant wheeled her out toward the lobby. There Johanna saw Serassan standing near the front door. Thorden held the door open as she passed through it.

"Serassan, what ..."

His eyes met hers for a brief second, then turned away indifferently. She heard him speak in gibberish to Thorden and the attendant, and then he was out of her sight.

In the parking lot, Johanna saw a white van parked at the curb. An orderly pushed an empty wheelchair back toward the hospital building as another attendant helped Radya into the van. Johanna saw that there were four other people already inside the back of the van, and they all looked out at her as she approached.

"Johanna!" Radya shrieked when she caught sight of her. The Russian girl looked frightened. The attendant turned to help Johanna board the van.

As she climbed inside, Johanna noticed Piedmont slumped in the middle seat near the window. His eyes were closed. She gasped and met the fear in Radya's eyes with her own bewilderment. The door slammed shut and then she heard the *kritchit* of the latch as it was locked.

Johanna embraced Radya on the seat. The young girl trembled and clung to Johanna. "Radya, are you all right?"

"Oh ... Johanna, I am so frightened." Radya would not let go. "So much has happened. I ... I wanted to see you. They ... they wouldn't let me."

Johanna stared at the unconscious Piedmont. "What's wrong with the professor?"

Radya withdrew, but still clung to Johanna's hand. "They were afraid he might cause trouble. They drugged him, I think. "

Johanna reached out her hand and stroked the stout man's head. She immediately became aware of the other four people in the van, who crowded the back seat behind her. Two men and two women stared at her and Radya.

"Who are *they?*" Johanna whispered.

"It's okay," one of the men said, "we're on your side."

Johanna breathed a sigh of relief. "Thank goodness. You speak English. I mean ..." She held her tongue. She didn't want to alarm anybody at this point. She was shocked enough herself. Instead, she introduced herself.

"I'm Vince Waldon," said the man who had spoken to her. He extended a hairy wrist over the back of the seat.

Johanna shook his hand, then squinted. "Wait a minute. Vince Waldon? The actor?"

He shrugged. "That's right." Then he turned to his colleagues and introduced them one by one.

The bald man with the dark mustache and brown eyes with bushy brows was a Greek sculptor named Stephen, "Steph" for short. The large, short-haired woman with beautiful blue eyes and a huge bosom was Rose. She had been jerked away from a promising career as an opera singer in New York. Then there was the tall, skinny, brown-haired woman with narrow eyes and high cheek bones. She was a singer, too, but had performed with a band. Although she could do just about any kind of performance, Jasmine, as she was called, had most recently been a recording artist.

"Well, what are we doing here?" Radya wanted to know. "Why are we on this bus?"

"They're taking us to another institution," said Vince. He seemed to be the spokesman for the other three passengers.

"How do you know that?" Johanna questioned.

"That's what they told us," said Rose.

"Who?" asked Johanna.

Jasmine pointed out the window toward the two men walking toward the van. "The doctors," she said. "Didn't they tell you?"

Johanna kept silent. Radya dug her nails into Johanna's flesh. "What's wrong with you?" Johanna asked her.

The Russian girl whimpered. "Him," she squeaked, "that ... man!"

Johanna glanced out the window. Serassan opened the door to the front seat and climbed into the driver's seat. Thorden double-checked the side door to see that it was locked. He peered in at Johanna and Radya, and a sly grin crept over his homely face. Radya buried her face into Johanna's shoulder, as if to hide from Thorden.

"Shh, it's going to be all right," Johanna reassured her.

"Doctor Serassan!" called out Vince from the back seat. "Can you tell us when we will arrive at the new hospital?"

"I'm telling you, we're not going to any hospital," grumbled the bald sculptor named Steph. "I demand that you take us back," he called out.

Thorden opened the passenger door and climbed in as Serassan stared at the men in the back seat. "We have a ways to go, Mr. Waldon," said Serassan in a calm voice. "But we will arrive tonight."

"I want to go home!" thundered Steph.

"You will be quiet!" It was Thorden this time who answered. His narrow eyes expressed anger and impatience. Johanna felt Radya quiver at the sound of the alien's voice.

Serassan started up the van's engine. Rose and Jasmine began mumbling in the back seat while Vince attempted to calm Steph. Johanna noticed Thorden looking back over his shoulder at Radya's slender form huddled against Johanna. By his lecherous look, she could guess why the young girl was so frightened. She remembered last night when Thorden had stolen into her room. What would he have done to her, she wondered, if Serassan had not interrupted him? What had Thorden done to Radya?

The van drove out of the parking lot and headed for the expressway. Johanna turned to Piedmont, who was still unconscious. Feelings of uneasiness overcame her, and she leaned forward to speak to Serassan.

"What have you done to Piedmont?"

Thorden smiled wickedly, but Serassan answered her. "It's all right, Johanna. It was necessary to sedate him. He'll come around shortly."

"Where are we going?" was her next question. "It's not a new hospital, is it?"

Thorden shot a threatening glare at Johanna, but again Serassan replied. "Let's not discuss it now," he said in a low voice. "I'll explain it all to you later. Trust me."

Trust him? Did she have any choice? A part of her wanted to trust him completely. Didn't he love her? She knew that she loved Serassan. He had been good to her so far. He had not lied to her. But another part of her was filled with doubts that plagued her mind.

She felt the tension and anxiety in the other people around her. They didn't seem to know that Serassan and Thorden were from the planet Estron, or that they were all headed for the *launch point*, wherever that was. Only Piedmont, who seemed to have put two and two together and figured out what the conspiracy was, had been drugged.

B arbara Wetzel dodged the patches of leftover ice as she headed for her car in the parking lot. It had been a blessing to see the sun yesterday, and to know spring was due to arrive. Freezing temperatures last night had made slippery sheets out of yesterday's melted puddles. So intent was she about watching her footing, Barbara failed to notice the two men leaning on her car. She stopped abruptly and her breath caught in her throat. Both men wore black coats and hats. Dark sunglasses and black gloves covered their pale complexions.

"Dr. Barbara Wetzel?" one of them asked. The voice sounded husky and unnatural somehow.

"What are you doing here?" Barbara sounded braver than she felt. "You're leaning on my car."

The men made no efforts to move away. The one who had spoken crossed his arms as they both continued to stare at her. "Are you Dr. Wetzel?" he demanded.

Barbara didn't want to get too close to them. "Yes," she replied.

"We have some questions."

"Who are you? The police? What do you want?" She began to tremble, and it wasn't from the cold.

"Where is Dr. Serassan?" the man asked.

"Well, he ... Listen, if you go inside and talk to somebody in the lobby, I'm sure they'll page him for you." She opened her purse and pulled out her set of keys. "Now, you must excuse me. I'm in a hurry."

The man with his arms crossed stepped toward her. "Not so fast. Tell us right now where Dr. Serassan went. We want to know where he's gone with those people."

"I don't know what you're talking about."

"Lying to us will surely bring trouble to you, Dr. Wetzel." The menacing edge in his words caused Barbara to take a step backward.

"It's vital we find Serassan and speak with him," the other man explained. His voice, Barbara noticed, had an unusual fuzzy quality.

"Well, I'm afraid he's gone," Barbara told them. "He left only minutes ago. He's transporting a group of mental patients to another hospital."

"*Your* patients," the first man accused.

"Some of them, yes." Barbara wondered how they knew so much.

"Tell us where this hospital is," the second man dictated.

"I ... don't ... know." As they moved toward her together, Barbara backed up. "Somewhere up ... upstate," she admitted.

"Where upstate?"

Barbara had a bad feeling about these men. She was determined not to give away any details. Whoever they were, they certainly did not look or act like policemen. "Listen, I don't know who you are or what you're after, but I don't think it's any of your business."

The second one poked his partner, and abruptly they walked away. Barbara watched as the two men slipped into a shiny black Mercedes, parked at the end of the row. She thought she'd get their license number, if she could read it, but as the car backed out of its stall, Barbara saw there was no plate.

They hadn't been on the road longer than half an hour when Johanna became aware of the discussion in the seat behind her.

"See? I'm not just imagining things," Rose, the opera singer, said.

"You know, I think you're right," replied Vince.

"That car's been following us for the last ten miles," said Rose.

"And look how close it is," Jasmine commented.

Steph only grunted.

"Do you suppose the doctors know?" Rose asked in a low voice.

"Shh," cautioned Vince. "It might be wise not to let on. There's a possibility ..."

"What?" prompted Jasmine.

Vince sighed. "Never mind."

Johanna turned around to catch a glimpse of what the other passengers were talking about. She gasped when she saw the black Mercedes on the van's tail. She could make out two men dressed in black in the front seat of the car. Both wore sunglasses and hats.

"What is it?" asked Rose.

Johanna shivered. "It's the same men," she replied.

Radya turned to have a look. "Johanna, what's wrong?"

Fearfully, Johanna leaned forward and got Serassan's attention. "We're being followed," she informed him.

Serassan gazed into the rear-view mirror. Without a word, he swerved into the passing lane and pressed the accelerator to the floor. The van thrust forward as its passengers gripped their seats.

Johanna saw the Mercedes change lanes and speed up, right along with them. By now, the four people in the back were all talking at once. Radya helped to steady the sleeping professor's lolling head as the van weaved in and out of traffic with its pursuer gaining.

Thorden yelled at Serassan, but with all the commotion Johanna could not make out what he said. A car horn blasted and faded as they continued to dodge the crowded highway. In the moments that followed, Johanna believed they were all going to die. She clung desperately to the back of Serassan's seat as he steered widely, causing the van to almost lose control.

She heard the screech of tires and once dared to look behind and see other cars that had turned off into the shoulder. The black car was still chasing them. She hid her face behind Serassan's seat and felt her body rocking side to side. Then, quite suddenly, the van stopped zigzagging. Johanna dared to lift her head.

"Don't let up," warned Thorden. "We've got to put miles between us and them."

"Did we lose them?" demanded Rose. "Why were they chasing us?"

"It doesn't matter now," Thorden growled back.

"I saw those men yesterday," Johanna revealed. "They tried to follow me downtown."

Serassan's concern showed as he slowed the van down to normal speed. "I'm not surprised. A lot of people have encountered M.I.B.s"

The other passengers exchanged puzzled looks. "M.I.B.s?" echoed Vince.

"What is this bull?" grumbled Steph.

"Yes. Men in Black," replied Serassan. "You haven't heard of them?"

"Why are we discussing this?" complained Thorden.

"Well, I've heard of them," spoke up Jasmine. She brushed back a lock of hair. "They show up, dressed all in black, driving black cars without license plates, and they harass people who make a big fuss about UFOs. I know because my boyfriend had this experience several years ago when he saw a UFO. But I don't see why they'd bother *us*."

"But who are they?" asked Vince. "The government?"

"Well, they tried to get my boyfriend to stop talking about what he thought he saw," explained Jasmine. "We thought maybe they were Air Force personnel dressed up to scare him."

"They are not from your government," Serassan told them.

"Then ... who are they?" asked Vince.

Thorden scowled. "Why are you indulging them?" he asked Serassan. "They were perfectly satisfied to think their government is keeping things from them."

"Wait a minute," said Vince. "What's all this talk? I don't see what Jasmine's boyfriend and UFOs have to do with any of us. Dr. Serassan, what is going on here?"

It was clear to Johanna that Vince Waldon still believed Serassan and Thorden were actually doctors, and that their destination was the promised hospital. Serassan seemed to realize then, too, that he had said enough.

"Mr. Waldon, I do not wish to upset any of you with any more of this talk. The danger is over. I suggest we all calm down. We still have a ways to go."

E vening was approaching when the van, which had been traveling north, finally left the main highway and headed west on a narrow country road. Radya had drifted off to sleep beside Johanna. Piedmont had stirred a couple of times, but was still out of it. Johanna noticed the terrain outside had become forest. Up ahead she could see mountains. The van drove on for another hour in the darkness. Soon the only light source was the van's headlights upon the desolate narrow road in front of them.

"There. Up ahead," Thorden told Serassan.

"Are you sure those are the coordinates?" The van slowed, then crossed over to the side of the road and slowly crept to a stop.

At the sound of the engine shutting off, everybody in the van stirred. Most of the passengers in the back seat had gone to sleep, and were now waking up.

"Where are we?" asked Steph.

"It's dark," said Rose.

"I need to get out and stretch," complained Jasmine.

"Why are we stopping here?" Vince asked. "We're out in the middle of nowhere. What's the matter? Did you get lost?"

Serassan and Thorden turned on a small beam of light in the front seat and appeared to be studying a map. They ignored the questions behind them.

Piedmont moaned, and Johanna reached over to him. "Oh ... bad dream," groaned the professor, to which Johanna replied, "Wake up now."

Piedmont lifted his head. She could not see his face in the darkness, but he shook his head. The others behind him began discussing their needs and discomforts.

"All right," Serassan said in a loud voice. Everyone turned to look toward the front of the van. The ceiling light came on inside and they could see. "You may get out, one at a time, to relieve yourselves."

"Where are we?" Vince called out.

"Can't we all get out at once?" asked Steph.

Thorden opened his door and proceeded to unlock the side door. Steph pushed his way toward the door first, but Thorden grabbed him as he swung out. "Didn't you ever hear of ladies first?"

Serassan opened his door and climbed out, then Johanna and Radya stepped out of the van. Thorden took hold of Radya to lead her away.

Radya wailed, "No! Leave me alone!"

"Where are we?" groaned Piedmont.

Before she could answer, Johanna felt Serassan take her arm. He gently moved her aside, then stuck his head into the van and coaxed the other passengers to get out. "You are safe here," he told them. "It is important that no one panic and try to run away, because if you do, there is the chance you will die of exposure. It is very cold, and we are miles from a telephone."

"Are we lost?" asked Vince again. "Did you run out of gas?"

"No. Nothing like that."

"Then what are we doing here?" Vince's voice rose in pitch.

"I have to go," Jasmine moaned. "Can I please get out now?"

Serassan let them out and directed them to a ditch alongside the van, where they could take care of their bodily needs. Serassan then handed out some sponge-like wafers that resembled bread sticks, only they were light and soft. "Here is your nourishment," he told the group. "These will replace food until we get to the mother ship."

At once, a cry of alarm erupted among the passengers.

"What! A *mother ship?*" cried out Vince.

"These men are aliens!" shrieked Rose. "Lord help us."

"I was afraid it was something like this," whimpered Jasmine. "Oh my

God, my *God!*"

"Don't listen to them!" shouted Steph. "It's a lie! Don't you see? They want us to believe that. They want us to really think we're insane."

"No!" This time it was Piedmont whose voice rang out in the darkness next to the van. "Serassan and Thorden are not joking. It was their plan all along."

"You are the chosen," Serassan responded. "All of you here, and many others from your world whom you will meet shortly."

"What is he talking about?" demanded Rose. "Somebody please tell me."

Radya clung to Johanna and shivered in the cold night air.

"Chosen? Chosen for what?" Steph demanded.

Johanna ate her wafer. It had no flavor, and seemed to melt right in her mouth. She, too, wondered what Serassan had meant about the chosen. Why had she, Johanna Dobbs, been chosen? She remembered Serassan and Thorden talking about breeding privileges in the doctors' lounge. Certainly that couldn't be why they had chosen her. Radya was young, as was Jasmine. Johanna and Rose were older, though, and Piedmont was in his 60s. If they wanted to kidnap humans and take them to their planet for breeding, why not choose only young specimens, and healthy, desirable persons to bring out the best attributes in the resulting progeny? No, there had to be another reason. What did she, Piedmont, and Radya have in common with the four others?

"Look! It's coming in!" shouted Piedmont. He pointed up into the sky.

Johanna and the others looked up and saw a bright star close to the horizon. It was brighter than any of the planets or stars that were visible in the clear, moonless sky. And it was moving—slowly.

Rose screamed. Steph began shouting, and Radya and Jasmine both broke down and wept. Thorden and Serassan took charge of the situation immediately as they gathered the affected passengers into a small circle and quieted them. Johanna watched, not exactly able to see what the aliens were doing, but it seemed to work. In a moment all was quiet.

Johanna asked Piedmont, "What did they do?"

"Used their hypnotic abilities to remove their fear," Piedmont explained. "How is Radya?"

"I don't know. Something's happened to her.'

"Dear Johanna, something is about to happen to each one of us," said Piedmont.

Johanna felt her lip tremble as she focused her gaze on the bright object, which stopped, then hovered, and began expanding as it moved in.

PART II

The Journey

— 14 —

The Abduction

Johanna felt Serassan close his arm around her shoulder. She stood, shivering in the dark. Everyone's gaze was on the bright sphere of white light in the sky as it descended slowly and expanded.

"You are cold," Serassan muttered.

Johanna drew comfort from his touch, but she couldn't take her eyes off the aerial object. She wanted to tell him she was excited. She had forgotten her fears. The warmth of his body revitalized her. "It's the mother ship?" she asked.

"No, not the mother ship," Serassan replied. "It's a shuttle."

Thorden turned out the inside light of the van and closed the door. Then he walked over to Serassan and Johanna. "They'd better get down here fast," he commented. "We're behind schedule as it is."

The shuttle approached slowly, then halted and seemed suspended several hundred feet in the air. Green and red lights blinked on and off in a circle along its bottom rim.

"Why doesn't it land?" asked Steph.

"It will," said Serassan.

"If only I had a camera," said Jasmine. "No one will believe this!"

Johanna was surprised that the others had lost their fear. She, too, felt strangely awed by the presence of the craft.

Thorden paced back and forth on the icy ground. He was growing more impatient with each passing minute. "Signal them," he barked.

"No, they will come at their own pace," assured Serassan.

"What's the delay?" asked Vince.

"Yah, it's freezing out here," said Rose.

Serassan remained calm. "They are just being cautious."

"Cautious?" scoffed Steph.

Piedmont sighed. "Even with all you are capable of, don't tell me you are at risk to land one of your small ships."

"We are at risk whenever we enter Earth's atmosphere. That is why we chose this spot. We did not wish to arouse suspicion or cause any unnecessary problems with other Terrans." Serassan found Johanna's hand and clasped it in his own. In the darkness no one seemed aware of her exchange with the alien.

"All this time," said Steph, mostly to himself, "I always thought UFOs were a figment of the imagination."

"Life," sighed Jasmine. "Imagine that. There is life out there among those stars."

Thorden grunted as he continued to pace back and forth. "You Terrans ... your ignorance dazzles me. Thinking you were all alone on your precious little planet. To think that you believed you were unique!"

"That's enough out of you, Thorden," chided Serassan.

Thorden ignored him. "We and hundreds of others have been visiting your world since civilization began on Earth. We've walked among you and learned much."

"Oh yah," chuckled Steph haughtily, "and now you're going to exploit us."

Thorden started to retaliate, but just then the shuttle began to move again. It hovered, and then lowered itself. Everyone watched as it expanded into a disc-shaped craft. As it maneuvered closer to the ground, they could see a line of tiny windows above its bottom half, which slowly revolved as the green and red lights continued to blink on and off. Finally, it gave off a bright flash of reddish light and came to rest on the paved road fifty yards in front of the van.

Radya was the first to react. She began to shriek. "It's a Yankee plot! It's a Yankee plot!"

Johanna pulled away from Serassan and rushed over to comfort the young ballerina as Serassan and Thorden advanced toward the ship. The others huddled together, not quite knowing what to expect.

Suddenly, an opening in the center of the craft appeared as two sides parted. A ramp was lowered in front of the door. They could see several figures standing at the entrance, but it was too dark to make out any details. As Serassan and Thorden approached, four of these figures emerged and walked down the ramp onto the street.

"We could make a run for it," Johanna heard Steph tell Vince in a lowered voice.

"I don't think so," Vince replied. "I can't move my feet."

"Johanna, I'm frightened!" cried out Radya.

Johanna, like the others, then realized that she could not move either. She was paralyzed. She stared as she watched Serassan direct two of the crew members toward her and the others. Then the figures walked over. As they drew closer, Johanna let out a gasp.

The beings that had walked out of the ship were humanoid. They were shorter than Thorden and Serassan, and they had grayish-white skin that appeared pasty. Their heads were a great deal larger in proportion to their bodies, and they had no hair. As they came into view, Johanna saw that their eyes were large and slanted toward the backs of their heads. She could see no ears on them, and their noses consisted of merely two holes. Their mouths were like a single line drawn straight across from their triangular chins.

"Do not be afraid," a male voice said. One of the beings looked right at Johanna, who was too startled to react. She had not expected to see such an exotic creature. He did not speak with his mouth, but seemed to be communicating directly inside her head, just as Serassan and Thorden had done on occasion.

But I can't help it, Johanna thought. Her impressions seemed to be communicated to the alien, who gently reached out to take her arm.

"I understand. Now come," she was told.

Another being took Radya and started leading the ballerina toward the ship. Radya whimpered, but she did not protest. Johanna found she could not resist following the alien either. It felt as though she were floating toward the ramp. The others behind her stood rooted to their places.

As she passed Serassan on the ramp, Johanna overheard him speaking with another crew member. "Thorden's plan should work. We passed a river about a mile back. There was a cliff where you should easily be able to push the vehicle. I think the safest idea would be to take it with us, though."

"We are crowded as it is," the being told Serassan.

Johanna heard no more as she entered the ship. She noticed more grayish-white beings seated at what resembled some kind of control panel in a circular room with windows. The beings escorted her and Radya down a curved corridor that arched toward the ceiling. They entered a small room without windows. The floor consisted of numerous colorful cushions which resembled stepping stones. There was nothing else in the room except walls that were white. A purplish light bathed the room, but did not seem to have a source. There the beings left herself and Radya, then departed quickly.

"Radya, it's all right," Johanna told the girl, "I know this is a lot to absorb. It is for me, too."

"That's easy for you to say," whimpered Radya. She glanced at Johanna with suspicious eyes. "You are part of it."

"Radya, what are you saying?"

"I saw you with him." Radya sniffed. "Why aren't you afraid like the others?"

Johanna knew Radya was referring to Serassan. She couldn't think of any way to explain to the girl. Besides, she had other concerns. Where was Piedmont? Would the others be brought into this room? It was not a big room. Looking around, she guessed it to be about eight feet by eight feet. How long would they have to be in this room?

Grayish-white beings appeared a few minutes later, bringing the other van passengers. Johanna went over to Piedmont, and they sat on the cushions on the floor close to Radya.

"Well, we may as well make ourselves comfortable." The older man sighed as he stretched out his legs. "Ah, that's better."

"Piedmont, Radya's in a bad way," Johanna confided in him.

"What did you expect?" he retorted.

Johanna didn't know. She certainly hadn't expected these death-colored creatures. As repulsive as they looked to her, she had to admit they had been gentle. Their voices had been soothing and very human-like. No one, as yet, had been harmed.

With the last of their group inside the crowded room, the last being out closed a door by lifting his slender fingers over the wall in the outer corridor. A door shot across and blended in with the wall.

"I think we're sealed in, folks," said Vince.

Now that they were alone without the aliens present, everyone began to talk. They were all astonished by what they had seen and heard and felt in the last half hour. Only Radya kept silent as she huddled in the farthest corner. She didn't even want to be near Johanna or Piedmont.

"How are you feeling now?" Johanna asked Piedmont.

The professor said he felt fine. He was fully conscious now, and the food wafer had revived him somewhat. "You managed to get away from them," he said to her. "How did you ever accomplish it?"

Johanna quickly went over the details of her escape the day before, how she hid in the laundry cart, and made her exit through the utility entrance on the first floor. She then told Piedmont about what she had overheard in the doctors' lounge, how Serassan and Thorden had been talking about meeting the mother ship.

"What exactly did they say?" he asked.

Johanna filled him in with as much as she could remember. "Well, first of all, Thorden told Serassan he wanted to see the ballerina. By that, I assume he meant Radya."

"Go on."

"Then Serassan said something about giving his word to somebody. I can't remember who it was." Johanna made a face. "Then Thorden got mad and told Serassan he had forgotten the purpose of their mission."

"What purpose?"

"I don't know. The purpose of their mission ... yes." Johanna looked around at the others, who were either talking amongst themselves or pensive as they rested on the floor cushions. "Thorden then got mad and said he wanted the ballerina. He had picked her, he said, and he wanted her. Now get this, Piedmont. Then Serassan told Thorden he didn't qualify for *breeding* privileges."

Piedmont stroked his beard and nodded. "I see. And? What else?"

Johanna strained to remember. "Let's see. They talked about the rendezvous with the mother ship. Thorden said he wanted to indulge just this once, and Serassan got mad again and told Thorden once was never enough for him." She looked into Piedmont's bloodshot eyes. "Do you know what they meant?"

"I have my suspicions," Piedmont told her, "but nothing concrete. I suspect our two friends have a rivalry going."

Johanna nodded. It was obvious that Thorden and Serassan did not always see eye to eye. She remembered last night when Serassan had come to her room and blown up when he found Thorden trying to seduce her, if that was what you could call it. She mentioned this to Piedmont as well.

Before Piedmont could comment, however, a vibrating rumble came from underneath them. Everyone looked up in fear as they felt themselves moving. The shuttle was apparently taking off.

Once again, Radya's fear overcame her confusion. The ballerina jumped up from her corner and joined Johanna and Piedmont. "It's the end, I know it." She covered her face and wept. Piedmont reached over and patted the ballerina gently on her back. Then he looked Johanna in the eye.

"Don't forget who you are, Johanna," he said. "Don't fall into a trap. You are blind to it now, but Serassan is setting you up."

— 15 —

The Welcoming Committee

Johanna hadn't realized she had been asleep. Suddenly she was awake inside the crowded compartment with the soft violet light and the six companions in a heap around her. A few of them began to stir as well. She remembered she was on board the alien shuttle carrier. How long she had slept, she had no idea, but she felt refreshed and alert as she roused herself from the soft, warm floor cushion.

Next to her, Piedmont slept on his back with his hands folded over his rounded belly. He still wore his glasses. Radya was curled up in the corner. The ballerina resembled a child as her long blond tresses fell every which way. Her pert little mouth was open.

The door in the wall slid open just then. Two grayish-white beings stood looking in from the corridor. Johanna sat up straight and stared at them. Her heartbeat picked up at the sight of their thin gray bodies and large, insect-like heads with the slanted eyes. Piedmont beside her stirred, and then awoke.

"Come with us," one of the grayish-white beings told Johanna. "You will be transferred now to the mother ship." Like before, the entity in the hallway used audible thoughts in his communication. Others in the room sat up then.

"We've arrived?" Piedmont pulled himself up.

"I don't even remember falling asleep," Johanna replied as she stood up. Turning to Radya, she reached down to help the girl up.

"Where am I?" the girl asked, blinking.

"You're with us," Johanna told her.

Piedmont took hold of the ballerina's other arm, and together they followed behind the other van passengers on their way out of the compartment room. A being outside the doorway held a tray containing small instruments. Another being gripped Johanna's shoulder and turned her around. Suddenly, she felt a pinprick in her arm.

With a jerk, Johanna spun around. She had just been injected by a needle-like device. She was gently pushed aside. A glance over her shoulder showed Piedmont receiving his shot from the alien technician.

Rubbing the spot above her elbow where she had felt the sting, Johanna let her strange-appearing escort lead her down the corridor. Piedmont and Radya were not far behind. Johanna noticed there were more people among them now—humans who appeared just as bewildered and mystified as Johanna and her friends. Searching within her line of vision, Johanna looked for Serassan, but saw no sign of him nor Thorden as she followed the crowd down the narrow, tunnel-like enclosure.

As they emerged from the tunnel, Johanna noticed they had entered a huge, well lit area with a high ceiling. She was in the middle of a crowd of dozens of people, and it was hard to see over their heads. There seemed to be a lot of commotion as the crowd murmured amongst themselves. Then a voice came over what must have been an alien loudspeaker system.

"Welcome!" the voice boomed. It was a female voice which echoed within the curved walls. "Welcome, Terrans. We greet you new arrivals, and extend our deepest hospitality. It is our intention that you enjoy your stay on the mother ship. We are very pleased to have you among us."

Johanna glanced at Piedmont, who frowned.

The voice continued to echo, "You will now follow your guides, who will show you to guest quarters that have been prepared for you individually."

"Who are you?" a man's voice thundered from the crowd.

A hysterical woman cried out, "Let us go! You have no right!"

"All of your questions will be answered," the voice over the loudspeaker replied. "You will find there is nothing to fear. Your guides will now come forward."

People began to talk at once. Johanna turned to Piedmont. "Let's stick together," she suggested. He nodded.

Just then, Serassan made his way toward them. He beckoned to Johanna, Piedmont, and some others. Johanna's heart beat faster. She felt relieved to see him. She and Piedmont helped lead Radya through the massive people. Before they could get to Serassan, Thorden stepped up to them.

"Radinka, come with me," he commanded.

The ballerina gasped in protest and backed away.

"Just a minute," objected Piedmont. "We three go together."

"Get out of my way, old man," sneered Thorden. He grabbed hold of Radya and attempted to pry her from Piedmont's grasp.

The professor was obviously no match for the alien. A scuffle followed in which Serassan immediately confronted Thorden and held him back. "The professor and Miss Dobbs, follow me," directed Serassan. He pointed to Vince and called out, "Mr. Waldon, you and Rose, too."

"But what about Radya?" cried Johanna.

"She's mine," snarled Thorden.

Serassan shrugged. "I'm afraid Miss Bjelkova is on her own now. Thorden will take good care of her."

"No! Johanna, don't let him take me," shrieked Radya. She burst into tears. Thorden managed to confront the ballerina, and in a moment had her under some kind of mind control. Her tears ceased as Radya let Thorden lead her away.

Serassan led Piedmont, Johanna, and the others out of the crowd and toward a passageway that was narrow but had a high ceiling. They made several turns and then came to a strange platform that resembled a tall, cylindrical chute with flowing beams of vertical light surrounding it. The lights flashed different colors and a soft droning hum could be heard coming from the platform.

Serassan waved his hand over a panel next to the chute, then motioned for them to step inside. Johanna waited until everyone else had crowded on, then she stepped on with Serassan behind her. He then activated a control of some sort. The lights completely covered all sides so that they could no longer see outside the chamber.

Piedmont asked what it was.

"This is the transport shaft," Serassan explained.

Immediately they felt themselves moving downward rapidly. Both Rose and Johanna gasped. Johanna's head swam, and she swayed a little. This was some kind of space-age elevator, she realized. The ride lasted a full minute, and the lights streaked in front of her as she felt her body suspended, almost weightless.

When it halted, she felt as though her body weighed ten times its amount, as if she had jumped off a fifty-story building and landed on her feet. Dizziness overcame her and she almost lost her balance.

Serassan caught her and steadied her. "I've got you, don't worry."

Johanna regained her equilibrium and replied, "Thanks."

Serassan dropped his arm and switched off the transport shaft. The lights shut off, and they all walked into another passageway. This one led to a wider hallway in which there were various doors that resembled the cabins on board a cruise ship.

"Mr. Waldon, these are your quarters," said Serassan. He stopped at one of the doors and waved his hand over the wall. The door retracted, and Johanna could not get a good glimpse of what was inside, but it appeared roomy and well furnished with familiar, contemporary-style furniture.

Vince turned to Serassan with a puzzled look. "But what am I ..."

"Your questions will be answered within."

"Now just a minute, I ..."

Serassan motioned for Vince to enter. The actor threw his hands up into the air and entered his cabin, and the door to his quarters slid shut again. Serassan beckoned to the rest of them to follow him further down the hallway. He stopped when he came to Rose's room. She went right in without protesting.

"How long are we going to remain on this mother ship?" Piedmont asked after the others had been delivered to their quarters. They walked along another corridor. Their footsteps made a soft shuffling sound on the padded floor. "And can you tell us where exactly we are headed?"

Serassan continued to lead them. "All of your questions will be answered," was all he said.

When they came to Piedmont's quarters, Johanna let the professor take hold of her hand. He squeezed it as if to tell her everything would be okay. Then he turned and went inside. Johanna stared at the wall, feeling suddenly scared. Now it was just herself and Serassan. She became aware of his eyes on her and glanced up at him. There it was—the longing look in those deep blue eyes that had been lacking since their departure.

"What's happening to Radya?" Johanna asked him.

"Don't worry about her," said Serassan. "You can see her later, if you wish." He read her mind and responded with a slight smile. "And Piedmont, too." Then he walked by her side as he led her further down the hall.

They came to a door at the end of the hall, and Johanna saw her name engraved above the entrance, J. Dobbs. Before he held up his hand to open the door, Serassan stared down into Johanna's face.

"Please, Serassan. I don't want to be alone," Johanna said. She was afraid he would leave her like he had the others.

"You will not be alone, Johanna." His voice had that soothing tone in it that seemed to draw her closer to him. In her mind she heard him speak even softer the words, "I still care for you." Like a magnet, she felt herself being pulled toward his face. She did not resist. She wanted him to kiss her again. She wanted to feel secure in his arms.

But before his lips touched hers, the door to her quarters slid open. Serassan quickly drew away from her, and Johanna turned to greet a metallic white object in her doorway. She was startled to see a creature about four feet tall with small, pointed ears on top of its artificial head, two glowing green eyes, no mouth or nose, embodied by a white, shiny casing.

"I leave you," Serassan said abruptly, and walked away.

"Enter," a mechanized female voice called out.

Johanna continued to stare at the form in front of her. She was reminded of a cat, then guessed that it must be some kind of robot. She watched the cat-like thing glide backwards to make way for her. When she glanced after Serassan, she saw he had quickly departed down the hall. She fought the urge to run after him and stepped timidly into her quarters.

"Oh!" Johanna was astonished at what she found. Before her was an apartment-sized duplicate of her own living room from her house. The same couch and chairs, coffee table—even her favorite painting of the seascape— were in place. The walls were papered with the same decor, and there against the wall was her old piano.

"Johanna Dobbs, welcome," the robot creature said.

Johanna crossed over to her piano and found the keyboard cover down. She ran her hand over the smooth wood, then looked up and took in the familiar objects she remembered and missed. Then she walked across the room to see that there was a bedroom in back, a bathroom, and even a kitchen. Although these replicas were not exactly like the ones in her own home, a lot of the furnishings were strikingly similar. Her head whirled and, for a few seconds, she imagined herself back home, in her own house.

"You must be tired from your journey," the mechanized voice said.

Johanna spun around to face the cat-like thing which had followed her. She swallowed to compose herself. Before she could think of something to say, the robot let out a human-like laugh, not unlike her own.

"I was told you might be in shock. Well, have no fear, Johanna Dobbs. I am here to wait on you. I am called Kameel-37, programmed to serve Johanna Dobbs, musician of the planet Earth. You may call me Kameel."

"Does ... does everyone have someone like you?" Johanna asked.

"Affirmative. I shall act as maid, companion, teacher, and assistant during your voyage. Other units have been placed in the other quarters. I have been programmed specifically for you, Johanna Dobbs."

Johanna continued to stare at the robot. She then noticed that Kameel-37 did not have any feet. The unit appeared to be suspended in the air.

Kameel spoke again. "Perhaps you should sit down, Johanna Dobbs. Does my appearance disturb you?"

Johanna sat on the couch. She didn't know what to say.

Kameel-37 laughed again. "Please be at ease. May I prepare you a meal? Do you wish a drink?"

Johanna looked around her quarters and remembered that she was thirsty, now that Kameel had mentioned it. "Uh ... yes. A drink would be fine."

The unit moved toward the kitchen area. "A cranberry cooler?" it asked.

"Why, yes." Johanna wondered how Kameel-37 knew her favorite refreshment. How had the aliens been able to furnish her quarters to resemble her own home? It was startling. She again got up and went over to admire the piano. It was a close duplicate of her own. Some of the scratches and stains in her own piano were not present in this model.

Kameel-37 rejoined Johanna with a tray containing a glass of red liquid with ice. "You will find I am knowledgeable in the history of music on your planet," the robot told her. "However, I am incapable of making my own."

Johanna accepted the drink and thanked the unit.

"You have many questions," prompted Kameel. "I am here to answer them."

Johanna sat down again.

"Are you pleased with your furnishings?" asked Kameel.

"Yes, delighted." Johanna took a sip. Not bad. Then she asked, "Am I a prisoner?"

Kameel responded, "You are free to move about the lower deck of the ship as you like. You may visit the other passengers, or if you wish you may remain here."

"Where is the ship going?"

"Your destination is the planet Karos," Kameel explained. "Karos is a newly colonized planet which is being populated by selected Terrans."

Johanna remembered Serassan had mentioned Karos once. But wasn't he from Estron? "Well, how long will it take to get to Karos?" she asked.

"The voyage will last approximately eleven of your Earth days," came the reply.

"Why are we going to Karos?"

"Karos has been designated as a new cultural center for the benefit of the planet Estron and other culturally deprived races in the galaxy," Kameel continued.

"Yes ... Estron." Johanna thought a moment. "Where is Estron?"

"Estron is a planet in the same star system as Karos. Your hosts are Estronian. I, Kameel-37, and other units on board the ship were constructed on the planet Estron."

"Really," commented Johanna. She took another swallow of her cranberry cooler. "Tell me, Kameel. Why have these Estronians taken us from our homes on Earth and made us prisoners like this? Some of us ... all of us, in fact ... wish to go back. Can we ever go back?"

"You will find the purpose of this mission is to bring peace of mind to all concerned," answered Kameel. "I do not understand why you would want to return to Earth. There is much ahead that you do not understand, but will. We have done everything in our power to make this voyage a pleasant one for all of you. My sole purpose is to keep you happy, Johanna Dobbs."

Johanna sighed. How could she be happy, knowing she may never see Earth again? "What about Serassan?" she asked the robot. "Can I see him?"

"There is no purpose in any further contact with Serassan at this time," Kameel told her.

"But there *is*. I wish to see him."

"He is not available. His task has been completed. He will move on to new assignments."

Johanna lay back against her couch. What did Kameel mean—Serassan had completed his task? What new assignments?

"You are bothered?" asked the machine. "You must not worry about Serassan. He is no longer your concern." Kameel took her empty cooler glass and started toward the kitchen with it. "Why don't you sit down at the piano, Johanna Dobbs? I know you would very much like to play."

Johanna declined. She was troubled about what Kameel had said about Serassan. "I don't feel like it right now," she said. She got up and wandered into the bedroom. "I think I'll take a nap."

"Then I will prepare you a meal," said the robot. "What do you desire?"

"You cook, too?"

"I do windows, too."

Johanna laughed for the first time. "A sense of humor. They've thought of everything, haven't they?"

"Shall I waken you at a specified time?"

"No, that won't be necessary." Johanna yawned and sank into her bed. "Fix what you want for dinner."

"Lasagna, then," said Kameel.

Johanna stared after the unit as it glided away. How did it know everything? Then she curled up on the warm bed and stared across the room at the familiar dresser and the bookshelves that contained copies of most her old books. Even the closet held replicas of all her clothes. Maybe this voyage wasn't going to be so bad after all, even if she was being held against her will.

— 16 —

He Loves Me Not

"I don't suppose I need to ask why you came to see me." Dr. Barbara Wetzel pushed her paperwork aside and folded her hands on top of the desk.

Manley Dobbs and his wife sat facing her in the office on the psychiatric wing. The man stared at Barbara with a reproachful expression while his wife, a rather squat woman with red dyed hair, squirmed uncomfortably beside him. "I demand some answers," he declared. "Where is Johanna?"

Dr. Wetzel's gaze fell from Manley to the desk top. "Certainly you must realize, Mr. Dobbs, that the authorities are doing everything they can to retrieve the bodies. The van they were riding in was recovered only this morning. Quite often in river accidents, the bodies are found many miles downstream."

"Doesn't it seem strange to you, doctor, that they were driving through such a remote area?" asked Manley. "I mean, what in God's name was that Dr. Whoever-He-Was doing, taking them into the mountains?"

Barbara sighed. She didn't understand the situation any more than Mr. Dobbs or anyone else. She could hardly believe the truth—that Dr. Serassan, his assistant, and those poor patients were all presumed dead. The van they had used to transport the group upstate had mysteriously driven off the side of the steep cliff and plunged into the falls below. Such a waste. Nine human lives terminated—not to mention the paper she could have written on their illnesses.

"I still think you should sue them," the wife spoke up.

"Be quiet, Doris." Manley leaned forward. "Dr. Wetzel, I had a very strange visit this morning by some fellows who were asking a lot of questions about my sister."

Mrs. Dobbs scrunched up her pudgy face. "Mean-looking dudes," she added. "I'd have slammed the door in their faces."

"What is your point?" Barbara rubbed her forehead. She wished the Dobbses would leave.

Manley continued. "I got the impression from these men that they knew something about Johanna's disappearance."

Barbara looked up at him, puzzled. "What made you think that?"

"Oh, he's as crazy as his sister," grumbled Doris. "Manley, if you had any sense, you'd sue this hospital for the negligence of Johanna's death."

"Doris, *please*." Manley appealed to Dr. Wetzel. "Well, for instance, the two men already knew about the van going off the cliff. You hadn't phoned us until later. And they kept referring to this doctor who was driving them. They were especially interested in where he was really taking them."

"Wait a minute." Barbara let go of a tangle of blond hair she had wound around her finger. "Where he was *really* taking them? What do you think they meant by that?"

"That's what I was hoping you could tell me," Manley replied impatiently.

"Say, what did these two look like?" she asked.

"They wore black clothes, sunglasses, hats and gloves," explained Manley.

Doris snorted. "Sinister chaps. They nearly scared me to death when I saw them."

Barbara's lips parted as she recalled the men in black who had confronted her in the parking lot yesterday.

"Doctor, are you all right?" asked Manley.

She wasn't sure. This whole thing was too weird. Something was going on that she did not understand—something more puzzling and frightening than a small group of normal people who had suddenly found themselves unable to communicate.

Johanna stood at Piedmont's door for a long moment. Then she pushed the alien doorbell. The wall was made of very solid metal. A soft buzzing sound came on, and a few seconds later the door slid to one side.

Piedmont stood in front of her, dressed in a red satin smoking jacket. His ruddy face bore a grin, revealing small square teeth as he beckoned her inside. "Well, Johanna. Come in. Do come in."

She stepped in and looked around at the professor's lavish surroundings. His apartment was well stocked with shelves and shelves of books. The decor was mid-twentieth century with old-fashioned furniture and birch paneled walls. A fireplace stood between the bedroom and kitchen, where a soft fire burned and crackled.

"All the comforts of home," remarked Piedmont. "They've thought of everything, Johanna. This is the perfect place for me to start writing my book."

113

Johanna noticed an old manual typewriter on the table in the middle of Piedmont's living room. "You'd think they'd at least have gotten you a computer."

Piedmont laughed. "I'd never use it. That typewriter you see there has been with me most my life. We go back a long ways."

"Where is your ..." Johanna wasn't sure what to call it.

"My servant, you mean?" Piedmont invited her to sit down. "I hear everyone on board has one. Why, you won't believe what Syben is capable of, Johanna. He's a walking thesaurus."

"How convenient. Where is this ... Syben?"

"He's off to the energy chamber," Piedmont explained.

"What's that?" asked Johanna.

"Well, as I understand it, all the units—as they wish to be called—must visit the energy chamber once a day for a couple of hours, in order to recharge themselves."

Johanna found this piece of information useful. She wondered when Kameel would be taking her two-hour leave of absence.

"I've already spoken with other Terrans on board." Piedmont shook his head and grinned. "You see? Already they've got me talking like them. Anyway, everyone else has had the same reaction. The accommodations are fantastic! How about you? Did you feel like you were home again?"

Johanna smiled, then frowned. "Have you seen Radya?"

Piedmont stroked his beard. "No, I haven't. Thorden's her guide. She might be on another part of the ship."

"Well, I can't help worrying about her."

"Oh Johanna, don't fret. I'm sure Radya is having a good time herself."

Johanna stared at Piedmont. He certainly seemed pleased about being here, which was a far cry from his behavior back at the hospital.

Piedmont leaned forward. "Johanna, you seem down. What is eating you?"

The truth was Johanna kept remembering what Kameel had said about Serassan. Piedmont had warned her about him. Hadn't he told her Serassan was setting her up? "Don't forget who you are, Johanna," Piedmont had said. And here the professor was, apparently forgetting who *he* was, where they were, and the predicament they were all in. Sure, it seemed like this voyage through space was a luxury cruise, but what would happen when they arrived at their destination? What then?

"Is everything all right, Johanna?"

"Yes, fine," she replied.

"Then nothing is troubling you?"

"Nothing." She stood up. "I just wanted to check on you and see how you were getting along." She walked to the door, then turned to face him. "Come by later and you can see my ... place."

"Why, thank you, Johanna. I'll do that."

On her way back through the corridor, Johanna passed a room that was open. She stopped and looked in. Four women in leotards were bending over a bar attached to the wall across the room. One of the young ladies was Radya, with her long blond hair twisted in a tight roll on top of her head. Radya caught sight of her, and immediately the Russian ballerina tottered over in her toe shoes. Her cheeks were flushed with color, and her blue eyes sparkled as she grinned. "Johanna! It's so good to see you."

"Radya, are you all right?"

"But of course. Why wouldn't I be? And you?"

As relieved as she was to find Radya well, Johanna was confused. "I was worried about you."

"Oh ... that." The Russian girl lowered her voice. "At first I was afraid. I have to admit it. Thorden did things to me that seemed terrible, that is true. But now! Oh, now, Johanna!" Her eyes lifted as she sighed, crossing her hands over her heart. "I have never been so happy. I have never known the taste of freedom. It feels wonderful!"

"Freedom?" Johanna stared at the girl.

"I never knew what it could be like."

"Radya, have you seen Serassan anywhere?"

"No. Just Thorden. Oh Johanna, he told me we are all going to a planet where everyone will exhibit their talent. Be it dancing, music, art, poetry ... isn't it wonderful?"

Johanna had suspected as much. "Is that what this is all about? You mean, we're all going to be in some universal talent show?"

Radya burst out laughing. "You Americans! You have such a sense of humor." Someone in the room called to her just then. "Excuse me now, Johanna. I must get back to my dancing."

Johanna watched a moment longer as the Russian girl resumed her place at the bar, and the dancers stretched. She noticed there was no music in the background. As she walked back to her quarters, Johanna recalled that she hadn't heard any music since they had met the shuttle and come aboard the mother ship. It seemed to be the one thing lacking in all the detailed furnishings.

When she was back to her own living room once again, Johanna went to the piano and sat down, then lifted the keyboard cover. She stared at the ivory keys as she thought more about what Radya had disclosed. Apparently the aliens had abducted only artists of one persuasion or another. Piedmont was an author and poet, Radya a ballerina, herself a musician. Johanna remembered that the other passengers in the van had also been artists. Vince was an actor, Steph a sculptor, Rose and Jasmine singers. But why would the Estronians abduct only artists? Why not Earth's finest minds, such as scientists, doctors, engineers?

"Obviously they didn't need those people," Johanna said aloud. "They've got their own scientists, doctors, and engineers, or how could they have built all this? Duplicated all this for our benefit? And somehow they've managed to outwit medical science by causing us to speak like them ..."

"May I assist you?" asked Kameel.

Johanna turned and saw the unit hovering behind her. "I was just talking to myself, Kameel."

"Why don't you play the instrument, Johanna Dobbs?" Kameel came closer. "I am equipped with recording equipment, in the event you would enjoy playing duets with yourself."

"I thought you said you couldn't make your own music," said Johanna.

"That is correct."

"But you would be if you recorded my playing, and then played it back."

"It would still be your music, Johanna Dobbs."

"Why do the Estronians want us?"

"It has been ordered," replied the unit.

"But why *us?* Why musicians? Why artists? Why dancers?"

"People living on the planet Estron require you," Kameel explained. "That is why they have colonized Karos and are turning it into an intergalactic cultural center. They now require musicians, artists, and dancers, as you stated."

"Well, why kidnap Terrans?" Johanna demanded. "Why can't they colonize Karos with their own artists? It is wrong to enslave others."

"Terrans have been found to demonstrate a high level of talent in the areas you mentioned," Kameel explained. "Estron has scanned many worlds, but your planet was found to be the best prospect. In answer to your second question, Johanna Dobbs, there are no artists on Estron."

Johanna's mouth fell open. "No artists? Not at all? Oh, that can't possibly be, Kameel. There must be people on Estron who like to sing and dance, who draw or paint, or simply entertain."

"Negative. There are no such ones on Estron."

Johanna couldn't believe she was hearing this. "But how can that be, Kameel? You're so highly evolved technologically ..."

"Why don't you play something?" urged the robot. "It's what you've wanted to do ever since you arrived here."

Johanna turned back to the keyboard. What she had just learned had baffled her so much, she figured only music could make everything right again. So she played. Surprisingly, the piano was in tune. She played for several minutes as images passed through her mind. She kept coming back to Serassan's face, his magnetic eyes glued to her own, his thoughts telling her he cared for her. But Kameel had said he was no longer her concern. His task was over, and he would now move on to new assignments. He had only been using her. She plunged down onto the keyboard and struck a sour chord.

"I do not understand," Kameel commented as the off-color notes continued to fill the apartment. "Johanna Dobbs, why are you unhappy?"

"Damn him!" Johanna cried. Her vision clouded as hot tears emerged from her eyes. "How could I be so blind?"

"What is wrong?" Kameel asked. "Does the music not make you happy?"

"I thought he loved me," Johanna blubbered.

"Who are you talking about?" asked the robot.

"Serassan," she revealed. She sniffed. "I thought he loved me."

"Come sit down where it is comfortable," invited Kameel. "I can see it is time for a 'woman-to-unit talk', Johanna Dobbs."

"I'll never see him again," she sobbed.

"Please come sit down. You will feel better," said Kameel. "I am programmed to help you in every way. I will listen to what troubles you."

Johanna did as the unit directed, and was surprised when, after a few minutes passed, Kameel brought out a cup of hot tea for her.

"Thanks, Kameel." She wiped her cheeks.

"You believed Serassan to be in love with you?" asked Kameel, and Johanna nodded. "That was the plan. It is one of his ploys, Johanna Dobbs. He has used it on several Earth women. It made it easier for you to go along with him. You must accept that now. It was his job."

Johanna sipped the tea. The soothing drink was relaxing, but the hurt inside remained. She wondered how many other broken hearts were sitting in their quarters somewhere on this same mother ship, drinking cups of hot tea their units had fixed for them.

— 17 —

The Risk of Love

Two days passed since they had been on board the mother ship. Johanna could not be sure of the days or nights because there was no daylight to set the hours. She went by her biological clock, and the regularity with which Kameel served her meals and prepared her bed. Once when Johanna had asked the unit for the time, Kameel had responded, "Time? Time, Johanna Dobbs, is irrelevant." There had been no further discussion.

Johanna remained in her quarters. Even the comfort of almost being in her own home could not lift her out of the depression she was in over Serassan. Try as she did, he filled her mind day and night. Sleep came fitfully. The memory of his face invaded her dreams.

"Kameel, tell me about the Estronians," Johanna mused. She lay sprawled on her couch, paging through a music magazine. The cat-shaped robot ran a silent vacuum tube over the oak floor.

"What is it you wish to know about them?" asked Kameel. The unit did not let up with its housework.

"What are they like? Are they all like Serassan and Thorden?" Johanna folded her magazine and sat straight up. "What am I saying? Serassan and Thorden are two different personalities."

"No two are alike, of course," replied Kameel, "just as no two Terrans are alike."

"Well, then, how are they different from Terrans? Oh, I already know they are more advanced. But tell me, do all Estronians possess the abilities that Serassan and Thorden have?"

"To a varying degree," the robot replied. The vacuuming was done. In an instant, Kameel caused the vacuum tube to slide up into a small box, which she

118

tucked away beneath a cavity beneath her metallic casing. "I notice you have not been practicing the piano, Johanna Dobbs."

"I don't feel like playing."

"I do not understand."

Johanna sighed, then changed the subject. "It seems strange to me that I haven't seen other Estronians on board besides Serassan and Thorden."

"If it seems strange, it is only because they felt you would be more at ease among your own kind, without ..." The unit stopped in mid-sentence while a shrill series of beeps suddenly filled the room.

Startled, Johanna stared at Kameel. The sounds had come from the unit itself. "What is it?"

Kameel shut off the sound by pressing a button. "If you will excuse me now, Johanna Dobbs, I must report to the energy chamber. I will not be gone too long. Is there anything you need before I depart?"

Johanna couldn't think of anything. She picked up her magazine again as the unit glided to the door. Kameel exited, and Johanna was alone in the apartment.

Throwing her magazine aside, she fell back against the couch. "Shoo! Nothing like a little privacy." Kicking off her shoes, she stared at the ceiling and basked in the luxury of being totally alone. This, as far as she knew, had been her unit's first energy chamber visit, unless Kameel had gone there while Johanna slept.

A knock on the door made Johanna flinch. "So much for privacy." She pushed herself up and went over to see who it was. She really didn't feel like any company right now. She wanted just to be left alone.

There stood Serassan, tall and overpowering with his deep blue eyes fixed on her. Her eyes swept over the white, one-piece uniform he wore. On the right side of his chest was an emblem comprising an eight-point star superimposed over a planet.

"Johanna, let me come in." There was an urgency in his voice.

She nodded. With a glance over his shoulder, the alien entered and the door closed again. Johanna was surprised to see him, but also glad. Then she remembered he had used her, just like he had used several other Earth women. She turned her back on him, and felt her lip tremble.

"I had to see you," he said. He placed his hand on her shoulder. The warm sensation almost caused her to slump forward. How she needed to soak up that wonderful energy he passed on to her.

Unable to resist, she slowly turned to face him. "Serassan, what are you doing here?"

He took her into his arms then. Her chin rested against his chest as she felt his strong hands softly caressing her waist. "I've missed you, Johanna. I waited until your unit was away to risk seeing you."

Johanna looked into his face. How smooth his tanned skin was, as though he had just shaved. Did the man shave every hour on the hour? "Risk seeing me? What are you talking about, Serassan?"

"Please, just let me hold you." He pressed her body against him.

She closed her eyes and basked in the flow of warmth that surrounded them both. Still, she remembered the hurt. "I don't understand."

"I love you, Johanna. Since the first time I saw you. Since I first heard you play—for the city holiday benefit two years ago."

Flashes of herself performing at the charity event came back to her. What did that have to do with Serassan?

"You didn't know it, of course," he continued, "but even then we were preparing you. Your future was already being plotted."

Johanna tore herself away from his embrace. "How could you?" she fired.

"Have I upset you?" He seemed surprised.

She folded her arms and pouted. "Don't pretend with me any longer. It was your *duty* to make me fall in love with you."

"Yes. Yes, you are right." Serassan strolled over to the piano and leaned against it. "That was what was supposed to happen. However, something else *did* happen. I was *not* supposed to fall in love with *you*." He looked at her. His gaze implored her to listen. "I couldn't help myself. You see, I discovered something. I found out that you are ... my special one."

Johanna backed away, confused. "What does that mean ... special one?"

He smiled. "It's not an easy thing to explain. To put it in terms you can understand, I suppose I could say you were meant for me."

"How am I supposed to believe you?" Already, though, Johanna could feel her will weakening. "I mean ... Kameel said you ... you weren't available, that you had ... new assignments."

"I am at great risk coming here like this." Serassan moved toward her.

"Why?"

"Involvement with Terrans from this point on is not allowed," he explained.

"Why? Why can't I see you whenever I want?" asked Johanna.

"We can meet during the unit's energy chamber visits," said Serassan, "and only then."

"So, Kameel mustn't find out you are here," confirmed Johanna.

"Quite correct." He drew her toward him once again, and smiled. "But it won't be so bad. Although I long for you near me at every moment, knowing that we can be together at least some of the time is worth the risk." He peered into her eyes and searched her mind.

Johanna felt as though she were under a spell. Sensations erupted not only in her mind, but all over her body as he held her tightly against his hard form. She became aware of the convergence of their breathing. She heard him speak of his love for her in his mind, how she was the only woman he loved or wanted, and always would be.

When he kissed her, his lips were tight and firm over her own. She clutched him in reply, and he opened his mouth and told her in his mind how she should do the same. Johanna felt so new at this, yet she somehow sensed he was not as experienced at this as she had expected him to be. *You are right*, his mind told her. *On Estron this form of affection is considered obscene, yet I find it highly arousing.* In her mind she laughed and told him, *Much has been made of it on Earth. I wish I were more expert so I could show you,* to which he replied, *The touch of an Earth woman ... you, Johanna ... is sending me into zones of delirious exultation.*

As his breathing accelerated and the lovemaking progressed, Johanna found herself encouraging him. His peculiar odor engulfed her as his kisses grew longer and their bodies entwined. The fragrance was like nothing she had known before she met him, and she found herself intoxicated by it. It thrilled her to know that this man, alien that he was, could possess her totally, mind and body.

When she broke away for a few moments of air, she asked him, "How long will Kameel be away?"

"Long enough, my beloved." Serassan stared down at her. "Johanna, please ... before we take the next step, I have an important favor to ask of you."

She smiled up at him, her soul in a magic rapture. There was nothing she would deny him. "What is it?"

His gaze shifted toward the piano. "Will you ... please play something for me?"

Johanna smiled. "Oh, is that all?" She squeezed his hand, then led him over, where she perched herself on the bench and thought a moment. Her head cleared in a matter of seconds, and then she began one of her own pieces. She was aware of Serassan standing behind her, so close. During the performance he did not even waver.

When she was through, Johanna slowly turned to him. There was a distant look in his penetrating eyes, as if his thoughts were far away. She could not hear his thoughts, but she sensed an elation in him, a high that sent him above the sensations she had known only moments ago in his arms. She didn't know what to make of it. "Serassan?" she finally asked.

His eyelids slowly closed, and then he opened his eyes and seemed to be aware of her once again. He reached for her, and she draped her arms around his neck. "You cannot know how fortunate your planet is," he murmured in her ear, "to possess such beauty. On Estron we would kill for such beauty."

This response startled Johanna, and she stared into his face. "But it was only music, Serassan."

He held her tightly. "Only music to you, my love. A narcotic to some of us."

This puzzled her even more, but she said no more as he lifted her face with his hand, and their lips met once again. *The time has come*, his mind told hers, *for you to be a part of me. No longer do I merely desire you, but I need you.* With that, he led her into the dark bedroom, where so many voices in her head conversed that she no longer listened. She knew he was going to make love to her, and even though she had fantasized it countless times before—and feared the unknown—Johanna's longing to be possessed by this man overrode all other thoughts.

Body sensations she had never felt before sent her into exhilaration so that only the urgency of the moment became important. His passion became her passion. Satisfying him became her ecstasy until—quite suddenly—she realized she had her own urgency. Heights she had never known before came into play for her as Serassan's body—alien though it was—drove her into a frenzied pursuit for fulfillment. She cried out in agitation, barely able to tolerate the latent enormity of his being, yet unable to resist him.

And finally they both collapsed, their bodies entwined on top of the quilt. Seconds passed in which Johanna listened to the pounding of her heart and his, and their breathing staggered to a normal rate. At last he withdrew, but she clung to him, the delicious experience still raging in her mind. She wondered if she had behaved according to his expectations.

"Well beyond expectation, my Johanna," he told her softly. "And what about you?"

She guessed he already knew it had been her first time. Sighing softly, she nestled against him and closed her eyes, feeling safe and secure.

The next thing Johanna knew, Serassan was gently shaking her awake. "I must go," he told her. He was already dressed. "The unit will return shortly, and I cannot be seen here with you."

Johanna pushed herself up. She grabbed for her clothes. "Let me come with you," she said.

"No. You must remain here."

"But why? We're free to come and go as we choose on this ship."

"There are limits," said Serassan, "at least for now."

Half dressed, Johanna sat on the edge of the bed. "I keep forgetting I'm a prisoner."

He reached for her. "Johanna, don't think that way." Then he added with a warm smile, "I love you."

She rubbed her cheek against his hand. "I know, Serassan. When will I see you again?"

"We must wait until Kameel-37 goes to the recharging station again." He explained that he knew how to check on the unit's maintenance schedule, and he would be in touch with her.

Johanna stood up as he started to leave. "Serassan, why is your involvement with Terrans not allowed?"

"I can't get into it right now. I must go."

But she followed him into the living room as he headed for the door. "Then tell me ... what did you mean when I heard you tell Thorden about *breeding privileges?*"

He looked startled, then bent over to kiss her. "It's very complicated, Johanna. Please ... if I don't go now, I risk being discovered."

She gave in, and they kissed once more at the door. Then he stole outside. She stood watching him as he hurried down the corridor. It had been some enchanted evening, and Johanna didn't want it spoiled by Kameel's metallic voice and ridiculous cat-like appearance. She switched off all the lights and retired for the night.

Everything in her life was good for once, and nothing was going to spoil that ... tonight, at least.

— 18 —

Radya's Flip Side

"Kameel, your cooking is out of this world." Johanna wiped her mouth with the napkin, then laughed out loud. "What am I saying?" She pushed the breakfast tray aside, and picked up her cup of black coffee. Now she could lie back and sip leisurely while she reveled in the memory of last night.

"Are you finished, Johanna Dobbs?" The unit hovered near her bed.

"I think I'll drink my coffee in bed," said Johanna, "but I won't stay too long. I've got a lot to do today. I'm going to start working on my composition."

The unit started to take the tray away, then stopped and turned to face Johanna. "Your cheeks are flushed. Shall I measure your body temperature?"

"No, Kameel. I feel fine. I feel ... wonderful!"

"I understand now. You are in high spirits."

Johanna sighed. "Very high spirits, Kameel." She spent the better part of the morning at the piano, where she worked, uninterrupted, until Kameel asked her about lunch.

"You are making progress at last," remarked the unit.

"I know. It's fantastic!" Johanna gathered up her music sheets and stacked them on top of the piano.

"I am curious about something, Johanna Dobbs."

"Oh? What, Kameel?"

"To what do you attribute this major change in your mood?"

Johanna couldn't tell her robot about Serassan's visit. She had to be careful what she said. "Oh, I don't know, Kameel. I'm a musician. We sometimes fall into unproductive phases. A lot of artists are temperamental."

"It does not make sense," protested the unit.

Johanna thought she had better change the subject. "Kameel, why haven't I seen any Estronians since I've been on board?"

"But of course you have."

"I don't mean Serassan and Thorden. I mean *other* Estronians."

"You have, Johanna Dobbs."

"Why can't I go talk to some of them?"

"They are not available now."

"Oh? Why not?"

"They are above, and you are below. I am Kameel-37. I am programmed to fulfill your needs, Johanna Dobbs. There is no reason why you should see your hosts."

"You mean my abductors."

"They have prepared everything for you to make your voyage a pleasant one. You are allowed to move about the ship's lower deck, if you like, and visit others of your kind."

"That's an excellent idea." Johanna stood up and stretched. She had been sitting at the piano a long time. "I need some exercise. If you don't mind, Kameel, I think I'll wait on lunch. I want to go pay a visit to Piedmont."

Johanna had not ventured outside of her quarters since that first day. She found it strange that no one else was out walking the halls right now. When she came to Piedmont's quarters, she knocked.

Within seconds, the professor opened the door to her. He was dressed in a brown bulky sweater. He seemed surprised to see her. "Why, Johanna! I'm pleased to see you." He invited her in.

A short mechanical form glided in from Piedmont's bedroom just then. Johanna was startled to see that it had a body similar to the shape of an insect, with glowing eyes like Kameel's, and no mouth or nose. A metallic deep male voice called out, "I see you have a visitor, Professor Piedmont."

"Yes, Syben." Piedmont glanced at his unit, then gestured to Johanna. "Johanna, this is my unit, Syben-86."

"Please have a chair," directed Piedmont's unit.

"Uh ... Syben," interrupted the professor, "would you mind leaving us for a few minutes?"

"I understand, professor. This is to be a private conversation."

"Something like that," grumbled the professor.

"Well, then, I will start that loaf of bread you requested." With that, the unit turned and glided off into Piedmont's kitchen.

Piedmont rolled his eyes as he led Johanna over to his couch. She saw that he had papers scattered in heaps everywhere around his typewriter. Apparently he had been busy at work when she had arrived.

"I hope I'm not interrupting you," said Johanna.

"Oh, not at all. Not at all, Johanna. I am glad you came by. I've been meaning to talk to you." Piedmont glanced off toward the kitchen to make sure the unit was not present, then turned back to her.

"What is it, Piedmont? Is something wrong?"

"It's just Syben. He's always around. Nosier than Mrs. Wilkins."

"Who's Mrs. Wilkins?"

The professor sighed, then smiled. "Oh, nothing. Mrs. Wilkins was my housekeeper back on ... Earth." The reminder that he was no longer on Earth seemed to upset him momentarily. He bent forward and lowered his voice. "Johanna, have you learned anything?"

"About what?"

"Where we're going, what lies ahead."

Johanna blinked. "Well, I know from my unit that we're being taken to a planet named Karos."

"Yes," said the professor. "That much I know. Tell me, have you been in touch with Serassan at all?"

Her silence gave her away.

The professor smiled reassuringly. "Never mind. I know it is forbidden. I tried to see the man myself. I didn't get very far."

"Why? What happened?"

"I like to take walks before I retire in the evening," explained Piedmont. "I've walked all over the passenger decks. Last night I wanted to see more of the ship. I found my way back to the transport shaft. I was denied access." He then told her that some kind of force field around the shaft prevented him or anyone else from gaining entry. "I have this fear, Johanna."

"Of what?"

"I can't be certain." He rubbed his chin. "Have you spoken with some of the others?"

Johanna confessed she had stayed cooped up in her apartment the last few days.

"Well, then you haven't heard about the Guild."

"What Guild?"

"Vince Waldon and some others banded together to form ..." He ceased talking when Syben-86 entered the living room. Piedmont gave Johanna a warning look that said they should change the subject.

"So tell me, Johanna," Piedmont said, "how's Radya? Have you seen much of her?"

"As a matter of fact, I've met her only once."

The professor turned toward the unit. "What do you want, Syben?"

"Am I intruding again, Professor Piedmont?" asked the metallic voice. "Perhaps I can fix you and the young lady some tea."

"Splendid. Do so." The unit retreated to the kitchen.

"So, have *you* seen Radya? How is she getting along?" Johanna prompted.

"Frankly, my dear, I'm more than a little worried about our Russian friend. She seems to be a totally changed person."

"When I spoke to her a couple of days ago, she seemed very happy," Johanna related. "She said something which I found very odd. It seems that for the first time in her life, Radya has known freedom. Can you believe it, Piedmont? Here we are, prisoners on this mother ship, heading for some distant planet in some distant star system, against our wills, and Radya is ecstatic to be *free*."

Piedmont shook his head. "I don't believe the girl knows what freedom is. She's lived in the U.S.S.R. all her life, after all."

Syben brought the tea on a tray then, and stood close by. The professor spoke of his book, and Johanna mentioned she was finally working on her music again. As soon as her cup was empty, she made up some excuse to leave, said goodbye to Piedmont, and walked on down the corridor.

She had learned a lot from Piedmont. For one thing, he was his old self again, no longer in a euphoria over the luxurious conditions the aliens had created for him. She wondered what else she might have learned from him if Syben-86 had not been within earshot. What had Piedmont been trying to tell her about Vince Waldon and this talk of a Guild?

She wandered the halls for a while, trying to find out where Radya was staying. Finally, hunger pangs won out, and Johanna retreated to her apartment. There she found Kameel setting her table. Johanna told her unit that she desired to visit with the Russian ballerina that afternoon, but didn't know where Radya was staying.

"I can find that out for you, Johanna Dobbs," said the unit. "Because your friend is under the custody of the guide Thorden, she is undoubtedly on another part of the deck. If you like, I can summon her unit and relay the message that you wish her to visit you."

"That would be lovely." Johanna picked up a spoon and started into her soup.

Later that afternoon, Radya came to Johanna's apartment. She wore a shiny fabric gown with a feathery wrap. Radya's blond hair was styled beautifully, and she had makeup on. Johanna thought the girl looked ten years older.

"Radya, you look ... beautiful." Johanna didn't know how else to describe it without hurting the girl's feelings. Actually, Radya seemed quite a bit overdressed, and a heavy perfume filled the apartment.

"How are you, comrade?" Radya twitched a smile and held her head high.

"That dress ..." Johanna couldn't help but gape. "It's so extravagant."

"Yes, I know." Radya sprawled herself out on Johanna's couch. "Tell your unit to pour me some vodka, will you please, comrade?"

"Well, I ..."

Kameel broke in, "Miss Dobbs does not possess liquor."

"Oh." Radya's face fell, but she shrugged. "Never mind. Anything will do."

The unit glided off to the kitchen, and Johanna sat down on a chair opposite the ballerina. "Radya, you're so ... different. "

The girl ignored her comment. "My unit said you wanted to see me. What's so important?"

Johanna was astonished at the bored tone in Radya's voice. "I just wanted to see you ... to see how you're getting along."

"I'm perfect, as you can see."

"Well, I'm certainly happy that you're no longer afraid. How's the dancing coming along?"

Radya fussed over her fingernails, which had been painted with a sparkling polish. "I dance. I do many things now that I never did before."

"That's good ... I think."

"I didn't expect you to understand," grumbled the ballerina. "After all, you were *born* free."

What was the girl talking about, Johanna wondered. Where was her head? "Radya, I saw Piedmont this morning."

Radya sighed indifferently.

"Don't you even want to know how he is?"

"He's just an old man. I have other concerns now," the girl retorted.

"What concerns?"

"None of your business."

Johanna saw that the Russian girl was not joking. She wrinkled up her nose as she studied Johanna's face. Johanna sighed. "Radya, something's happened to you. Something has changed you."

"That's nonsense."

"It's Thorden, isn't it?"

Radya smiled in a sophisticated fashion as she looked on Johanna with superiority. "He's really not as bad as people think, Johanna."

"After what he's done to you? How can you say that?"

"He has promised me many things," said Radya. "I dance for him ... and a little bit more ... and whatever I desire is mine."

Kameel brought in the drinks, two cranberry coolers on a tray.

"It can't last, Radya," Johanna warned. "This is all just a fantasy. Can't you see?"

Radya laughed. "Oh Johanna, you don't know the half of it. Why they picked you—a spinster—is beyond me. You're old enough to be my mother!" She reached for her drink, sniffed at it, then made a face and placed it back on Kameel's tray. "Besides, Piedmont is a fool."

Johanna stood up. "I think it's time for you to leave now, Radya."

The ballerina sat up straight on the couch and looked perturbed. "Are you telling me to leave? What have I done? I thought you asked me over here to gossip about Piedmont and the others. Well, don't bother, Johanna. I have better things to do with my time." She strutted to the door and struck a pose. "On Karos, I'm going to be the prima ballerina."

Johanna stood staring at the door after Radya left. It was unbelievable. How could a person change so drastically? How could the frail young girl who had clung so timidly to Johanna only days ago have transformed into a selfish prig? Johanna was convinced Thorden had something to do with it. If Serassan was visiting Johanna during Kameel's energy chamber visits, it was likely Thorden was doing the same thing with Radya. Either that, or the Russian girl had suffered an emotional breakdown brought on by the stress of her abduction.

Serassan came again that evening while Kameel was visiting the energy chamber. It was late. To keep from arousing suspicion, Johanna had pretended to retire. She fell into Serassan's arms and clung to him as he nuzzled the top of her head with his chin.

They made love in fervor, then lay in bed afterwards. Even though she knew their time together was brief, Johanna wanted to hold onto this moment forever. She felt secure and content in his presence, with his shroud of warmth and tenderness that seemed to emanate from his very being.

"We decided to colonize the planet Karos rather than take you to Estron," Serassan explained to Johanna as they discussed the mission. "Estron is not as habitable as Karos. I'm afraid you Terrans would find the conditions on Estron less than ideal."

"How many of us are there?" Johanna wanted to know.

"Quite a number of you. I'd say close to a thousand."

Johanna had expected a couple of hundred, at the most. She stared at the man beside her. "That many? I should think a thousand artists would be missed on Earth."

"We were careful to select only certain ones," replied Serassan. "You will notice that most of the Terrans are single, reclusive people. We would not risk taking the most conspicuous among you."

"I see, so you settled for second best." Johanna pouted.

"Not so, Johanna."

"But if you had found a way, you'd have picked Van Cliburn."

He stroked a wisp of dark hair that had fallen over her bare shoulders. "We chose the cream of the crop," he said.

"Serassan, how did I get to be this way?" Johanna asked.

"You mean ... so bold as well as beautiful?"

She scowled. "You never did explain. Why am I speaking Estronian? What happened to my English?"

"A simple surgical technique," he replied, and began twisting a lock of her dark hair around his finger. "For your sake, it has been blocked out of your conscious memory. Remember the night of the ballet? I did it then."

"Did what?"

"While you visited the powder room, I abducted you for a short time, and implanted a filter scrambler mechanism into your speech center."

Johanna laughed. "What? And you expect me to believe you performed brain surgery on me in the ladies' restroom?"

"Believe me, Johanna, it's best that you don't remember."

"But ... brain surgery! Serassan ..."

"A simple technique for us," Serassan replied seriously." I opened your nasal passages and ..."

"Please!" Johanna touched the tiny scar beneath her nostrils. "Spare me the details."

"It left barely a mark," he said. "Can your Earth doctors be that precise?"

Johanna was still puzzled. "But I didn't lose my speech until the next morning."

"True. I inserted a triggering device near your Hodarian gland."

"My ... what?"

"Never mind. You don't want to know."

"But why can't I speak both languages, like you and Thorden? I can understand why you would want us to communicate in Estronian, but why wipe out all that we knew before?"

Serassan reclined and rubbed his forehead. "Well ... we needed a way to unite all Terran emigrants chosen for this mission. Rather than simply abduct a thousand people at the last minute, we felt it would arouse less suspicion by altering your communication."

"In other words," mused Johanna, "you made us look crazy, so we'd be thrown into mental hospitals."

"Disguising your altered state as a form of mental illness has had its drawbacks," Serassan admitted. "Many of you have suffered needlessly. The trauma of a quick abduction may have been the better solution."

"But then how would you explain a thousand people disappearing from the face of the Earth overnight?" Johanna challenged.

He studied her face for a moment. "It's happening, but on a smaller scale. People vanish every day. Think of all the missing children."

"Estron is to blame for all those poor kids?" demanded Johanna.

Serassan shook his head. "No, not Estron. There are others—many others in this galaxy and beyond—who are responsible for a great many events. I am sorry to report that many of them are not acting on behalf of Earth's best interest."

Johanna laid her cheek on Serassan's shoulder and basked in the warmth of his hand as it massaged her back. "I wish you had just come and whisked me away from the very beginning," she murmured. "I would have come willingly, had I known all you have told me."

"If only it could have been so," he replied gently. "The trouble was there were vast preparations to be made—accommodations for you on the mother ship. All of that took time, dear Johanna."

"What will happen when we arrive on Karos?"

"You will start new lives. You will do what you've been doing all your lives—making the universe a more beautiful place in which to exist."

"Why is there no art on your planet, Serassan?"

He sighed. "I don't know."

Johanna drew her legs up and snuggled against him. "I just don't understand. I can't imagine a world that ..." She shook her head. "You don't even have music?"

Serassan was silent for a long moment, then he explained. "When my planet reached out into the galaxy, it discovered that other worlds, other peoples, had something in common that Estron did not. When we discovered what that something was, we were not content to do without it."

Serassan went on to say that when astronauts returned to Estron with samples of culture from alien worlds, the people of Estron became enraptured. Art, in all of its forms, was such a hit on Estron that it could not be imported fast enough or in large enough quantities to satisfy the majority. As a result, ulterior methods came into play and a kind of black market was set up. The world was on the verge of a civil war when the councils came together and several plans were sought to put an end to the deceit and resulting violence.

"Well, once you found out what you were missing, couldn't your people imitate it?" asked Johanna. "I mean, how else does one learn?"

"Of course there were attempts to make art of our own," Serassan grumbled. "We failed ... miserably."

"Oh ... how?"

"We lack your talent."

Johanna frowned. "Not everyone on Earth has talent either. That never stopped anyone from trying."

"Talent is something you are born with, Johanna. We know that much. And that is why we are hoping you and the others will introduce new genes into our progeny."

"You're going to use us to improve future generations?" Johanna stared at him. "That's ridiculous! While there may be some of us who are young, several of us are well beyond the child-bearing years."

"You?" Serassan laughed. "Come on, Johanna. You're more capable than you give yourself credit for."

"And what about Piedmont?" she asked.

"What about him? Men older than Piedmont ... much older ... have fathered babies."

"And how is this baby-making experiment of yours supposed to be carried out?" Johanna demanded.

Serassan hung his head. "Our methods are crude but will work, and without any discomfort to the Terrans."

"What if I don't want to have a baby?"

"You won't even know about it, Johanna."

"What are you talking about?"

"Do not get excited, Johanna. Perhaps I have told you too much. I did not mean to alarm you." His deep blue eyes looked on her with a compassion that touched her heart.

Johanna relaxed and smiled up at him. "Oh Serassan, I want *your* baby."

He continued to gaze at her. "Once we reach Karos ..." He turned away.

"Once we reach Karos, *what?*" Johanna demanded. "Serassan, tell me."

"How I wish I had been chosen for the breeding program," he revealed. "I have not."

Her mouth dropped open. "You mean ... some other alien ..." A horrid thought struck her. "Oh, no. Is Thorden ..."

"No, Johanna. Thorden was not chosen either."

She threw her arms around him then, and felt his powerful grip as he embraced her. In her mind she felt the overpowering love he held for her, and she closed her eyes and prayed somehow their relationship could continue, even after they reached Karos.

"I think I understand one thing now," she murmured.

"What is that?"

"Why we aren't allowed to go on the upper level of the ship." Johanna withdrew to face him. "You mentioned your planet would not be habitable to us. Is that why I haven't seen any other Estronians? Because you need certain conditions in which to live?"

Serassan nodded. "That is so."

"And you and Thorden ... why are you immune?"

"We are guides. We have taken on human bodies in order to fit into your world and pass off as one of you. When we reach Karos, I will submit to a surgical procedure that will allow me to inhabit Estron once again."

Johanna gazed at him curiously. "And what did you look like before?" she asked.

"Is it important?"

"I just wondered."

"Well, I was ... different." That's all Serassan would say about his appearance. When she prodded him for a detailed description, he shrugged it off and reminded her that soon Kameel would be returning. He asked if she would play him something on the piano before he left, and Johanna complied.

"I don't care what you looked like, Serassan," she teased as they got dressed, "as long as you didn't resemble one of those frightening, skinny, gray beings from the shuttle craft." A minute later she added, "Or Thorden!"

"Yes ... Thorden." Serassan nodded. "Thorden was not happy about the results of his transformation. He still complains about his looks, how they misshaped his nose."

"Well, if looks reflect an individual's personality, whoever did the surgery knew exactly how to make you and Thorden."

Serassan put a restraining hand on her shoulder. She turned to him and resigned herself to another deep kiss. Then he held her tight. "Things, Johanna, are never what they seem."

— 19 —

Seed of Enlightenment

"Thanks for meeting me like this, Dr. Wetzel." Manley Dobbs poured cream into his cup of coffee. "I hope it's not an inconvenience to you."

The blond woman psychiatrist had expected to find the plump man in a neurotic state. The last time she had seen him, he had been grief-stricken and overwrought. She was surprised at his placid manner. "I'm sorry I missed your sister's memorial service. Now that we are a doctor short, my schedule at the hospital is back to its normal madness ... excuse the pun." She sipped at her mug. "What did you want to see me about?"

"I had a dream," Manley said. "Usually I'm not one to dwell on such frivolities. However, this dream was so vivid."

"What was it about?"

Manley stirred his coffee with a spoon. "It was about Johanna."

"I see." Barbara put down her cup. The man was obviously too cheap to make an appointment. Some people had a lot of gall, seeking free advice.

"Wait, this isn't what you think." Manley shook his head and smiled. "I didn't invite you here during my coffee break to have my head examined. You see, the dream made me realize something. My sister did not drown in that river accident last week."

Barbara tried not to show her feelings of concurrence. "Just because none of the bodies have been recovered yet, Mr. Dobbs ..."

"She's alive! They're *all* alive," Manley insisted. "I saw it in the dream."

Barbara's curiosity was now sufficiently aroused. "What exactly did you see in your dream?"

Manley smiled excitedly. "A huge ship," he began with gestures. "I saw a spaceship come down out of the sky and land. Then Johanna got on, and it took her away."

Barbara stared at him. "A spaceship?"

"Yes."

"In your dream?"

"Yes, but here's the clincher. The night after I had that dream, I happened to be out walking the dog. It was a clear night, and there were lots of stars. I saw something up there that moved, then stopped, then moved again. It changed colors. Well, I went back to the house to get my wife and the binoculars. But of course, by the time we came out again, it was gone."

Barbara took a long gulp from her mug. Her fingers trembled.

"Don't spill on yourself, doctor." Manley had noticed her reaction. "I had never seen anything like that in my life. You've got to believe me. And after that dream! What do you think it means?"

Barbara wiped her lip with a napkin. If it had been anyone else or had happened any time before last night, she'd have long written him off as crackers. But the coincidence was too uncanny. She started to speak, but her voice cracked.

"Is something wrong?" asked Manley.

Barbara took another quick sip of the hot brew. "This is unreal."

"I swear, it was there."

"No, I don't mean your sighting," she said. "I'm talking about what *I* saw last night."

Manley leaned toward her. "What did you see?"

Barbara cleared her throat. "I used to treat people who told stories like this. Now ... I just can't believe that, but what I saw last night was very real. Either I've been working too hard and I'm going insane, or ..."

"No!" cried Manley. "No, you're quite sane. And I'll tell you something else. I think Johanna was quite sane as well. Tell me, doctor. Do you believe Johanna and those others died in the crash?"

Barbara stared into her lap, where her hands had crinkled up the paper napkin with its wet stain. "Well, actually ... no. I've had a lot of doubts about it."

"I think that's significant." He relaxed against his seat and studied her. "Were you scared?"

"Of what?"

"Of ... you know ... the UFO."

"There were three."

"What? Really?" He sighed. "That's fantastic. They must be watching you closely."

"Who?"

"I don't know." He frowned. "The occupants, I guess. It's funny, doc. I used to be a fairly simple guy. I used to think in simple terms, but I always had a lot of feelings … especially toward my sister. Now, suddenly, I have these wild and exciting ideas. They just pop into my head. It's like I have tapped into this source of knowledge. For instance, I never used to care what went on in the world. I went about my daily tasks like anybody else. Got up, went to work, dragged through the day till quitting time … you know what I'm talking about. Today I'm beginning to see things a lot differently."

Barbara felt the shiver of fear dissolve as she watched him. "Go on," she urged.

"Our world, our Earth, is in trouble," he continued. "So much is wrong in the world, so much ill-will, violence, disease, hunger, the threat of nuclear war … How can we go on this way? Sooner or later, something's got to give. You know I'm right. We feel so safe and snug in our little cubby holes of life that we've made for ourselves. We live, day to day, with our heads buried in the sand, like ostriches. One day the stress is going to be too much, and something's going to give." He paused as his eyes rolled sideways. "Forgive me, doc. I didn't mean to ramble on. Lately I've been doing that. It's driving my wife Doris buggy."

Barbara smiled. "No, you're making a lot of sense. I understand what you're saying. I, too, have been going through a lot of personal changes since the accident happened. I can't tell you how logical your words sound."

Manley shrugged. "They're not my words … I don't think."

Barbara studied him closely.

"As I said," Manley explained, "all these weird thoughts have been just coming to me."

"Channeling," she said.

"What? Yes, I think you're right."

Barbara rubbed her chin. "Funny," she murmured. "That word just popped into *my* head."

Johanna had worked on her music composition for two solid days. More than a week had passed since she and the other Terrans had boarded the mother ship. Weary but satisfied with her progress, Johanna relaxed with a glass of iced tea. She yawned as Kameel entered the living room.

"Why don't you take a nap, Johanna Dobbs? You've been working very hard."

"No, I'm okay." Johanna had been working hard, but it was those late nights with Serassan during Kameel's absences that were the true cause of her fatigue. "Anyway, I want to visit Piedmont today."

"You do not mingle much with the other Terrans," remarked Kameel. "Why is that?"

Johanna stretched. "I guess I'm a bit of a recluse. Some of us are, you know. I think Piedmont's the same way."

"I perceive you are fond of the professor."

"He is my closest friend, Kameel. I'd trust him with my life."

"And your other friend, Radinka Bjelkova … do you trust her?"

Johanna sighed. "She's confused right now, Kameel. She's been through a rough time, and she's still a girl, barely nineteen."

"And do you trust her?" the unit asked again.

Johanna stared at the cat-like robot. "That's hard to say, Kameel. Can I trust you, or any of the Estronians?"

Kameel hovered next to the coffee table. "Trust is a human characteristic. Please define trust, Johanna Dobbs."

"Well … trusting is sort of believing in someone … knowing they will stick by your side, even when things get rough. That's what a friend does, Kameel. Aren't you my friend?"

"I am programmed to serve you. I am a companion to you, if you desire it."

"When you have a friend," Johanna resumed, "a real friend, you trust that person. I think I can trust you, Kameel, even though you are not human."

"If trusting is an ingredient of friendship, then yes. You can trust me, Johanna Dobbs."

When Johanna paid a visit to Piedmont's quarters, the professor greeted her enthusiastically. As she sat down in his living room, the professor went to his desk and attempted to lift his typewriter.

"Piedmont, what you are doing? You'll hurt your back," chided Johanna.

"It's not that heavy, Johanna, really." The old man groaned as he managed to lift the heavy machine off the table. Turning to her, he gritted his teeth, his ruddy face flushed, then threw the typewriter onto the floor.

"Piedmont!" Johanna jumped to her feet at the crash of metal.

The professor stood back and shook his head in dismay. "Oh dear, now look at what has happened."

At that moment, Syben-86 glided in and approached them. "Are you harmed, Professor Piedmont?" asked the ant-like unit.

"No," grumbled Piedmont.

Johanna knelt beside the machine, which had lost its carriage in the impact with the floor. "Oh Piedmont … your typewriter! It's ruined!"

Syben-86 came right over, and lowered itself to the floor. Extending its steel arms, the unit raised the broken machine up into the air. "Do you wish me to repair this apparatus, Professor Piedmont?" it asked.

"Can you, Syben?"

"I am capable of almost anything. I can repair typewriters. Your apparatus is alien and primitive, but I will effect restoration immediately, if you so desire."

"Then, please, take the damn thing and fix it," ordered the professor.

Syben-86 moved toward the door. It turned to them and asked, "Is there anything you wish before I leave?"

"Oh, we'll be just fine, Syben. But I must have my typewriter in good working order."

"Very well, professor. I will return shortly." The unit departed.

"And good riddance," the professor called out after Syben had left. He turned to Johanna, who still knelt beside the desk. "Oh, don't fret about it," he told her. "I did it on purpose. I wanted to have some time alone with you to talk." He led Johanna back over to the couch, where they sat down. Suddenly, Piedmont caught the look on her face. "Why, Johanna, you're blushing. What is it?"

She shrugged. "Nothing."

"Are you feeling all right?"

"I'm perfectly fine. In fact, I've never been happier in my life."

"Yes." He scratched his red beard, but continued to glance at her suspiciously. "And I can guess why. Our fraudulent doctor is the cause of those glowing cheeks, without a doubt."

Johanna started to protest.

"But never mind," interrupted Piedmont. "I have matters much more urgent to discuss with you now. I know you've been shut up in your rooms for several days. You probably haven't heard about the demonstrations."

"Demonstrations?" Johanna was puzzled.

"There have been a few minor uprisings," explained Piedmont. "The Opposition Guild is responsible."

"Opposition Guild? What are you talking about?"

"It's a small group ... right now. But we're growing. Before we reach Karos, we hope to have swung the majority to our side."

"We?" She stared at him. "Piedmont, are you a member of this Guild?"

"I know this is hard for you to believe, Johanna, but there are still some of us who would like to get back to Earth. We are protesting the captivity of all Terrans by Estron."

"It sounds dangerous."

"No. We won't use violence. Ours are totally passive measures. We cannot hope to gain our freedom by force, not when Estron holds all the cards."

"But do you really think they will turn the ship around and take us back to Earth?"

"I don't know. I only know this, Johanna. I know that human beings were not meant to live as slaves. That's what we'll be when we get to Karos."

"That isn't so!" She then told Piedmont about some of the things Serassan had disclosed, about the Terrans colonizing the planet and helping the Estronians develop a new race with inbred talent. "Once we get there, we will be free to lead our lives as we always have—be it writing, painting, dancing, or making music—and the audiences and the people who come to admire our art will be the most appreciative, devoted patrons you could ever imagine. That's what Serassan told me."

"Dear Johanna, he has painted an impossible dream for you. Can't you see it?" Piedmont stood up and paced back and forth. "They want to force us to use our talents. Well, dash it all, nobody can force poetry out of me! I haven't written anything in days. I've lost my enthusiasm. And a lot of other people feel the same way."

Johanna was silent. She remembered how she had been the first day or two aboard the mother ship, depressed and unproductive. Serassan had been the reason she had been inspired. Piedmont had a point. She found out that Vince Waldon, the actor, was self-appointed leader of the Guild. He had some strong ideas, but so far Piedmont had managed to mellow him with logic, and had succeeded at convincing him that peaceful demonstration was the only way to proceed.

After she left Piedmont's quarters, Johanna strolled down the corridor, deep in thought. She didn't recognize Radya, whose sharp footsteps echoed on the floor, until the ballerina stopped in front of her.

"Well, hello, Johanna." The Russian girl seemed more cordial than she had the other day. Her dress was still extravagant, and she was plastered down with makeup.

"Radya, hi."

"Have you come from Piedmont's?" asked the girl.

"Well, as a matter of fact ..."

Radya's whole figure tensed up as a storm crossed her face. "He's a fool, you know. He's a member of that *Guild*. If you value his friendship, Johanna, you'd better talk him out of it, and soon! They're going to get themselves killed."

Johanna stared the girl in the eye. "I take it you don't approve of the Guild, Radya."

"I'm very much against it! Where is it going to lead us? We're all going to have to be hypnotized! They'll have complete control over us all. Do you want that?"

Johanna glanced in both directions of the hallway. She wasn't sure if it was safe for herself and Radya to discuss the Guild in public. Obviously, it was no secret if Radya knew about it. Johanna was sure that Thorden must know about it. And now Serassan would know—by reading Johanna's mind—if he and Thorden hadn't already discussed it. "Piedmont told me the Guild is peaceful. They don't want to cause trouble."

"It's too late! They already have." She eyed Johanna critically. "Why don't you get Serassan to furnish you with a wardrobe? You know … something a little more … flattering."

Johanna's heart raced. So Radya knew about Serassan coming to her apartment. She wished the girl would keep her mouth shut. Anybody could be listening. "I have to go now, Radya." She started walking.

"Peace. Peace!" the girl called after her. "Everybody wants peace, yes! But where did it ever get us?"

Oooooh, she's hard to figure out, Johanna thought as she returned to her quarters. Radya had certainly gone over the edge.

"Yes, I know about the Guild," Serassan disclosed that evening during his visit to Johanna's quarters. "It is nothing to be too concerned about. They are few in number. Of course, we expected this."

"How long now before we reach Karos?" asked Johanna.

"An estimated two days."

Johanna rested contentedly against Serassan's shoulder. "What are we going to do, Serassan? What's going to happen to you and me after we reach Karos? How are we going to see each other?"

"I wish I had some answers, Johanna. Right now, the situation looks grim."

"Then, you haven't spoken to anybody yet? What about your superior?"

"It's unlikely she will understand."

"She?" Johanna looked at him. "Your superior is a woman?"

"Now you see why it is difficult for me to even think of bringing up the subject."

"Well, certainly another woman would understand about love," stressed Johanna.

"Females from Estron do not differ that much from males," Serassan explained. "They are so unlike Terran women. Perhaps the centuries of our advanced technology over Earth's has caused our women to succeed so well. Our roots are not unlike your own. At one time, Estronian women bore children, raised them, and were the cores of their families. When we reached that point in our development where women were no longer needed for such tasks, they found they could concentrate on uninterrupted lifetime careers in a vast number of fields. Many of our women are leaders. They have proven themselves highly competent intellectually and mechanically. Many of them are what you on Earth sometimes refer to as *work*-aholics."

Johanna was fascinated. "The women on your planet don't give birth?"

"No."

"But what about the sex drive?"

"Rarely have I encountered such an Estronian female," replied Serassan. "It's as though the women are so wrapped up in their accomplishments, they have no desire. We've taken away their need for fulfillment as wife and mother, and in its place we have over-achievers."

"Well, what do the men do?" Johanna was almost embarrassed to ask, but she couldn't help being curious. She knew how virile Serassan was.

"Are you sure you really want to know?" He smiled playfully.

Johanna felt her face redden. "Don't tell me the majority of Estronian men have lost their sex drive."

"No, I'm afraid that is one trait we have not been able to overcome."

"So ... what you're saying, Serassan, is that men and women do not fornicate on your planet?"

"You can now understand how difficult it is for an Estronian man to qualify for breeding privileges on Karos," Serassan said sadly.

"Why were *you* disqualified?"

"On the basis of sperm count, most probably. They also wanted the best prospects for a successful hybrid. Although we are humanoid, there are still many elements that deviate from the Terran physique."

"And I would have to let some stranger rape me?" Johanna's eyes grew wide with disgust.

"You won't even remember," he assured her. "Don't worry, Johanna."

"They'll hypnotize me first? Well, they can't make me forget a thing like that! How can they expect any decent woman to ..."

He quieted her with a burst of warm energy from his hands as he stroked her thigh. "You are so beautiful, Johanna." His words soothed her to silence as her heart slowed down. "Forget now. Forget about what I have told you. We have only two nights left together. Let's not waste them." His lips met hers then, and she succumbed to his embrace as they wrestled passionately beneath the sheet.

— 20 —

The Upper Level

"Miss Dobbs, wait up."

Johanna spun around. Vince Waldon caught up with her in the hall. She had been on her way to Piedmont's with a recording of her completed piano composition.

"How are you?" The actor smiled.

"I'm fine," she replied. "I was just on my way to see Piedmont."

"I'll get right to the point." Vince placed a hand on her shoulder. "We're planning a raid this afternoon. Some of us are going to sneak up above and try to get at the ship's navigational computers. We need all the help we can get."

"Are you nuts?" Johanna stared at him.

"If we can somehow alter the navigation, we have a chance of getting back to Earth. Won't you join the Guild?"

"Well, Vince, I don't see how you can hope to stand up against the aliens."

"We have a good idea of what we're doing. I'm convinced we can do it," he said. "But we're going to need as many people on our side as we can get. Are you in?"

"I-I don't know."

Vince's expression darkened. "Where does your loyalty lie, Johanna? With Serassan?"

Johanna could feel her face growing hot. Did everyone on board the ship know about her secret meetings with the guide?

Vince didn't wait for an answer. "Either you're for them or you're against them, Johanna. They've abducted hundreds of innocent human beings. All of us are here against our wills. We know no other way to stop them."

"You speak as though they've harmed us," she countered. "They haven't."

"Maybe not yet," he said, "but what about after we reach Karos? Certainly you've heard about their plans for us." Before she could comment, he waved his arms. "I don't have time to argue with you, Johanna. If you don't want to actively participate, I can understand. But do one thing for me. Just give Piedmont a message for me, will you? Tell him we've got the green light, and he is to meet us at the first level junction in one hour." Vince walked away before she could even protest.

Piedmont was not in. Syben-86 greeted Johanna and relayed the message that the professor had gone for a stroll. The unit invited her to stay and wait for him, but Johanna declined. She felt uncomfortable in the presence of Piedmont's robot. Instead, she walked back to her quarters.

What was Piedmont getting himself involved in, Johanna wondered as she walked on down the corridor. This did not sound like a peaceful demonstration the Guild was planning. It sounded like sabotage, or worse—suicide! How could the Guild members possibly expect to match wits with the Estronians, presuming they could get at the upper level in the first place? What would happen to them once the Estronians caught them?

Back in her apartment, Johanna sat and listened to her music recording, but she couldn't concentrate on it. She was worried about Piedmont. Perhaps by finding the older man not in his apartment, she had prevented him from going off on some foolish escapade that could only end in failure—perhaps doom. She finally convinced herself that he would be all right because of her lack of action. He would have returned to his quarters by now, and was safe in his ignorance of what Vince and the other members of the Guild were planning.

Kameel served lunch and commented on Johanna's lack of appetite. "What is bothering you, Johanna Dobbs?"

"I went to see Piedmont earlier," Johanna divulged, "but he wasn't in."

"And you are worried about your friend?" asked Kameel.

"Well, I did want him to hear my composition recording."

"Then why don't you go down after your meal and see if he is back?"

Johanna decided to take Kameel's suggestion. Grabbing her recording, she left once more. When she arrived at Piedmont's, Syben-86 answered the door.

"It is you again, Johanna Dobbs. I am sorry, but Professor Piedmont has left again. When he returned, I told him about your visit, but he said he had to leave. I thought you would have spoken to him by now, for he mentioned he would be seeing you."

"Syben, did he say where he was going?"

"Negative. It is not necessary to keep tabs on your whereabouts."

Thank goodness for that, Johanna thought. In fact, there were many things for which she was thankful the units did not know about. "If you see him again, Syben, tell him I was here."

Slowly, Johanna walked on down the corridor, not toward her quarters this time, but toward the hallway she knew led to parts of the ship that were off-limits to Terrans. She noticed the deck was unusually quiet and vacant for the middle of the afternoon. Where was everyone?

She feared that Piedmont had gotten word of the Guild's expedition by some other means. Perhaps at this very moment he was lurking in danger with other Terrans as they attempted to reach the upper levels. She found herself heading toward the transport shaft. She hadn't been in that area since the day they had arrived. The strange chute, surrounded by colored light beams, seemed to beckon her as she approached it. No one was in sight. She remembered, though, that Piedmont had told her he had tried to get on it once, and had been denied access. How? What triggering device kept the Terrans from boarding the unusual elevator?

Someone was coming. Quickly, Johanna looked around for a place to hide. She ducked behind a large metallic tub just as Thorden rounded the corner. With him was Radya, dressed lavishly in a pink lounging suit with sequins. The alien stopped and drew the ballerina's slender young body up against his own. Johanna turned her eyes away in disgust as the hook-nosed alien moved his mouth along the contour of Radya's face, up to her ear lobe. Suddenly, Radya cried out, "*Ow!* You bit me."

"Let's swirl up to my cubicle," Thorden said as his hands began to fondle the Russian girl's breasts.

"Now?"

"Why not, sweet thing?"

"No, Thorden, not now." Radya struggled to get away. She glanced over her shoulder. "Someone might see."

"Who? Serassan?" Thorden laughed. "He's not going to report us. He has his own sweet dark secret. Let's go up."

They kissed fervently, then Radya pulled away and groaned. "I must go. Remember the jade toe shoes you promised me."

"I have not forgotten, my little dancer. And tonight, when you perform for me, the slippers will be the *only* thing you need to take off."

Thorden let her go and stood next to the transport shaft. Johanna, in her hiding place, watched as the square-faced alien waved his hand and the light beams parted for him to enter. Suddenly, they closed again and a hum sounded. In a flash of colors, Thorden was gone.

Radya started to walk away when Johanna emerged from behind the tub.

"Radya!" she called out.

The ballerina gasped, then relaxed when she saw it was Johanna. "What did you do? Why do you spy on me?"

"Radya, I wasn't spying. Have you been up there?" She pointed to the transport shaft, which had now returned to its unoccupied state.

Radya eyed Johanna suspiciously. "I don't have to answer any of your questions." She started to walk away.

Johanna caught up with her. "Please, Radya, I have to know. I think Piedmont and some members of the Guild have gone up. They might be in trouble." She implored the ballerina, "Please tell me how to operate the transport chute."

"I do not know what you are talking about."

"I think you do, Radya."

"And so what if they are? They won't last up there long."

"What do you mean?"

"It is nothing, Johanna."

"But I heard Thorden say ..."

"You *were* spying on me, Johanna!"

"You've been up there before, haven't you, Radya?"

The ballerina shrugged. "So what if I have? He's always injected me first. That's the only way I can tolerate it."

Johanna wanted to know more. "What? Is it cold? Hot? Why can't we stay up there for very long? What injections does Thorden give you?"

"Shhh." Radya frowned. "Nobody's supposed to know about that. It's the oxygen levels. They aren't high enough for us ... not for very long, anyway. If the professor got up there, he's passed out by now."

Johanna turned toward the transport shaft. "I've got to go up there and find him," she said. "Please tell me how."

Radya sighed with impatience. "I'm late for my exercise. You're a fool, Johanna, if you go up there."

"Are there guards?"

"No, of course not."

"Then, please tell me how to get onto that thing. I'll find Vince and Piedmont and the others, and convince them to stop whatever they're trying to do. Before it's too late!"

With a loud sigh, Radya stepped in front of the transport shaft and held up her hand to the triggering device. "I'll hold it while you get on," she told Johanna, "but I cannot help you to get back. You must figure that out for yourself."

The beams parted at Radya's touch. Johanna stepped inside the light cylinder. A moment later, flashing colored lights surrounded her, as before. Suddenly, her body and the platform she stood upon were thrust upward at a tremendous rate of speed. She couldn't catch her breath, and her head swam. She fought to keep from losing her balance. Finally, the ride was over. The beams parted and Johanna stepped off. She teetered a few steps, then regained control. She was alone in the deserted corridor.

Aware of distant voices, Johanna started walking. She still felt dizzy from the elevator ride ... or was it the thin oxygen Radya had mentioned? Perhaps it had been a foolish gesture to try and come after Piedmont. But how was she going to get back down to her deck?

Johanna heard footsteps. On an impulse, she swung into a room where a door was open. Several grayish-white beings, exactly like the ones from the shuttle craft, sat around a long table. One of them saw her.

"Look, a Terran," said a female voice.

"Oh!" The others reacted in surprise, and two of them immediately stood up.

Johanna didn't know what to do. Her first instinct was to turn and run, but she felt too weak. Clutching her head, she blinked and tried to clear her head. Two beings rushed toward her as black dots swam in front of her eyes. Then she passed out.

When Johanna came to, she found herself lying on a cot in a small room with no windows. Another grayish-white being, with some kind of instrument in its hands, stood over her. For the first time, Johanna was able to examine one of the creatures in detail. She recognized the familiar white uniform with the emblem. It was the same one Serassan and Thorden wore. As alarming as this creature appeared with its swollen gray head, large slanted eyes, and slitted mouth, Johanna sensed an intelligence and felt a warmth surrounding her that assured her she would not be harmed.

"Good. You are coming around finally," the being said to her. It was a woman's voice in her head as the being's mouth did not move. "I have injected you, so you should be able to sit up and tell me what this is all about in just a matter of minutes." The woman alien moved the instrument over Johanna's body. A soft buzzing met her ears.

Johanna wanted to ask where she was, but she felt sluggish. Before she could even attempt to sit up, Thorden entered the room.

"Is this one of yours?" the being asked Thorden.

A cruel smile spread over Thorden's square jaw as his narrow eyes swept Johanna's legs. "Ah ... the musician," he crooned.

The woman alien stared at Johanna in admiration. "You are musical? Oh, how superior! How I would enjoy some Terran music right now ..."

"You know the rules, Plipquum." Thorden frowned at the grayish being.
The gentle-voiced alien cowered in shame. "I did not mean ..."

"*Where is she?*" Serassan crashed into the room just then. He saw Johanna lying on the table, and pushed his way past Thorden. "Johanna ..." Serassan turned to Plipquum. "What happened?"

"She walked into the evaluation room about ten minutes ago," explained the being. "That's all we know."

"Another rebel," accused Thorden.

"Undoubtedly," agreed Plipquum sadly. "Shall we send her to the pacification chamber now?"

"No." Serassan turned to the gray alien. "I will see that she gets back to her quarters. There is no further need for your service. Thank you, Plipquum." With that, the grayish being left with her instruments.

Thorden remained. He studied Serassan and folded his arms. "You'll arouse suspicion, you know."

"I don't care," mumbled Serassan. He stroked Johanna's arm.

Slowly, she began regaining control of her muscles, and rolled her head back and forth. She still could not speak.

"Leave us now, Thorden."

The ugly man seemed reluctant to leave. "You risk much, Serassan. You had better watch what you say. Your behavior is being questioned."

"I am growing sick and tired of your hypocrisy, Thorden. Now *go!*"

When they were at last alone in the room, Serassan helped Johanna sit up.

"Oh, Serassan, have I put you in jeopardy?" she asked.

"Forget that. We all do what we must. What were you doing on this level? How did you gain access to the transport shaft?"

Johanna quickly explained her situation. She told Serassan how she feared Piedmont had followed the Opposition Guild up in order to find the ship's navigation computers.

"Have no fear, Johanna. There was a raid, about half an hour ago, but the members were caught, and Piedmont was not among them."

"Caught?" Johanna looked into his eyes. "What will happen to them?"

"A little time in the pacification chamber, and then they'll be returned to their quarters."

"But ..."

"Their motives were anticipated, Johanna. We would not think of harming any of you Terrans. Do you believe me?"

She nodded. Of course she believed Serassan. He would never lie to her. She breathed a sigh of relief that Piedmont was not involved.

"Now come." Serassan helped her to her feet. "I will take you back where you belong."

"I'm feeling much better," said Johanna. "Can't I see this part of the ship first? Where is your cabin?"

"The injection is only temporary," Serassan explained, "but if you promise to play the role of one who is undergoing pacification, I think I can give you a rare peek."

Together they left the room, then Serassan gripped her shoulders and gently pushed her down the hall. Several grayish-white aliens passed and stared in their direction. Serassan made some remarks about taking Johanna to the "P.C.", how she was a member of the Guild, and had to be dealt with. Johanna stared straight ahead and tried to act intimidated.

When they were alone, Johanna asked Serassan about Radya and Thorden. "How do *they* get away with it?"

"Thorden is well known for keeping concubines," said Serassan. "Of course, it is forbidden. Miss Bjelkova, I'm afraid, is just another one of Thorden's many conquests. He favors dancers in general. The reason why he can get away with ..." Serassan broke off as another alien approached them in the hall. Serassan and the alien exchanged signals.

"Where are you taking that Terran?"

Serassan halted. Johanna felt his grip tighten on her shoulder, and she assumed a blank stare. "One for the pacification chamber," he replied.

The being glanced at Johanna. "So it has come to this, has it? I hear the Preejhna Chiyuub is not pleased. It will now be necessary to post patrols."

"I see no benefit in that," argued Serassan.

"The Guild is growing stronger," replied the being. "They have confiscated some medical supplies. We have reason to believe they can inject themselves."

"I was not aware of that," said Serassan. Johanna wiggled, and he toughened his grip. "Be still, Terran."

"Proceed," ordered the being, and watched as Serassan pushed Johanna along.

"Who was he?" whispered Johanna as Serassan loosened his grip on her.

"A ranking officer. I'd better show you back to your quarters now. It's beginning to look a little odd. That is my cabin up on the left."

Johanna glanced at the number above Serassan's door—71752—and she quickly memorized it. Then he led her toward the hall and the transport shaft. They passed several more aliens, so they were silent until after they boarded the chute. Johanna wondered why there were so many beings from the shuttle craft. Where were the Estronians?

She shivered as he signaled for the device to engage. "I won't cause you any more trouble, Serassan."

"Don't speak of it," he said soothingly and smiled at her.

"Tell me," said Johanna. "How can you and Thorden survive the different oxygen conditions? How can you slip back and forth?"

"We are conditioned for instantaneous adjustment," he replied.

"Then, why didn't any of us pass out after we boarded from the shuttle craft?"

Serassan patted her hand. "The shuttle crew injected you before you came on board the mother ship. Remember?"

Yes, the shuttle crew, thought Johanna. She shuddered. She hadn't expected to run into so many repulsive members of the shuttle crew. She clutched Serassan and she closed her eyes and waited for the strange feeling of swift movement to pass. *I hate this thing*, her mind said out loud.

You'll get used to it, his mind answered her. *It has been a traumatic afternoon for you, my beloved.*

Traumatic it was, she agreed, *especially waking up in that little room, and finding that horrible gray face staring right into my eyes!*

"You mean Plipquum?" he said aloud.

"Oh, Plipquum was nice enough," Johanna replied with her voice. "She has such a gentle manner. But I can't help it, Serassan. I find those creatures *loathsome*. I prefer to stay down below from now on."

His mind seemed to shut to hers suddenly. The chute stopped. Again she felt as though she had fallen several stories from the top of a tall building, only to land safely on her feet. Serassan let go of her as the light beams ceased, and they faced the corridor of the Terran deck.

Stepping out, Johanna turned to thank him. She wanted to risk one last embrace. Nobody was around to witness it. Instead, she saw pain in his blue eyes. He did not look at her. "What is it?" she implored.

"It is nothing." He closed the transport shaft with a wave of his hand. In a flash of movement and colors, he vanished.

Johanna stood and stared at the empty chamber for a couple of minutes longer. What did it mean? The sharp pang of foreboding seemed to pierce her just then. She wasn't quite sure what it was, but she sensed a wedge had come between herself and Serassan.

— 21 —

Serassan's Revelation

Kameel met Johanna at her door. "Johanna Dobbs, where have you been? Your friend, the professor, was here several times inquiring about you. He said it was very important that he speak with you."

"Then I must go there at once," said Johanna.

"Wait. Please come inside and rest first. You appear distraught. Tell me your concern."

The last thing Johanna wanted to do was discuss her experience on the upper level. "But Piedmont is probably ..."

"He said he would come back soon. I will fix you some tea." The unit glided into the kitchen.

Someone knocked on the door just then. "I'll get it. It's probably Piedmont."

"Johanna, thank heaven." Piedmont entered the apartment. Kameel came in, carrying a tray of hot tea. Piedmont seemed startled when he saw the unit. "Are you all right?" he asked Johanna. "I was worried sick." He eyed the unit again, and glanced uncertainly at Johanna.

"It's all right. You can trust Kameel," she said, and invited the professor to sit down. "Kameel, please get another cup for Piedmont."

The unit left again, and the professor turned to Johanna. "It's getting out of control, just as I feared it would."

"What are you talking about?" she demanded.

"The Opposition Guild. Vince Waldon is obsessed with the idea of overthrowing the Estronians and turning this ship around."

Johanna quickly filled him in on what had happened to her that afternoon. She was still explaining when Kameel entered from the kitchen. "Serassan said some members had been caught and were spending some time in the pacification chamber." She turned to her unit. "Kameel, do you know anything about a pacification chamber?"

"Yes. It is a holding cell in which deviant behavior is corrected."

"How?" asked the professor.

"Through stimulation of brain waves, the subject is taught through the aid of a cerebral device to maintain alpha state for several minutes. Thus the name pacification chamber. Once the subject has learned not to deviate, he or she is then released."

"Biofeedback," put in Piedmont.

"Is it painful?" asked Johanna.

"Only in difficult cases," replied Kameel. "To put it in your terms, a visit to the pacification chamber is much like a retreat to a meditation center. There is no pain administered unless the offender is an habitual problem."

Suddenly, a whining sound penetrated the room. Both Piedmont and Johanna fixed their gaze on Kameel, who appeared to be the source of the alarm.

Then the whining ceased.

"What is it, Kameel?" asked Johanna.

"A summons," the unit said. "I must visit the energy chamber. I will return shortly." With that, Kameel glided toward the door and disappeared into the hallway.

"I wonder what that is about," said Johanna.

Piedmont sighed. "It's started."

"What has?"

"Johanna, won't you please join us in the Guild? We need every available person."

"But it's a futile cause!"

"It's our only hope for returning to Earth. Our only hope for freedom."

Johanna sipped her tea and listened as Piedmont tried to sway her to his side. She tried to convince him the effort was a waste of time and energy. They were never going to see Earth again.

"I can see it's useless to argue with you any further, Johanna." The professor drank up the rest of his tea, then started to get up.

Just then, Kameel entered the apartment. They turned to gaze at the unit.

"Well, what was all that about?" Johanna asked.

"New instructions," replied Kameel. "Professor Piedmont, Syben-86 awaits you outside, and will escort you back to your quarters."

"I can take a hint," grumbled the professor as he set his empty cup on the tray. "I was just leaving anyway." At the door he turned and waved to Johanna, then left.

"From now until the time we reach Karos, patrols will be posted in all corridors," Kameel continued to say as the unit picked up the tea tray. "We are instructed to keep track of all your comings and goings, and whom you visit, where, and for how long."

"I don't understand." Johanna followed the unit into the kitchen.

"When I must go tonight for my energy chamber visit, another relief unit will come in my absence, Johanna Dobbs. You will not be left alone any longer."

Horror flooded Johanna's mind as she realized what this meant. There was no way Serassan could come to her with a substitute unit in the apartment, or patrols posted in the hallways. "I don't believe this, Kameel. I value my privacy! I don't want to be baby-sat by some strange hunk of metal and wires that ..."

"I am sorry, Johanna Dobbs," the unit interrupted. "This makes you unhappy. I am programmed to keep you happy on this voyage, but I have received my own instructions and cannot disobey the orders given."

"Who gives such orders?" Johanna wanted to know. "Serassan?"

"That is not your concern."

"Tell me, Kameel. Was it Serassan?" Johanna's heart pounded at the thought of Serassan turning against her.

"Higher authorities have given the command," replied Kameel. "Why is it that Serassan interests you so much?"

Johanna did not want to discuss it, and said so.

"You can trust me, Johanna Dobbs. You said you could. You wanted me for your friend. I am your friend."

Johanna's mind was in a whirl. She didn't know whom to trust. She sat down at the kitchen table and held her head in her hands. "What does it matter now, anyway?" It took a few seconds for her to prepare her confession. Finally, she sighed and began. "I happen to be deeply in love with Serassan." She paused, then slowly admitted, "We have been meeting here at night during your absences." She glanced over at the unit, then said, "I suppose you think I'm a delinquent, don't you?"

Kameel cleared the tray in the sink, then joined Johanna at the table. "I do not think anything of the sort, Johanna Dobbs. I do not understand love, but apparently it is something you share with Serassan. He has obviously taken great risks to see you. His need for music has been his weakness. Now it will be his downfall."

"Oh, Kameel, you're not thinking about reporting this, are you? I trusted you."

"I will not report what you have told me," assured the unit. "I was merely stating the facts."

Johanna wanted to ask what Kameel meant about Serassan's impending downfall, but her heart felt heavy. His look when he had left her at the transport shaft haunted her. Had she ruined him today? Had she ruined everyone's chances by going on the upper level and exposing herself without even considering the consequences of her action? And now, with patrols guarding the corridors, there was no chance of seeing Serassan tonight, or tomorrow night. By then it would be too late, anyway. Tomorrow they were due to orbit Karos.

L ater that evening, Johanna tried to play the piano, but she couldn't make the music sound the way she wanted it to. She was surprised when Radya dropped by.

"Radya, come on in. Sit down."

Radya did not smile. She seated herself on Johanna's couch and crossed her legs. "I told you it was a mistake to go up the transport shaft, Johanna. However, I am glad you survived it. What happened to you up there? Thorden can no longer visit me, so I didn't find out."

Johanna sensed a hint of insecurity in the ballerina's voice. Radya was obviously trying to cover it up with an air of superiority, but Johanna could tell the girl was frightened. "Is that what you came here for, Radya? To wheedle information out of me, for ... God knows what reason? For all I know, you'll go straight to Thorden and betray Serassan."

Radya's blue eyes flashed in anger. "I would do nothing of the sort." She glanced around the room. "Where is your unit?"

"Don't worry. Kameel can be trusted," said Johanna. "It's too bad some people can't be."

"You refer to me?"

"Well, somehow word got around about myself and Serassan."

A silence followed in which Radya hung her head. "He promised me jade toe shoes," she said.

Johanna squinted. "What's that got to do with anything?"

"When I was a little girl, practicing ballet in Moscow for long hours each day, I used to dream about having fine things." The Russian girl examined her elaborately manicured nails. They had been polished with an iridescent coating. "My family was very poor. My father was a street sweeper, and my mother a maid. I almost didn't get into the ballet school. When I did, I thought it was a miracle. But I realized, even then, that I would never have the fine things the others had—beautiful clothes, a different leotard for each day of the week. I was the best dancer in class, but the last girl to finally earn her toe shoes. Not because I didn't deserve them, but because my family was so poor."

She looked into Johanna's eyes with moisture forming on her lids. "Even when we came on tour to North America, I was the underdog. It meant so much when they asked me to perform the night ... the night that ... it-it happened." Sobs choked her voice.

Johanna's tone softened. "A lot has happened to all of us," she said. "People change sometimes when they are under stress."

"Now you despise me." Radya wiped her cheeks. "I know it. I see it each time you look at me."

"You've had a hard life ..."

"You can't possibly understand how hard," sniffed Radya. "I didn't realize it myself until ... until Thorden ..." She looked up at Johanna with tear-stained red cheeks. "Oh, Johanna, I do not want to go back to what it was like. I do not want to return to Earth."

"But Earth is our home," protested Johanna gently. "What about the people there? Don't you miss your mother and father?"

Radya blinked. "Of course I do. I miss them very much. But I must now try to forget about them. Because none of us are ever going back."

"What about Thorden? You would rather stay with him?" Johanna could not understand what the girl saw in the repulsive alien with the sinister voice and crooked nose.

"No," admitted Radya. "Well, yes ... maybe. I don't know anymore." She stood up. "It's time for me to go. Please excuse me for barging in. I don't know what has come over me." Without another word, she left.

Johanna sat on the couch and stared into space. She felt sorry for the Russian ballerina. Radya was obviously in a confused state right now, but at least that was better than parading around the ship as though she were the Prime Minister's wife. Johanna wished there was some way she could help the girl, but she had her own problems.

As expected, Serassan did not come to her apartment that evening. When Kameel left for her energy chamber visit, another unit arrived. Johanna went to bed but was restless. Events kept flashing through her head. When sleep finally did overcome her, she awoke with a cry during a dream in which Plipquum, the alien whose gray face had bent close to hers, filled her with terror. As she lay in bed, panting, Johanna remembered Serassan on the transport shaft. That look—had it been despair? It continued to haunt her.

The next day Johanna was in a terrible mood. Every time she tried to sit down at the piano and get some work done, frustration set in. Once, Kameel accidentally knocked over a vase across the room. Johanna flew into a rage because it was just like the one Manley had given her for her eighteenth birthday. Soon every little noise and disturbance wore on Johanna, and she gave up and slammed the keyboard cover down.

"That does it. I'm going." She marched toward the door.

"Where are you going, Johanna Dobbs?" called out Kameel.

"Never mind!"

"I must remind you, Johanna Dobbs, rules dictate that you must report to me where you are going. It must be verified."

"That's ridiculous." Johanna tried to open the door, but the wall remained shut. She spun around and frowned at the unit. "Kameel, open the door."

"First, tell me where you are going. It is necessary."

Johanna sighed impatiently. "If you must know, I'm on my way over to see Professor Piedmont. I can't get anything done here."

"What is wrong? Why are you upset?"

"Everything. Why the third degree?"

"I'm sorry, Johanna Dobbs. Believe me, I sympathize, if that is at all possible. Your hosts feel it is for your own safety. It is only a matter of hours before we are in orbit around Karos."

"Open this door, Kameel!"

"Please be brief, Johanna Dobbs." The unit caused the door to slide open and Johanna escaped.

Out in the corridor, Johanna was appalled by the number of robot units in sight. She quickened her pace until she was just outside Piedmont's quarters. When she knocked, he let her in right away.

"Johanna, is everything all right?" Piedmont asked.

"I hate all this," she snarled.

"I was wondering when you would come around," he retorted. "Have a seat, my dear."

Johanna didn't see Syben-86 anywhere in the room. "Are we alone?"

Piedmont lowered his voice. "I've got him in the bedroom, counting adverbs on my manuscripts." He smirked.

"What's happening to the Guild?" Johanna wanted to know.

"It's still intact."

Johanna sighed. "I'm frightened, Piedmont. In just hours ..."

"I know." He patted her hand and smiled. "The Guild is attempting one last demonstration of resistance this afternoon. With martial law in effect, they have become desperate. They will stop at nothing."

Johann's jaw dropped. "What are they planning to do?"

Piedmont shook his head.

"You must tell me, Piedmont. Is there going to be violence?"

"Not so loud," he hushed her. "Remember Syben ..."

"Well, what are they going to do? I want to know. I have a right to know!"

"The Guild now comprises the majority of the Terrans on board this ship," Piedmont explained in a low voice. "They've decided to launch an attack."

"What!" Johanna forgot to keep her voice low. "How? Without weapons?"

"Remember Steph, the sculptor?"

She nodded.

"He has some rather nasty tools of the trade—for starters. They've armed themselves with knives, clubs, ropes ..."

"Oh, I can't believe they'd be that foolish!" cried Johanna. "They can't stand up against Estron. The aliens cannot only read minds, but you've seen how they've demonstrated hypnosis to control their captives."

"Nonetheless, Johanna ... they're an angry mob. There are close to a thousand Terrans on board this mother ship, and we suspect only about a hundred Estronians."

"And what about the robots? There are also a thousand of them."

"True. But the Guild is determined to fight."

"This is insane!" Johanna left and started back to her quarters. Vince Waldon and his followers couldn't possibly accomplish anything. At the very least, people would suffer—both the Terrans and perhaps some of the Estronians.

As she passed an open doorway, she heard angry voices from within. Slowing down, Johanna overheard a woman inside yelling, "Death to Serassan! I'll kill him with my bare hands, if I get a chance."

"Has everyone had their injection?" called out a man's voice. It was Vince Waldon. Johanna peeked in. Several people were gathered.

"How's your unit coming along?" someone asked.

"It's almost dismantled," came the reply.

At that moment, someone in the room spied Johanna and came over. "Come on in. We need all the help we can get."

"Oh, hello, Ms. Dobbs," called out Vince. "Jasmine, give the lady an injection."

"It took me all morning to short out my unit," Johanna heard another woman telling someone.

"Death to Estron!" cried out the first woman.

"Come over here, Johanna." Jasmine helped her in. "This will only take a second."

"I'm glad you came to your senses," Vince said. He was sharpening a large chef's knife with a whetstone. Some people crowded around him, cutting off her sight.

Suddenly, Johanna felt a sting in her arm. She flinched, and watched as Jasmine withdrew an Estronian hypodermic instrument. "What did you do that for?" Johanna asked.

"Everyone has to have it, Johanna. Here, let me get you a piece of cotton." Jasmine walked away.

People were swarming, many of them carrying knives or clubs—makeshift weapons of one sort or another. Johanna saw some robot units that had been disassembled in a corner. Panic gripped her suddenly and she began to fight her way toward the entrance. All around her, people talked excitedly. The crazy woman kept yelling, "Death to Serassan! Death to Estron!"

Finally, Johanna was out in the corridor. Before anyone could stop her, she took off down the hall, astonished that several of the units that had been on patrol before now were missing. She was out of breath when she arrived at her quarters. Inside, Kameel stopped dusting when she entered.

"Kameel, I need your help."

"Why, Johanna Dobbs, you are out of breath. What is wrong?"

Johanna stared at the pinprick of blood on the inside of her arm, then looked around her wildly. "You've got to help me, Kameel. They're going to hurt him."

"Hurt whom?"

"Never mind. I've got to get up to the top of the ship."

"That is not possible," protested the unit. "Certainly you know by now that humans cannot exist very long in the atmosphere above. Even if you could, there are patrols."

"Kameel, if we don't leave now, it will be too late!" She started for the door.

"Where are you going, Johanna Dobbs? You must report to me. It is the rule."

"Kameel, this is serious!" Johanna found that the door would not open. She pounded on the wall, then turned to frown at Kameel. "Let me out. If you don't, a lot of people are going to be hurt—maybe even killed! I don't know how to make you understand."

"Desperation," said Kameel. "Yes, I am programmed to handle your desperation, Johanna Dobbs. Won't you please sit down, and I'll fix you a cup of tea?"

"No!" Johanna screamed. "I must warn Serassan!" She clawed at the metal wall, then turned to Kameel. "If you don't let me out of here, I'll disassemble you. The others did it to their units. I'll do it to you!"

"What others? What are you talking about, Johanna Dobbs?" Kameel glided over.

"Look for yourself—the patrols! They're gone!"

The door opened then, and Kameel moved into the corridor after Johanna.

"I do not react to threats, Johanna Dobbs. But I am your friend. In case you don't remember, we made a pact of friendship. I will follow you now. I will help you get to Serassan, if it is so important to you."

Johanna ran blindly down the hallway. "Is there another transport shaft we can use, Kameel? By now, the others ..."

"This way." Kameel-37 turned into another corridor, where several patrol units glided out in front of their path.

"Explain!" one of the units demanded.

Kameel-37 did not stop. "Urgent!" she warned with Johanna at her heels. "This Terran is in trouble. You must let us pass."

Johanna was surprised when the patrol unit did not interfere. Kameel led her down another narrow passageway. They seemed to be moving through tunnels that led nowhere. Johanna also became aware of a loud hum.

Finally, they came to another transport shaft, and Kameel made the beams open up to let them get on. A moment later, they were flung upward, with Johanna clutching her fists to maintain her stance. Then they came to a stop, and Kameel led Johanna on another maze journey. All the time, Johanna prayed that this winding around was not wasting precious time. At last, they came out in a corridor that looked familiar.

"Where is everyone?" Johanna asked.

"They are probably viewing the planet," Kameel replied. "We are now in orbit around Karos." The unit led Johanna toward Serassan's cabin. Johanna remembered passing this way yesterday. "I do not know which cubicle he is in," the unit said. "He is probably not even here."

Then Johanna saw the number above Serassan's quarters. She stopped at Cubicle 71752 and knocked on the door. "He's got to be here," she prayed.

Seconds later, the hatch opened and she faced Serassan. Both joy and fear seemed to grip him as he immediately pulled her inside. Kameel remained in the corridor.

"Why are you here?" He embraced her then. "Never mind. I am happy to see you."

"Serassan ..." Johanna pulled away. "I've come to warn you ..."

"Johanna, there is something I must tell you first."

"No. Serassan, listen to me." Johanna stared into his face. "The Guild is on their way up. I'm afraid for you!"

"What are you talking about?" he asked. "Who is on their way?"

"Guild members! They are after blood! Oh, Serassan, you've got to stop them. If you don't, a lot of people will be killed."

Serassan laid a calm hand on her shoulder. "Relax, Johanna. Nobody is going to get killed." How could he say that so calmly? Serassan led her over to a desk. "Johanna, listen to me. There is something I need to tell you. I am not the man you think I am."

What was he saying? And how could he discuss their relationship at a time like this, when at any moment violence could erupt on the upper level of the ship? "But we've got to *do* something," she insisted.

"Yes, you are right." He nodded his head sadly, and gazed into her eyes. She saw pain in his. "Johanna, you must leave ... now."

"But what about you? You're in danger!"

"I am where I belong. You, however, cannot last much longer in this part of the ship."

She explained about the injection, but he interrupted.

"It does not matter. It will wear off soon enough. There is no way you could ever love me ... the way that I love you. You must leave." He turned away sadly.

Johanna reached out to him. "Serassan. How can you say that? You know that I love you. I want to spend the rest of my life with you."

"That is not possible."

"But it is."

"How?"

"Well, I don't know. You survived on Earth for long periods of time. Can't you work out some way to do the same thing on Karos?"

He spun around to face her. "You mean, you would stay on Karos ... *now?*"

She stared at him. "Does that surprise you?"

"The other Terrans ..."

"The others are not me. I want to stay with *you*. I want to live my life with the man I love." She reached out to him.

"No." Serassan's voice was firm. He stopped her. "I can't go on deceiving you."

"What is wrong?" demanded Johanna. "One minute you say you love me, and the next you're telling me to go. Serassan, I don't understand!"

"You love the man you *think* I am. Well, Johanna, if you saw me for what I really am ..." He reached over the desk for something.

"I do love you," she insisted. "How can you question it?"

Serassan stared into a small crystalline dish he held in his hands. "But will you still feel the same when you see this?" He handed the glass object to her. "Look at it."

She took the sparkling, gem-like object in her hand, and was startled to see a face. It was a three-dimensional picture of a tall grayish-white creature, very much like the ones on board the ship and shuttle craft. She recognized something deeply familiar in the blue eyes.

Suddenly, she realized what it was he was trying to tell her. She blinked, then glanced up at him. "This is *you*, isn't it?"

"Yes. It is I. This is my true Estronian appearance." He turned away. "Now do you see why you cannot love me?"

— 22 —

The Guild Raid

The last trace of twilight had disappeared by the time Barbara Wetzel climbed the ridge that overlooked the major portion of the city. She stopped to stare down at the cluster of lights and traffic. Up here the air was fresh and cold. Only a few crusty patches of ice and snow remained. She lifted her eyes to the heavens and marveled at the many constellations she was just starting to learn.

Footsteps startled her. Turning around, she saw the figure of a large man walking toward her. She hadn't noticed the car parked several yards away. Not until he was near did she recognize Manley Dobbs. "I wondered if you'd be out here tonight," said Barbara.

Manley came and stood next to her. He lifted a pair of binoculars which hung around his neck. "Hello, Barbara. Nice night, isn't it?"

"Very," she replied. "Seen anything?"

Manley sighed, lowering the binoculars. "Not yet."

"Have you had any more dreams lately?"

"A couple." He sat on the rail of the fence where the hill sloped steeply downward. "You know, Barb, I keep thinking Johanna will come home."

She leaned against the fence and crossed her arms. The night air was nippy. "What have you been picking up?" she asked.

"Probably nothing, really." He wiped the end of his nose with his hand. "I get the feeling things aren't right out there in space." He lifted his head and gazed up at the stars. "I get this feeling that Johanna is having a lot of trouble adjusting to … whatever it is she's adjusting to."

"What about your dreams?" asked Barbara.

Manley handed her the binoculars. "Well, a couple of nights ago, I dreamed about an evacuation. I think there's going to be an evacuation in the near future."

"You mean ... ships landing? Removing people from the planet?"

"Exactly."

Barbara studied the stars. "I'm just trying to understand it all," she confided. "By the way, I had another sighting."

Manley looked at her. "You did? When?"

"The other night." She found Arcturus in the lens and rolled the focus knob with her index finger. "I woke up and felt compelled to go outside. It was 2:30 AM, and I really didn't want to get out of bed. I was tired, and it was cold. But I just had to get up and go outside and have a look."

"And you did?"

"Yes, finally." She handed the binoculars back to Manley. "I stood on my porch for several minutes, wondering what I was doing out there, freezing to death. I was turning to go back inside when, suddenly, this ship passed over the neighbor's house."

"How big?" asked Manley.

"Huge," said Barbara. "Probably as big as the house. There were a few lights, but it wasn't all lit up or anything. It just hovered there over the neighbor's house for ... I don't know how long. It was really strange, Manley. Everything had quieted down, even the neighbor's dog barking. Then, the ship slowly moved away. I stood there and watched it rise. Then, suddenly, it took off until it was a tiny speck of light in the night sky. It blinked out, and I didn't see it anymore."

"What did you do?"

Barbara shrugged. "I went back inside. I went back to bed, but I couldn't really sleep."

"Did you report it to anyone?"

"No." She stared down at her boots. Her toes were beginning to feel numb from the cold. "Who'd have believed me?"

"I wish you'd called me. Why didn't you?"

"It was the middle of the night." Barbara nudged him. "What would your wife have said?"

Manley lifted the binoculars again. "Boy," he sighed, "I wish I had seen it."

"Do you know what modern psychology thinks about UFOs?" Barbara asked him.

"No. What?"

"I read an article the other day," she said. "People who see UFOs are supposed to have this psychological need which UFOs themselves provide. In other words, modern psychologists believe that what we are seeing is fulfilling some kind of emotional requirement."

"Is that what you believe, Barb?"

She sighed. "I don't know, Manley. I've been very confused lately."

"I'll tell you what I think is happening," he said. "I honestly believe there are higher intelligences that have been coming to this planet for centuries. Maybe longer. My dream seems to say that the time we have left here on Earth is very short. Something's bound to happen. I don't know whether it's going to be a pole shift, or a nuclear holocaust, or what. But whatever it is, *they* know about it." He glanced up at the heavens, then back at her. "They are concerned about us for some reason. I don't know. Maybe they're our ancestors."

Barbara stared at him incredulously.

"Forgive me. There I go again, Barb—letting words just tumble out of my mouth." He shook his head. "I don't know where I get these ideas." He lifted his binoculars again, and searched the sky.

Johanna ran her finger down the hologram imprinted on the gem she held in her palm. The man beside her was silent. A torrent of shame swept over her as she recalled the way she had reacted to the appearance of the aliens. The grayish-white beings were *Estronians*. Serassan was one of those grayish-white beings.

"Oh, Serassan ... I feel terrible ... I had no idea ..."

"Don't hide your feelings, Johanna. I know you find my former appearance hideous." He turned away.

Still clutching the crystalline dish, she reached out for him. "And you thought this would matter to me?" She studied his portrait again, then smiled. "It's totally miraculous," she finally said. "What you must have gone through to look the way you do now ..."

She stared up at him. He still had his back to her. "Serassan, listen to me. I love the man inside of you. Don't you see? I don't care what you looked like then, or in the future."

He walked to a window across the room and beckoned to her. "Look, Johanna ... out there."

Outside the small cabin window, she saw a large, curved object that reflected white and orange, with the black of space behind it. "Karos!"

"Yes, Karos. What would have been your new home."

Johanna lost herself for a moment as she continued to gaze at the planet the mother ship orbited. She had seen television shots of Earth taken by the astronauts aboard the space shuttles, but never had she laid eyes on anything so awesome, so spectacular.

"You would have loved it," Serassan murmured. "It is so much like your Earth in many ways. A perfect place to breed artists in our galaxy. It's regretful you will never set foot on it."

Johanna stared at him, puzzled. "What? Why not?"

He faced her with sympathy in his blue eyes. "If what you say is true—if the Opposition Guild plans to attack—then my people have no choice but to abort the mission."

A surge of fear rose within Johanna. "Abort the mission! What does that mean?"

"It means, my love, that we were wrong." He led her by the hand over to a couch near the door. "It means Estron is totally challenged by the repeated occurrences that have arisen on board this ship the past eleven days. We expected some acts of protest, but we never bargained for the violence that you have brought upon us. We are a peaceful civilization. Such acts are unpalatable to even those as lower minded as Thorden."

Johanna stared up at him, still unsure. "Are you saying ... we're all going to die before we even land on Karos?"

"Violence obviously breeds more violence," Serassan started to say. "Indications show ..."

Before he could finish, the door opened. A flood of voices from the corridor poured in. Johanna and Serassan popped up from the couch as a crowd of Terrans rushed into the room, waving knives, clubs, and began yelling in anger.

"Get him! *Kill* him!" they shouted.

"Pirate! Kidnapper! *Liar!*" roared the voices.

"Free us! We'll *never* perform on Karos!" others called.

"*Death* to Serassan and Thorden!"

Johanna screamed as she saw a woman with a large blade streak toward them. "No! Don't touch him!" She stepped in front of Serassan to ward off the attacker.

"Johanna, *no!*" Suddenly, Piedmont pushed his way through the crowd. Johanna screamed as the professor's glasses got knocked off his ruddy face. "Johanna! Stand aside, for God's sake!" he called out.

Johanna caught glimpses of grayish-white aliens at the entrance. Several Terrans began to moan, and the din started to subside as a high-frequency whirring sound pierced throughout the room. Johanna continued to throw herself between Serassan and the others who had not yet been affected by the aliens' sonic weapon. Piedmont was close enough to touch her now, and she reached for his hand.

"You slime! You *maggot!*" shouted the woman with the knife behind Piedmont.

"*Traitor!*" somebody shouted. Johanna saw a flash of metal.

At that very moment Piedmont jumped in front of Johanna, and a second later the blade slipped into his side. Johanna screamed as the older man crumpled to the floor in front of her. Several aliens had made their way into Serassan's quarters and raised a white box that was the source of the whirring sound. The woman who had stabbed Piedmont closed her eyes and collapsed to the floor.

"Don't harm her!" Serassan ordered. The box was lowered before Johanna could be affected by it.

Johanna stared in horror as Piedmont knelt at her feet. A pool of warm blood seeped from his sweater as he tried to raise his head to search her face. His eyes bulged as he attempted to look at her, and no sound came from his lips. She knelt down beside him, and attempted to hold him up, but he only slumped against her.

Serassan helped lift the professor as several Terrans crowded around, still dazed from the frequency weapon. Grayish beings herded subdued people out of the cubicle into the corridor.

"Help him!" Johanna gasped as she struggled to her feet. "Oh please, can't you help him?"

Serassan and another alien dragged Piedmont to the couch. The professor was now unconscious, and his once red-complexioned face was drained of color. Already the lips bore a tinge of blue.

"The wound is extensive," the grayish being told Serassan. Johanna recognized the healer, Plipquum. "Look at the amount of blood he has lost," she said. She immediately injected something into the professor's neck.

"I'm afraid it's already too late," replied Serassan, who had placed both of his hands over the professor's prostrate body. "Many vital organs have been severely damaged."

"It can't be too late!" yelled Johanna. "Can't you *do* something? You, with all your advanced surgical techniques! Can't you save him?"

Plipquum held a small instrument out to Serassan to indicate some kind of reading, and he nodded at her. "Johanna, come with me," he said. He gently helped her over to another chair across the room.

"Piedmont! Oh, Serassan, please! *Please* help him! Save him!"

"I wish we could." Serassan spoke in a quiet voice. "We are not gods."

"But you can do wondrous things! You said so. Look what you did to me." She felt the scar beneath her nose. "Oh, you *must* be able to save Piedmont's life." She jumped to her feet. "Plipquum, please! Can't *you* do something?"

Serassan put a restraining hand on her. "There is such a thing as mortality, Johanna."

"Then ... then bring him back to life! We ... we can't just leave him this way." Johanna broke into sobs and buried her head in her hands. It was too late, however. She knew Piedmont was dying. He had thrown himself in harm's way in order to save her life—and that of Serassan's. Johanna continued to cry as Serassan held her. Moments later, dizziness set in. She remembered a circle of grayish heads bending over her, and then blackness overcame her.

"Someone is here to see you," announced Kameel later that afternoon, when Johanna had retired to her quarters. She lay in her bed with her knees drawn up, trying to shut out the agony of all that had occurred on the upper level.

"Tell whoever it is to go away," she ordered.

"Miss Bjelkova insists on seeing you, Johanna Dobbs."

Johanna slowly sat up and rubbed her swollen eyelids. It took a couple of seconds for her head to quit throbbing. "All right, Kameel. Show her in."

Just at that moment, Radya barged into the bedroom. "Is it true? Piedmont is gone?"

Johanna turned to the ballerina, and her look gave it away.

Radya plunged into tears. "Oh no! I didn't want to believe it!"

"I know," Johanna murmured in reply. "I still can't believe it myself. He was such a kind, sweet man. He was against the violence. He was just … in the way."

"Oh, the *fool* …" Radya sobbed. "I warned him. I knew no good would come of the Guild. And now … oh, *now,* Johanna …" Radya looked up at her with mascara-stained cheeks. "I-I don't know myself anymore. I am ashamed." Radya reached out for her.

Johanna took the young ballerina into her arms as the blond mass of hair shook with the heaving shoulders. "You are so young, Radya."

"That is inexcusable." Radya lifted her head. "Oh, when I think of how I … oh, how I despise all of this! I wish I were in Piedmont's place." Radya fell into a new series of sobs.

"You mustn't talk that way," chided Johanna. "We've got to hold on. Be strong. Piedmont told me once to remember who I was. Radya, you must remember who *you* are—a talented dancer with your whole life ahead of you."

"I will never dance for *them*." A hateful glare filled her face. "I'll fall off a tall building and paralyze my legs before I'll ever perform another *pas de deux.*"

Johanna looked alarmed. "Shhh." She patted the ballerina's back as Radya continued to sob on her shoulder. She didn't know what to say. She couldn't help it, but she felt the same way. Suddenly her music and her entire purpose for living meant nothing to her. It was like Piedmont had said —Serassan had just been painting an impossible dream, telling her about life on Karos and the endless exhibitions of art and culture. Somehow that life did not appeal to her now. She didn't care if she never touched a piano key again.

A piercing whine met their ears as Kameel approached from the other room. The robot unit stood at the door to the bedroom. "This is a summons to all the Terrans from above. You are to go immediately to the transport shaft, where you will be taken to the loading dock."

— 23 —

The Last Ship to Earth

"Kameel, what is it?" Johanna asked. "Why are we being summoned?"

"Please follow orders, Johanna Dobbs. I do not wish to use force. We are still friends, after all."

Johanna started to get up, but Radya pulled her down. "No! We can't, Johanna. They want to take us down to that planet, don't you see?"

It certainly sounded like that was the case, but Johanna could see no way of delaying the inevitable. "Come on, Radya. We'll stick together."

"I don't want to go." The girl's lips quivered. "I'm afraid."

Johanna couldn't help but smile. The old Radya was back. She managed to help the girl up, and together they followed Kameel to the door. Johanna stopped and faced the unit. "I suppose this means goodbye, Kameel."

"I do not understand goodbye," admitted the unit.

Johanna wiped a tear away and smiled. "I'm going to miss you, Kameel. It's been pretty nice having a … chamber maid."

"I hope I have been useful to you, and made your voyage more pleasant than otherwise," replied Kameel. "Now, you must hurry. You are both wanted on the loading deck."

Reluctantly, Johanna and Radya turned toward the corridor. The Russian ballerina clung to Johanna just as she had when they had boarded the mother ship.

There was a mass exodus going on in the hallways. Reassembled patrol units were supervising Terrans on their way to the transport shafts. Johanna and Radya lost themselves in the crowd of excited passengers. Many were fearful, some angry, some in tears. Yet everyone moved toward the transport shafts, perhaps a little hopeful, too. Curiosity seemed to prompt them, and that overshadowed the doubts and fears that plagued them all. Johanna felt a pang of sadness when she remembered that Piedmont would not be accompanying them to this final stage of their voyage.

A long line stood in front of the transport shaft. Robot units administered oxygen injections to each Terran before they were permitted to get on. This time Johanna did not feel the same disorientation as she rode the transport shaft up to the loading deck. For one thing, so many people were crowded into the chute that there was no way she could fall over in a faint. Sweat and human body odors flooded the small area. The murmur of confused voices sounded distant to her as she thought about Serassan and Piedmont.

Radya still held onto Johanna as they got off the shaft and moved with the crowd toward the loading deck. Swarms of Terrans stood in the wide-open area in which they had first arrived. Johanna noticed several Estronians standing on a platform overlooking the crowd. She strained to see if Serassan was anywhere in the crowd, but she did not see him.

It was several minutes before a female voice came over the loudspeaker as it had that first night they had arrived on the mother ship. As the voice demanded their attention, the Terrans quieted down.

"We address the Terrans, our honored guests. I am Preejhna Chiyuub, commander of the Earth Star mission. It was our intention that this voyage be a pleasing and relaxing experience for all of you. We have never wished any of you any harm. Yet, now that we have come to the transition stage of our mission and are in orbit about Karos, we have made a final decision."

People began to murmur among themselves once more. Johanna glanced at Radya, whose eyes darted suspiciously back and forth.

"Please let me finish," the voice over the loudspeaker continued.

Immediately the crowd hushed.

"It is with great grief that we of Estron admit the failure of this mission."

A chorus of cheers rang out, and then people began talking at once.

The voice boomed over the loudspeaker. "We underestimated your violent tendencies. We realize now that our breeding program will not work. Estron is a peaceful civilization. It has taken our planet centuries to evolve to where we are now. We do not wish to pollute future generations with your primitive vices. It seems that human beings, when held in captivity, must rebel. We were mistaken in assuming that, by giving you all the comforts and pleasures in life, you would be content to go on with your lives, creating the beauty for which you were chosen."

"You can't force creativity!" a man shouted from the crowd.

"We have to be free to do our work!" a woman yelled.

Radya let go of Johanna, but said nothing.

"We of Estron thought we could acquire talent through you. For decades our ships have scanned your planet, and others. Why our civilization has lacked the talent you possess remains a universal mystery, but we hoped to find a way to better ourselves. You were our most promising hope. We will not force talent out of anyone. You are free to return to your planet Earth and your homes there."

The loudspeaker clicked off, then people exploded with laughter, yells, hugs, and cheers. Arms and elbows bumped Johanna's side, and her toes got stepped on. She stared at Radya, and found the ballerina to be in as much shock as she was.

"Did you hear that?" Radya finally asked. "We're ... free."

"Wait! Before you return to your decks!" A male voice came across the loudspeaker. Johanna turned and saw Serassan standing on the platform. "Ladies and gentlemen, please! Be silent! I must speak! Please let me say something!" He raised his arms and waited for the din to subside enough so he could be heard.

"I wonder what *he* wants," Radya grumbled.

"I am authorized to make a request," Serassan announced. His deep voice echoed the far walls of the loading deck. "Most of you—maybe all of you—will want to return to Earth right away. But the Preejhna Chiyuub has omitted one important fact, and I feel I must tell you." He fought off an Estronian who tried to take away the microphone. "Your planet is very close to upheaval. There are forces in effect that are beyond your control. If you return to Earth, you may perish. But, as spokesman of a culturally deprived planet, I beseech any of you who wish to remain and colonize Karos ... you will be welcomed and honored. We offer you life and freedom and the pursuit of your art for the benefit of millions who are underprivileged."

"Go to hell!" someone called out.

"I don't care about anything else," a woman next to Johanna said. "I just want to see my family again. I want to go home."

Again, people's voices rose and drowned out Serassan's request over the loudspeaker. Johanna watched anxiously as a couple of grayish Estronians escorted Serassan off the platform. He then disappeared from her sight.

"I can't talk now."

"But, Manley, I need to see you," Barbara cried into the phone. "Can you leave the house?" In the background, she could hear Doris Dobbs yelling at her husband to get off the phone.

"Sure," Manley replied. "Where?"

"I don't care. My place, I guess."

Barbara made out a scuffle, as if Manley's wife was trying to take the mouthpiece away from him. The next thing she knew, the connection had been broken. With a sigh, Barbara hung up her end. She wasn't sure if he was coming over or not. She glanced uneasily around her apartment.

Ever since they had become involved in seeing UFOs, Manley had met with a lot of hostility in his marriage. Barbara had hoped she was not the cause, but after hearing Doris just now, she realized the plight Manley was in. Yet, he was the only person she could confide in.

Twenty minutes later, the doorbell rang, and she let Manley into her apartment.

"You sounded desperate over the phone," he said. "What's wrong?"

Barbara paced back and forth. "I'm sorry I caused Doris to get upset," she replied. "It's just that I think I finally figured something out."

He fell into an armchair. "Don't give Doris a second thought. The fact that I've found new meaning and purpose in my life makes her feel very insecure. What did you figure out?"

"It just all fits," she said. "The patients with the syndrome ... then Dr. Serassan showing up from practically nowhere ..."

"You're talking about the abduction," affirmed Manley. "Johanna and the others on that van."

Barbara nodded, and sat across from him. "Not only that, but several talented people have been reported missing from around the world. Explain that." When he shrugged, she asked, "Wasn't your sister a musician?"

"She was once a concert pianist," he said. "Just before she got sick, she did some composing."

"Then I'm right. And Dr. Serassan and Dr. Thorden were impostors." She grew excited. "That's how they did it, then. Somehow, aliens disguised as doctors caused your sister and others like her to appear insane. Then, when they had everyone gathered, they took them away."

"To the stars."

Barbara nodded.

"In the ship I saw in my dream." Manley smiled at her. "An interesting theory, doc. It makes a lot of sense to me. Unfortunately, people like Doris will never buy that explanation."

"No one else will either." She shook her head sadly. "There's no way to prove my theory, unless those missing people are returned to Earth."

"Do you think that's possible?"

"No." Barbara smiled at him. "Even if it were, Manley, who'd believe them? If someone who had spent months in a mental hospital, who had been missing for weeks, suddenly showed up and claimed they had been up in a flying saucer ..."

"I see your point." Manley got to his feet. "Well, Barb, I'd better be going."
She walked with him out the door. "Thanks for coming over."

"Anytime." Outside, in the darkness, he looked up into the sky and stuffed his hands in his pockets. "Doesn't it make you wonder sometimes?"

Barbara inspected the stars, interspersed by wisps of cloud cover. "I wish you'd stop worrying," she pleaded.

"I have," he said. "I had another dream last night."

"And? What did it tell you?"

Manley took Barbara's hand in his, and squeezed it. "I know Johanna is never coming back."

In the confusion that followed the announcement made by the Estronian commander and Serassan, Johanna and Radya found themselves moving with the crowd back toward the transport shaft. Celebration cries continued to ring out around them as people discussed plans for the future, and shed tears of joy and relief.

"Johanna, you're so quiet," Radya said at last.

"I was just thinking about home," Johanna replied, "and my brother Manley. He'll be so happy to see me."

"I know it doesn't make much sense," said Radya. "*Oof!*" She grimaced as someone bumped into her. The man apologized, then turned his back. Radya shook her head. "You'll think I'm crazy, Johanna, but I think I will go home ... to Moscow." She smiled. "I do want to see my mother and father again. I miss them."

"But, Radya ... you could have your freedom. You could live in the United States, or anywhere else in the world."

Radya shook her head stubbornly. "I know what freedom *is* now," she told Johanna. "I'm not an expert at it, that's for sure, but maybe I can do some good over there. In my own small way." She looked at Johanna. "Do I make any sense?"

Johanna smiled to herself. "In your own small way," she repeated, then looked around. "It makes a lot of sense, Radya. A lot of sense." She started to push herself through the crowd.

"Johanna, what are you doing? Where are you going?"

"I have to see someone," Johanna called back. Without waiting for a protest, Johanna wormed her way through the pressing bodies. She had to see Serassan. She had made up her mind. How she could cut her way through this crowd was foremost in her mind. But, fortunately, people let her through.

Then Johanna ran into a grayish-white alien who grabbed her wrists. "Terran, where are you heading?" asked the gentle voice.

"Serassan. Please let me talk to him."

"This way." The being led her along a corridor.

"Johanna!"

Johanna stopped, and both she and her escort turned around. Serassan hurried toward her. Then the Estronian slipped away. Johanna stood facing Serassan.

"You've come to say goodbye, haven't you?" There was great pain on his face.

"Oh ... you mean you won't be guiding the Terrans back to Earth?" Johanna was surprised. "I ... I thought that was your job."

Serassan took her into his arms then, and held her tightly. "Johanna, oh my special one, how I've dreaded this moment. Even up to an hour ago, I had hoped there was still a chance we could be together. It was a false hope. I must return to Estron, and you to your home and your brother."

Johanna broke away. She trembled as she looked him in the eye. "But that's what I came to talk to you about, Serassan. I'm not going back."

His reaction was like an electric charge had passed through him.

She didn't wait for his reply. "Oh, I'll miss Earth. By now I'm sure Manley's given up on me, though, and besides ... I'm not the same person I was. You've changed that." She drew the tip of her finger up over his chin and smiled. "I'm a real woman now. I can't go back to what I was."

"Oh, Johanna ..." He embraced her again.

Then she thought of something. "But, if you're returning to Estron, then ..." She took a deep breath. "Never mind. It doesn't matter. I'll still live on Karos, and ..." She remembered Radya. "And maybe I'll do some good there. Maybe in my own small way."

A group of excited Terrans broke out in song somewhere nearby. Serassan led Johanna toward a wall where they could speak more privately. "All I know," he said, "is that I've changed, too. I'm not the man I was before we left Earth." He rubbed his forehead and stared at the floor. "This body ... it's been a burden to me. The mission has ended, and I have the option of returning to Estron."

Johanna's eyes filled with tears. "Oh, Serassan, I'd love you in any form. Go back to being what you were. It doesn't matter to me. We can still be together, at least part of the time, on Karos. That's a hundred times better than going back to Earth and never seeing you again. I couldn't bear it!"

"And neither could I." He smiled sadly. "But I'd rather inhabit a Terran body half a century and have you for my wife on Karos. I don't know that much about art or music, but I know I want to be surrounded by it forever." He kissed her. "Collect your things. I'll make the arrangements. We can be on the first shuttle to the planet's surface."

Johanna promised to do as he said, and meet him later. She wanted to break the news to Radya first, though. When she passed the ballerina's quarters, Johanna was startled to find Thorden just coming out of the apartment.

"Thorden!" She gasped.

The alien sighed in a bored fashion. He carried what resembled a small surgical kit under his arm. "Haven't they taken care of you yet?" Rolling his eyes, the beak-nosed alien walked on down the hall.

Johanna knocked on the door. As the wall parted, she stepped inside. Radya sat on her couch and grinned when she saw Johanna.

"Radya! Guess what? I'm staying."

Suddenly Radya's face went blank. She stared at Johanna, then placed her hands on her skinny waist and said, "*Orfwanveelsh strixculk gomjad purfyam biolreikwurb.*"

Now it was Johanna's turn to go blank. She stared at her Russian friend. "Radya?"

"*Yeeb daquid voolf grumbwik.*" A giggle escaped Radya's lips.

Johanna burst out laughing, too. "Oh Radya, you've got your speech back."

The blond girl spat out a series of gibberish.

"Good luck to you, too, Radya." Johanna turned to leave, but Radya sprang from the couch. Then she came and embraced Johanna.

"I'll miss you, Radya. But I know I'm doing the right thing." Johanna wiped a tear from her eye.

Outside in the corridor, a lot of jargon was exchanged as people scurried back and forth. Johanna passed Piedmont's door and she lingered a moment. "I wonder what Piedmont would have done," Johanna reflected.

"*Meeshchur gowax glimbpblar fufvgom xeegli,*" somebody called out as they passed by.

Johanna lingered for a long moment, then turned away with a smile on her face. "Yes." She nodded as she turned away. "He probably would have." She smiled to herself as she continued on down the corridor.

About the Author

Ann Carol Ulrich was the name under which the author wrote her first novel and several that followed. *Intimate Abduction,* published in September 1988, was expanded from a writing assignment while taking a course in Supernatural Literature at Michigan State University in 1975. After graduating with her bachelor's degree in English with a Creative Writing Emphasis, the author moved to Colorado with her first husband and  their toddler son. She believed that one day she would turn the short story into a science fiction novel, but had not realized that three novels would comprise The Space Trilogy. *Return To Terra* was published in 1995, followed by *The Light Being* in 2005.

By then, other books were in the works, and subsequently she remarried and took the name of her new husband, changing her name to Ann Ulrich Miller. She has published more than 20 books, most of which are novels—many with a paranormal theme. Her interest in UFOs and metaphysics, sparked in the mid-1980s by the UFO coverup movement, stimulated her imagination and also prompted her to become involved in UFO Contact Center International, a nonprofit that was founded to promote research and to assist contactees and abductees who are often ridiculed and not believed. The author claims she may have had contact herself and admits to several sightings of UFOs. In 1987 she began a monthly metaphysical publication, *The Star Beacon*, which has had subscribers around the world and continues to this day,.

She met her second husband, Ethan Miller, after he read *Intimate Abduction* and drove to Colorado from Ohio to meet her. They were together 19 years before his passing from a long illness in September 2008. She is a grandmother and lives near her three sons in Western Colorado.

She has written two memoirs and four romantic suspense novels, along with a series of Young Adult mysteries set in her native state of Wisconsin during the late 1960s. You can find out more by visiting her author website, *AnnUlrichMiller.com.*

Titles by the Author

The Space Trilogy series
Intimate Abduction
Return To Terra
The Light Being

Romantic Suspense/Mystery
Night of the November Moon

Under the name Ann Ulrich Miller

Rainbow Majesty
Sonata Summer
The Dream Chasers

The Annette Vetter Young Adult Mystery Series
Under the name Ann Carol Ulrich

The Mystery at Hickory Hill
The Secret of the Green Paint
The Pouting Pumpkin Mystery
The Legend of the Lantern
In the Shadow of the Tower
The Ground Hog Mystery
Spring Break at the Lake House
Prom Night

plus for Pre-Teens: **The Root Cellar Mystery**

Memoirs
Throughout All Time, A Cosmic Love Story
Stepping Forth, An American Girl Coming of Age in the '60s
A Dog Named Ranger

Animals/Humor
The Back Yard of Clara the Clutz

Co-authored with Shirlè Klein Carsh
Permutation, A True UFO Story

Don't miss the sequel to *Intimate Abduction*...
RETURN TO TERRA

and the final segment of The Space Trilogy...
THE LIGHT BEING

Both from Earth Star Publications
and available in eBook format

Johanna and Serassan

Ann Carol Ulrich

Enjoy reading Chapter 1 of the second book in The Space Trilogy,

Return To Terra

by Ann Carol Ulrich

— 1 —

Strange Encounter

The car cruised east on I-80, exceeding 68 mph. Dorothy Myers sat behind the wheel of her Toyota Celica, undisturbed by the passing vehicles to her left. Her mind was in a passive state as the car's CD player filled the air with soothing tones of Narada.

What now, she wondered, as her thoughts skimmed over the summer events and the various places she and Ellen had visited. It had been an adventure taking three months off to tour the West. They had thrown a tent and sleeping bags in the car and saved money by roughing it.

Now she had to face reality and get on with her life. Ellen had college to finish, so they were on their way home. Dorothy just wasn't sure what she was going to do. She'd had more than enough education, that was for sure. She could always go back to her work in massage therapy, but something nagged at her. She felt she should be doing something more, but what on earth could it be?

A stir of movement from the back seat broke Dorothy's train of thought. Ellen sat up and stretched. "Oh, where are we?" She yawned.

Dorothy glanced at the clock on the dash. The glowing digits seemed to blur. It was just past 11:30. "Grand Island's just up ahead." She glanced over her shoulder. "Go back to sleep. It's not your turn to drive."

Ellen leaned over the seat. "I know. Gee, I must have slept. Any rest areas in sight?"

"We passed one turnoff a while ago," Dorothy replied. "I don't know what's ahead."

Ellen sighed. "Nebraska must be the longest state in the country."

"That's why we're driving at night. And South Dakota's no picnic either. Plus it's the shortest route for getting home. You have only three days before classes begin."

"You had to remind me." Ellen rode in silence for a while, then said, "But it was a fantastic summer, wasn't it?"

Dorothy agreed. "It was what we both needed, that's for sure."

They rode in silence for a while and Dorothy thought about the ups and downs of their trip. Ellen had proven to be moody and Dorothy probably would never take another vacation with Ellen.

"Dorothy! Stop the car," Ellen cried.

"Why?" Dorothy took her foot off the gas. She looked at Ellen, who was pressed against the side window of the back seat.

"I see something odd." Ellen continued to stare out the window. "Stop the car. I think you should see this thing."

Dorothy pulled over into the shoulder of the interstate. As soon as the car rolled to a halt, Ellen opened the door and jumped out into the dark. Dorothy put on her emergency flashers and kept the engine running, then stepped out.

The air was thick and moist but cool. A slight breeze blowing some brush next to the highway was the only sound. Dorothy took in the wide expanse of the starry sky, with foggy wisps of cloud cover scattered here and there. The moon had not risen yet.

"Look!" cried Ellen. She pointed at the southern horizon, where Dorothy noticed a bright speck of white light. At first it resembled a bright star or planet, but as they watched it became obvious that the object was in motion.

Dorothy stood beside Ellen. Cars whooshed past them on the road. "It's an airplane."

"No," said Ellen. "It's not an airplane. It doesn't have any blinking lights."

Dorothy squinted. The binoculars were in the trunk, packed beneath their sleeping bags and clothes. She didn't feel like digging them out. She watched with Ellen as the bright object made a dip in the sky, then curved upward and made a semi-circle. Suddenly it came to a stop and just seemed to be waiting.

"Now do you still think it's an airplane?" asked Ellen.

Dorothy knew it wasn't anything like that. "Unbelievable ..." Dorothy could feel her heart beating faster. Why had she stuck her camera away? She started toward the trunk.

"Where are you going?" Ellen sounded nervous.

Dorothy realized her keys were still in the car, which she had left running. She turned around. Just then the object began moving in a straight line, slowly, toward the east. Dorothy and Ellen watched the object until it grew smaller and then finally disappeared behind some cloud cover.

"Well, so much for getting a picture of it." Dorothy sighed. "Come on. Let's go before somebody hits us."

Ellen climbed into the passenger seat in front. She began to chatter about UFOs and how she had always thought people who saw them were imagining them, or seeing airplanes or helicopters or weather balloons. Dorothy continued to drive, and after a while Ellen grew quiet and soon nodded off beside her.

Dorothy stuck in another CD. Soft relaxation music filled the car. She noticed the car's clock said 12:10. That meant they would reach Omaha sometime after 3 AM—if she managed to stay awake. Dorothy approached an exit up ahead and remembered Ellen's request for a rest stop. She took the exit and glanced at her friend beside her. "Ellen, do you still need to stop?"

There was no answer from her passenger. Dorothy turned onto a road and began looking for signs that indicated a gas station ahead. Ellen slept and Dorothy continued to drive. The music seemed to have a numbing effect on her. She hummed along so she'd stay awake.

After a while it dawned on Dorothy that she was not headed in the right direction. There were no gas stations ahead. She was going out of her way to appease Ellen, who was sound asleep. With a sigh of frustration, Dorothy waited for a semi truck to pass her, then slowed down so she could turn the car around and head back toward the interstate.

Suddenly something caught her eye. Out the windshield was the strange light again. It was directly ahead, just over the eastern horizon, and seemed to be staying within her line of vision.

"Ellen, wake up." Dorothy stopped the car and reached over and nudged her friend. "It's back."

Ellen groaned but did not awaken.

"Ellen... *Ellen*, wake up. Come on." After another minute, Dorothy gave up. Ellen was really out of it.

Dorothy noticed the light growing bigger. She rubbed her eyes and wondered if she was imagining it. It seemed to have acquired a tinge of red around the edges, and was definitely larger than a star by now. Before long she began to feel tired—really groggy.

"Ellen... *wake up.*" Dorothy grabbed the other woman's slumping shoulder and shook her. "Come on, Ellen, it's time to wake up." When there was still no response, Dorothy pleaded, "Ellen, *wake up,* what's *wrong* with you?"

The light in the sky was brighter now—and much closer. Dorothy grew frightened. The object was low and flying toward her. As it neared she could see its shape more clearly. It was a huge boomerang, with a red glow around the convex bottom.

Wth a hammering heart, Dorothy spun the steering wheel and stepped on the accelerator. She started speeding back toward the interstate. The next moment she slammed on her brakes and skidded to a stop. Above her was the object, which was as large as a house. Its width filled the entire windshield as it descended over the highway. She could now see a single red light on the end, where the boomerang came to a point. Dorothy marveled at how Ellen could possibly sleep through this.

Suddenly the engine killed and all of the dash lights went out, leaving them in darkness except for the brilliance from the UFO. Dorothy tried to start the engine, but it wouldn't even turn over. In a panic, Dorothy started shaking Ellen, demanding that she wake up.

Then a blinding yellow light flashed into the car from the left window. Dorothy gasped and covered her face. She felt sure she was going to wet her pants.

A man's voice called out, "Roll down the window, ma'am. Roll it down."

Dorothy huddled close to Ellen, but then noticed the alternating flash of red and blue lights behind her car. It dawned on her at that moment that the man outside her car was a policeman and he was shining a flashlight in her face.

Ellen stirred then and began to mumble.

Dorothy reached over and rolled down the window. The policeman lowered his light so she could see him.

"May I see your driver's license, please?" The trooper had a husky voice. His manner was calm and collected.

Dorothy fished her billfold from her purse and managed to spill everything out onto the floor. She handed him her license as Ellen opened her eyes. "Oh no, did we get a speeding ticket?"

"Dorothy Myers. You're a Florida resident?"

Dorothy's voice came in uncontrollable little gasps. "Yes, but w... we're headed for De... DeKalb, Illinois. We've just been to C... California."

The officer shone the light at Ellen, who grimaced and shielded her eyes. "Are you all right, ma'am?"

Ellen blinked and looked around. "I'm fine."

The policeman gave Dorothy back her license. "Do you realize your car is sitting out in the middle of the highway?"

"Yes, but officer, I... I had to st... stop. The thing... my engine died, and then... and then... it wouldn't start. *Oh my God*!" Dorothy realized there was nothing hovering in the air in front of the car. The boomerang object had vanished, but she didn't remember when.

"Just a minute," said the trooper. "What thing are you talking about?"

Dorothy told him about Ellen spotting the UFO, and how they had stopped and watched it until it disappeared. Ellen's eyes were wide as she concurred with Dorothy's story. Then Dorothy told him how she had seen the object out the windshield and how it had come in so close that she had to slam on her brakes. Then the car had died.

Ellen said nothing.

The officer sighed. "People who usually report these things are overtired. I suggest you get some coffee. There's a café just off the highway about seven miles ahead."

Dorothy felt confused. Had she imagined the boomerang? Ellen was looking at her as though she were a freak, yet she had tried to rouse Ellen and couldn't. Dorothy felt frustration set in, but decided the officer had been more than fair not to ticket her, so she politely told him she would follow his advice.

"And if I were you, ma'am," the officer added, "I wouldn't mention this to anyone."

Dorothy frowned as he walked back to his flashing patrol car. How could he remain so nonchalant? There had been no inflection in his voice at all, as though he were simply bored by it all.

Dorothy turned to Ellen. "I don't believe this is happening."

Ellen yawned. "When do you want me to take the wheel?"

Dorothy had recovered from her fatigue. In fact, the blood was racing through her system with the anger she felt. "He didn't believe me!" She started up the engine and then continued east, griping to Ellen about how it felt to be treated like some nut.

"Hey, if you say it happened ... I believe you." Ellen nodded off a short while later and Dorothy continued driving.

The next thing Dorothy knew, the light of dawn was rising up ahead. She felt a wave of relief that it was going to be daylight soon. After breakfast Ellen could drive and she could sleep.

"Good morning, are we there yet?" Ellen sat up and frowned. "Now I've got a stiff neck."

Dorothy asked, "Why didn't you climb into the back seat where you could stretch out?"

"I don't know. I should have." Ellen looked right and left. "We should be close to Iowa City by now. Wait a minute. This isn't Iowa."

"We're coming up on Lincoln," replied Dorothy.

"Nebraska?" Ellen cringed. "What happened? We should have reached at least Des Moines by daylight."

Dorothy shook her head. "I don't know. I don't remember stopping anywhere to sleep. I've been driving all night." She glanced at Ellen. "We only stopped twice, remember? Once when you saw that UFO, and then with the policeman."

"What policeman?" Ellen stared blankly at Dorothy.

"The state trooper. Ellen, don't you remember?"

"No."

Dorothy was too stressed out from driving to sort it out. She clutched the steering wheel and drove the final stretch to Lincoln. She and Ellen did not speak of the policeman or the UFO the rest of the trip.

To read the rest, you can order *Return To Terra*, the second book in Ann Carol Ulrich's *Space Trilogy,* available in either paperback or Kindle from Amazon.com. Visit *www.earthstarpublications.com* for ordering information.

The Space Trilogy
by Ann Carol Ulrich

INTIMATE ABDUCTION

RETURN TO TERRA

THE LIGHT BEING